The woman was

Annja felt her heart le everything changed.

Time became the enem Annja's shoulders. Every minute counted now. Annja needed to get the woman covered up and back to the top of the ledge, then to a medical facility as fast as humanly possible.

"I don't know if you can hear me, but I'm going to try to get you out of here. Don't struggle. Just lie still and let me do all the work. Understand?"

She leaned in close, but didn't hear a response.

"All right. Hang on. I'm going to free your arm, then roll you over."

Annja looked down at the woman she'd come to rescue. Her face was as pale as the rest of her, but even in her present state Annja could see that she was beautiful. Beauty, true beauty, always brought the predators out of the shadows.

One of the woman's eyes was swollen shut but the other opened.

"Don't worry, I've got you. You're going to be okay," she told her. "I'm taking you to the hospital."

The woman blinked, then moved her lips slightly. *"Krv…Grofka."*

Startled, Annja pulled back. That was one Slovakian phrase she did understand.

Krv Grofka… Blood Countess.

Titles in this series:

ROGUE Angel

Alex Archer

BATHED IN BLOOD

A GOLD EAGLE BOOK FROM

WORLDWIDE®

TORONTO • NEW YORK • LONDON
AMSTERDAM • PARIS • SYDNEY • HAMBURG
STOCKHOLM • ATHENS • TOKYO • MILAN
MADRID • WARSAW • BUDAPEST • AUCKLAND

Recycling programs
for this product may
not exist in your area.

First edition March 2015

ISBN-13: 978-0-373-62173-6

Bathed in Blood

Special thanks and acknowledgment to
Joe Nassise for his contribution to this work.

Printed in U.S.A.

THE
LEGEND

...THE ENGLISH COMMANDER TOOK
JOAN'S SWORD AND RAISED IT HIGH.

The broadsword, plain and unadorned,
gleamed in the firelight. He put the tip against
the ground and his foot at the center of the blade.
The broadsword shattered, fragments falling
into the mud. The crowd surged forward,
peasant and soldier, and snatched the shards
from the trampled mud. The commander tossed
the hilt deep into the crowd.
Smoke almost obscured Joan, but she continued
praying till the end, until finally the flames climbed
her body and she sagged against the restraints.

Joan of Arc died that fateful day in France,
but her legend and sword are reborn...

1

The castle door stood partially open, as if in invitation.

From his hiding place amid the shrubbery half a dozen yards away, Count György Thurzó eyed the door cautiously.

He didn't like it.

He had planned every detail of this mission, for failure could not only doom his career but bring reprisals the likes of which he'd never seen. Thurzó had informed no one of his intent to visit the castle; the king had merely ordered that he investigate the accusations, a task he could have assigned to one of his own court functionaries. But Thurzó had decided to investigate himself. If the claims proved to be unfounded, he would cull favor with the countess, the widow of his old friend, for having saved her from public embarrassment.

If the accusations proved to be true... Well, then, he would be in a position to handle the situation with the delicate hand it would surely require.

He and his men had traveled from the capital only at night, hiding out in abandoned barns and empty groves each morning so that none might see their approach and send word ahead to the castle's mistress, Countess Elizabeth Báthory. The success of their venture depended entirely on surprise; the countess might not be cut from the same cloth as her deceased husband, Ferenc Nádasdy—a man whose ruthless ferocity on the battlefield had earned him the moniker the Black Knight of Hungary—but Thurzó knew her to be extraordinarily intelligent and cunning, a combination that was apt to make her dangerous.

His group had reached the village of Csejte just before sundown and hidden in a narrow canyon half a mile outside town until full dark. Then and only then had they passed through town and headed up the narrow road that led to the castle proper, sitting atop a hill that overlooked both the town and the surrounding territory. Nearing the castle, they'd dismounted before the final bend in the road, tied the horses to nearby trees and crept forward to their present position: a clump of shrubbery that allowed them to see the castle without being seen.

That door looked like trouble to Thurzó. He hadn't come all this way to be ambushed.

Why leave it open?

Thurzó watched the entryway carefully, his gaze returning again and again to the narrow triangle of light spilling across the floor tiles just beyond. If someone was waiting inside the door, they would eventually shift their position, and their shadow would dance across that space, even if only for a second.

But the light on the floor remained steady; no shadow disturbed it, even after waiting several long, tense moments.

Not an ambush, then? A careless servant, perhaps?

If that was what it was, they were in luck. Before setting out for Csejte, Thurzó hadn't known how he was going to gain access to the castle. He'd run through various scenarios, but each and every one of them, aside from clandestinely scaling the walls, had required help from someone already on the inside. He'd had his men pack grappling hooks and ropes just in case, but he'd spent the better part of the journey here praying for another solution.

It seemed his prayers had been answered.

He glanced back at his men, gave the signal and then rose from his crouch and headed for the half-open door at a brisk walk, drawing his sword as he went. If it came to fighting, he would be ready, as would his men; the handpicked fighters following at his heels were some of the best in his retinue, never mind the most trustworthy. They'd been sworn to secrecy for the duration of the mission, and he was confident that each and every one of them would keep their word. He heard more than one blade slide from its sheath behind him, and smiled at the sound.

Thurzó didn't stop when he reached the door but strode in, an excuse about his concern for the countess's safety ready on his lips. The excuse turned out to be unnecessary, though, for the foyer was empty and quiet.

Too quiet.

Thurzó waved his men forward. Perhaps it was just a misperception caused by his own unease, but every single man that followed him inside seemed to hesitate, as if aware that crossing the threshold put them on a path from which there was no return.

Real or imagined, Thurzó didn't blame them. What they'd come here to investigate would chill even the most hardened of hearts. And if it was true...

If it was true, then God help us all.

The men quickly split into two groups. The first would sweep the upper floors while the second, led by Thurzó himself, would cover the main floor and then descend into the dungeons.

If the rumors were true, that was where he expected to find Elizabeth. Word had reached the king a week hence that she would be gathering tonight with her confidants for one of her dark rituals. Thurzó had come to catch her in the act.

Better me than someone else, he reasoned. At least I will show restraint.

They found the first body less than five minutes after separating from the others.

The young woman lay sprawled facedown against the side of the passageway. She was naked, with long blond hair that was caked with drying blood. A thin, wavering trail of the same stretched out behind her, as if she had been crawling forward on her stomach before her strength had given out.

Thurzó rushed to her side, but when he rolled her

over it was clear he was too late; her unseeing eyes stared up at him from her slack face.

He noted absently that she'd probably been quite pretty, but the majority of his attention was drawn to the extreme pallor of her skin and the multiple wounds that covered her chest and abdomen. He stopped counting at twenty. The sheer violence of the act sickened him; who would do this to a woman?

He knew the answer, of course. He didn't want to admit it.

Elizabeth, what have you done?

At first, Thurzó thought the injuries had been made with a knife or dagger, but upon closer examination he could see the wounds were rounded, like those delivered with an auger or some other tool designed for puncturing. They were also deep and had no doubt led to significant blood loss. That alone made him think she hadn't crawled here on her own; someone had been dragging her and dumped her here when they had no more use for her.

After she'd been drained dry…

He shook the vile thought from his head and rose from the body, knowing this wouldn't be the last corpse they would find within these walls.

"Nothing we can do for her," he said quietly to his men. "We'll take care of the body once we've secured the countess. Let's keep moving."

The group continued deeper into the castle. The halls were well lit but eerily empty, and the strange silence lay about the place like a shroud.

Thurzó was familiar with the general layout—one

of the reasons he'd been chosen to lead the fact-finding expedition. He had been friends with Nádasdy, Báthory's deceased husband, and had often played within the castle walls as a child. He used that knowledge to lead his squad through the various rooms that made up the lower floor with relative quickness until they neared the stairs that led to the dungeons. There they found a second body.

This one was also a woman, though slightly older than the first. She was a brunette and she, too, was naked, making it obvious that the two women had been treated similarly. Thurzó could see the same rounded wounds, the same pale hue to the skin that indicated massive blood loss, the same refined beauty in the woman's features.

His men muttered darkly at the sight, and he knew their mood was changing from apprehension and fear to anger. It was one thing to accidentally kill a woman in the hot blood of battle. It was quite another, however, to ruthlessly murder a woman in one's home. The noble class was not known for its gentle manner toward commoners, but this…this was just obscene.

Thurzó rose to his feet, intending to speak to his men, but before he could do so the door to the dungeons proper, just a few feet away, was shoved open. He spun around, sword at the ready, to find himself staring at two older women dressed in dark garments, carrying an injured and bloody girl between them. The way they were holding her, dragging her up the stairs by her wrists, made it clear they weren't concerned with her welfare in the least; she was just another piece of garbage to be disposed of, no doubt the sooner, the better.

The two groups stared at each other for a long second, both nonplussed at being interrupted.

Thurzó recovered first, springing forward and pushing the point of his sword against the throat of the woman on the left, whom he recognized as Dorotya Semtész, one of Elizabeth's personal servants.

"Put her down, gently," he told them.

For a moment he thought Semtész might actually try to argue. She glared at him, pretending to dismiss the blade at her throat, but a glance over his shoulder at the rest of his party, all heavily armed and no doubt as angry as he, must have convinced her that arguing was a waste of time. Without a word she lowered the injured girl toward the floor and her companion followed suit.

Thurzó kept his blade on Semtész'z throat as he said, "Bakoš, Kollár, help that young woman. Szabó, keep your eye on her—" he indicated Semtész's companion with a nod of his head "—while I talk to this one."

As his men did as they were ordered, Thurzó nudged his captive off to one side, away from the others, with the point of his sword. When they were far enough away for his men not to overhear, he asked, "Where is she?"

Semtész didn't bat an eyelash as she lied through her teeth. "At her estate in Vienna. She'll be there for a fortnight."

Thurzó knew that wasn't true; he'd had men watching Báthory's other estates for three days, and he knew she hadn't left Csejte.

Kollár interrupted him from behind.

"She's dead, sir."

That made three victims so far.

God help them.

"If Lady Báthory is out of the country, then I suppose this was all your doing?"

Báthory's servant was smart enough to see the trap he'd laid for her—admitting to the crime would mean she was as good as dead, since murder was a capital offense—but she surprised him by nodding in agreement.

"Yes. The girl's death is my fault."

He didn't believe that for a moment, but he also realized the futility of trying to get information out of her when she was all too willing to confess to murder. Anything she said would be suspect, and all of it more than likely designed to delay him from carrying out his real objective—locating and arresting the countess.

He didn't have time for this.

Thurzó grabbed the woman by the arm and led her back to Szabó, who was keeping an eye on her companion. "Put them in irons," he told his lieutenant. "We're taking them both back to Bratislava to stand trial."

"Yes, sir."

Semtész glared at him, but he ignored her, his thoughts on who he'd take with him into the dungeon for Elizabeth's arrest and who he would leave behind to guard the prisoners.

He never got the chance to make a decision. Cries for help erupted from down below.

Thurzó didn't hesitate; gripping his sword, he rushed down the steps. The stamp of booted feet on the stone behind him let him know that several of his men were following. At this point it didn't really matter who it was, just that he had some backup.

Torches burned in sconces set into the walls, lighting the way before them, and the group of men quickly found themselves standing in a narrow passageway with rows of cells on either side.

The cells were full of women.

Some held the living. Some held the dead. Some held a mix of the two, and it was often difficult to tell the difference given the terrible state many of the prisoners were in. One glance was all it took to recognize that the women had been tortured. They had been beaten and battered and in some cases bitten, though by whom or what Thurzó didn't know.

He had his suspicions, though, oh, yes.

Unlike the women they'd found upstairs, some of these prisoners needed immediate assistance, and he couldn't just pass them by without giving aid. Leaving the dead to fulfill their mission was one thing; abandoning the living was something else entirely.

Thankfully the doors to each cell were made of wood, rather than iron. That meant there'd be no need to wait for a blacksmith. Thurzó had anticipated the need to smash through a few doors once they were inside the castle, so several of his men were carrying battle hammers.

"Break them down!" he called to his men. "Break them all down. Get these women upstairs and give them what aid you can!"

His men immediately got to work, the wood resisting

at first and then splintering beneath the repeated blows. The noise drew the other half of his party from the halls and chambers upstairs, where they'd been searching for the countess, and the added manpower made the job go that much quicker.

Soon his men were entering the cells, leading those who could move up the stairs and into the great hall, where they received as much care as Thurzó's men could provide. Those who were too injured to walk were carried upstairs by one or more of his soldiers; the gentleness these hardened warriors showed to the wounded struck Thurzó deep in the heart.

When the last of the prisoners were upstairs, the bodies were carried out of the cells and lined up in the passageway one after another. Thurzó stopped counting when he reached forty-three.

He'd checked the first few corpses—those that were reasonably intact, at least—and noted the same kinds of injuries as they'd discovered upstairs. They'd been bled dry like animals brought to the butcher's for slaughter.

His disgust now in full bore, Thurzó stood back and let his men work, his mind wandering to all-but-forgotten days, trying to figure out just where the countess was hiding.

The upper floors were vacant, and they had covered every inch of the lower floors, as well. Lady Báthory had been inside these walls when the night had begun, and Semtész's behavior seemed to indicate she was still here somewhere.

But where?

He cast his thoughts back, back to the days when

he and Ferenc had run wild through these tunnels, and as the images rushed through his mind, one stuck out. A faint memory of Ferenc showing him a hidden door in one of the cells, a door that led to an unfinished tunnel...

Thurzó slipped away from the others and entered the cell in question. Holding a torch, he walked over to the back wall and pressed on it several times, trying to remember how his childhood friend had done it all those years ago.

Something about putting pressure on the right slab while standing...just so?

The wall slid open silently, revealing the passage he remembered from his youth. At that time, the tunnel had led to a dead end, but he could see now that improvements had been made over the years, widening the tunnel and lengthening it, as well. Torches had been lit at regular intervals. The tunnel took a couple of sharp turns and then opened up into a wide chamber.

In the center of the room, a large rectangular sunken bath was surrounded by half a dozen braziers. Each had a fire blazing inside, no doubt to help ward off the room's chill.

In the flames' lurid light, the bathwater had an unusual crimson tint.

Thurzó stepped forward, moving closer, and as he did so the smell finally hit him.

A thick, coppery scent—one he was intimately familiar with from the time he'd spent on the battlefield.

With slowly dawning horror, Thurzó realized the

bathwater wasn't truly water at all. It was blood, a vast pool of blood hot enough to give off steam.

He'd never seen anything like it.

And while he stood there, the surface of the pool suddenly rippled and a figure rose out of its depths, shocking him so much that he stumbled backward.

A hearty laugh—a laugh he recognized—filled the chamber as the woman rising from the bath caught sight of him.

"What's the matter, György? Surely you've seen a naked woman before?"

Elizabeth!

He stood there staring—he couldn't help himself. The countess stood thigh deep in the tub, the fluid slowly sliding down her curves and back into the bath, allowing her pale skin to peek out from the crimson flow. Her usually raven-black hair was highlighted with streaks of color, and her blue eyes peered out of a face that seemed to be camouflaged in red paint.

When she licked her lips, he was reminded that it wasn't paint at all, but blood.

Human blood.

"My God, Elizabeth, what have you done?"

She laughed again, longer and harder this time, and he realized that asking what she hadn't done might have proved a more useful starting point.

Even so, her answer surprised him.

"What have I done? I've found the very thing man has spent centuries searching for, the very thing he thought forever out of reach. I've found the secret to immortality!"

Thurzó couldn't believe what he was hearing.

"Immortality? You're insane! Look at yourself, Elizabeth. You're covered in blood, for heaven's sake!"

"Yes, look at me, György. Look at me!" she exclaimed, spreading her arms to draw his attention to her body. "I'm fifty years old and I look like a girl of twenty-five! I'm getting younger with every treatment."

Thurzó *was* looking; as morbid as the scene was he couldn't take his gaze off her. He told himself he was looking for evidence to back up her claims, preposterous as they were, but deep down he knew the truth. Countess Elizabeth Báthory was a beauty, even as she appeared now; Thurzó couldn't deny that. He'd found her attractive when they were younger, when she'd been betrothed to his friend, and the years had only done her justice.

He looked because he wanted to look. It was as simple as that.

Rounded wounds, like those caused by a pike or an auger...

The thought slipped in like an enemy from the shadows, reminding him of just how the countess and her companions had obtained all the blood currently steaming in the sunken bath and Thurzó was suddenly ashamed.

He focused his gaze just beyond her, so he could see her movements but wouldn't be so tempted to stare. Thurzó tried to figure out just how many bodies it must take to fill a tub of that size. And she had mentioned multiple treatments...

"I don't care what you claim to have discovered," he

said through a jaw stiffened with anger and distaste. He waved with his free hand at the bath before him. "You should be struck down where you stand for this...*this abomination*!"

Elizabeth walked forward slowly, swaying slightly as if listening to some sensual rhythm only she could hear. Thurzó tried to keep his gaze focused over her shoulder, but the closer she came, the more difficult that was, until he had no choice but to face her.

By now she was only a few feet away.

His gaze found hers, and then, as if by its own volition, dropped to her body once more.

Catching himself, he looked back into her face and saw her smirking at him.

"Oh, but you're not going to do that, are you, György?" she asked softly. "There are other things you'd much rather do than strike me down."

She was right; he could no more hurt her than he could grow wings and fly. The sad truth was that he'd been in love with Elizabeth Báthory for years.

Elizabeth moved closer, until her blood-slicked body was just inches from his own. He could feel the heat rising from it as she said, "So what are you going to do, György?"

Thurzó stared deep into her eyes, letting her see the storm that raged within him, and then, steeling himself, said, "In the name of His Majesty, King Matthias II, and under the authority granted to me as the palatine of Hungary, I place you under arrest for the torture and murder of multiple young women under your care..."

Bytča, Hungary
January 1611

THE TRIAL WAS a madhouse.

Thurzó had been observing the proceedings from the balcony overlooking the judges' box for the past several days. He'd watched witness after witness take the stand and condemn the three women and one man on trial for the evils conducted at Csejte and elsewhere.

Elizabeth herself was not on trial; she remained at Csejte Castle under house arrest, guarded by ten of his most trusted men. It had taken considerable effort on his part to convince King Matthias that putting a member of the upper nobility on trial would serve little purpose. Báthory came from a wealthy and influential family; angering them by trying and executing her, which was precisely what Matthias wanted to happen, would have caused no end of difficulties. Thurzó had hoped to convince the king that Elizabeth should be spirited away to a nunnery for the remainder of her days, but that possibility became less and less likely as word of Báthory's involvement in the atrocities quickly spread.

Just the day before a journal was produced as evidence by one of the maids, listing six hundred and fifty victims who'd died by Elizabeth's hand. Thurzó hadn't seen it himself, so he couldn't vouch for its authenticity, but at this point it really didn't matter. Elizabeth was responsible for killing young women and stealing their blood. Thurzó had witnessed her crimes firsthand.

Commotion spread through the courtroom below, breaking into Thurzó's thoughts. Leaning over the banister, he could see that Royal Supreme Court Judge Theodosius Syrmiensis was returning to his seat while his twenty co-judges took their places in the judges' box.

Thurzó felt his pulse race; a verdict must have been reached.

Judge Syrmiensis sat down and waited for the wardens to restore order to the room. When all was quiet, he faced the defendants.

"Dorotya Semtész, Ilona Jó, Katarína Benická and János Fickó, this court finds you guilty of eighty counts of murder."

A roar went up in the courtroom, and the judge had to wait until the wardens could quiet everyone a second time.

"Defendants Semtész, Jó and Fickó shall be put to death, sentence to be carried out immediately. Defendant Benická is sentenced to life imprisonment. The court has spoken."

Commotion erupted again, but Thurzó had lost interest. The verdict was exactly what he'd predicated; Benická had been bullied by the others and therefore deserved a lesser sentence, an opinion he had stressed during his own testimony a few days earlier.

Justice had been served.

A memory of Elizabeth rising out of the pool of blood reminded him that one aspect of this whole mess still needed to be resolved. Thankfully the verdict would give him the opportunity to see the king and plead his case again.

Perhaps this time the king might listen…

Forty minutes later he was ushered into the king's

meeting chamber, where he found Elizabeth's eldest son, Paul, already in conference with His Majesty.

"Ah, welcome, Thurzó," the king said when he arrived. "How goes the trial?"

"Judge Syrmiensis returned a guilty verdict less than an hour ago. The three sentenced to death have little time left in this world."

"And thank God for that," the king said with a grim expression. "A nasty business all around."

Thurzó glanced at Paul, but the other man wouldn't meet his eye. A tremor of concern shook Thurzó. Had Paul been negotiating with the king behind his back?

Thurzó suspected he had, and the king's next words confirmed it.

"Young Báthory has a rather unique answer to our other problem."

"Is that so?" Thurzó replied, glancing at Paul one last time—still no response—before giving his full attention to the king.

"You made it clear that a public trial and execution of Countess Báthory would be a mistake."

"Yes, I have and…"

The king held up a hand, silencing him.

"I happen to agree with you. As does the countess's heir."

This time Paul met Thurzó's gaze and nodded briefly before looking away again.

"We cannot, however, allow the countess's monstrous actions to continue."

Here it comes, Thurzó thought.

"I have agreed to grant Countess Báthory my pardon and absolution for the crimes she has committed against my subjects. In return, her son will consider my debt to the Báthory family repaid in full."

Thurzó knew the family had loaned the king considerable amounts over the past several years. But Countess Báthory controlled that debt, not Paul. And she would continue to control it until her death. Then, and only then, would control pass to her son.

The king wasn't finished, however.

"Paul agrees that the countess must pay for her crimes. It is only just. To that end he has suggested that she be imprisoned within her suite of rooms inside Csejte Castle, there to remain until she passes from this earth. Since she would be unable to carry out the myriad duties her position as head of the Báthory family requires, I would have no choice but to declare her legally dead and pass control of her estates to her heir."

Matthias and young Báthory smiled at each other, and Thurzó knew in that moment it was already decided. The king wanted his debt excused and Elizabeth's son wanted her out of the way. The solution was elegant and simple. Everybody would win.

Everybody, that was, but Elizabeth.

At least she'll be alive, he told himself.

Pasting on a smile, Thurzó told the king he approved of the solution.

"Good," the king replied. "I'm putting you in charge of the masonry work."

It took a moment for the king's words to register. "Masonry?"

"Yes, of course. Did you think we would just guard the door?"

That was exactly what Thurzó had pictured. Post a guard, allow her to spend some time in the fresh air every day—the civilized approach.

But too late Thurzó remembered that Matthias had a cruel streak, and this was his way of getting back at the countess for holding that debt over his head.

"I want the entire suite of rooms bricked up. Doors, windows, everything! We'll leave a few slots in the walls through which she can receive her food, and so the guards can keep an eye on her, but she will remain a prisoner—a real prisoner—until the day her vile countenance passes from this earth! Do you understand, Thurzó?"

He nodded and waited for the king to dismiss him with a toss of his head. As he moved toward the exit, one final question occurred to him.

"If I may, Your Majesty, why me?"

The king didn't even look at him as he delivered his answer.

"You should have killed her when you had the chance, Thurzó, and saved me all this nonsense. Since you didn't, I'm leaving it in your hands."

And that was that. In trying to save her life, he'd ended up bringing her a fate worse than death.

Love certainly was blind.

2

Csejte Castle
Present day Slovakia

Annja Creed eyed the camera for a moment, and then stepped forward to adjust the angle of the lens an inch or so to the left. Satisfied, she nodded to herself, moved back to her former position and keyed the remote in her left hand.

"As you can see, behind me lies the ruins of Csejte Castle, home to one of the most beautiful, and most villainous, women who ever lived—the Blood Countess herself, Elizabeth Báthory."

A shake of her head, a double click of the remote to stop and restart the recording, and then she tried again.

"The crumbling walls you see behind me are the ruins of Csejte Castle, once home to Elizabeth Báthory, a woman some consider one of history's greatest monst... Gah!"

She stopped the recording and turned away in frustration. Creating the opening to the show should have been a piece of cake. She'd done hundreds of such takes during her time as cohost of *Chasing History's Monsters*, the cable television show she'd worked for these past few years. Yes, normally she would've worked with a cameraman and wouldn't have to worry about framing and proper exposure, but she was a steady hand at this by now and probably could have shot, edited and produced the entire show on her own.

Which was exactly what she was intending to do for this one.

The whole thing was a bit of a lark, she had to admit. She'd been with her regular crew in the Czech Republic, filming an episode on Faust and the mysterious creatures that still supposedly haunt his house, but the shoot had wrapped early. With a few extra days suddenly on hand, Annja decided to make the jaunt across the border into Slovakia to do some rock climbing and maybe even visit Báthory's legendary castle.

She'd caught a flight into Bratislava, took a train northeast into Košice and drove the short distance to the small village of Višňové. Annja could see the castle's ruins on the hill above the village as she'd driven in, and that was when the idea had struck. She'd checked into her hotel, fired up her laptop and searched the database.

For some strange reason, *Chasing History's Monsters* had never done an episode on the world's most notorious serial killer, Countess Báthory herself.

Don't look a gift horse in the mouth, Annja, she'd reminded herself, and decided then and there to see what she could put together on her own. Selling a complete episode—shot, cut and edited—to her producer, Doug Morrell, would net her some extra cash and give him an episode he could deliver to his own bosses seemingly overnight. That would make him look good, and he could even hold on to it for an emergency situation when some other episode's filming went south. It was a win-win situation.

She was pretty certain Doug would take the show; the subject matter was right up his alley. It would make a great episode.

If she could get the opening right, that was.

Annja turned and surveyed the ruin of the castle. There really wasn't much to look at, truth be told. A few sets of crumbling walls, an extended tower or two, but not much more than that. The castle had been sacked and plundered by Ferenc II Rákóczi in 1708 as part of the Hungarian uprising against the Hapsburgs. It had been left to fall into ruin, and a ruin it had become.

And yet something still drew people here.

She knew what it was, of course.

The lure of history.

Annja understood that; she'd felt that same thrill, that same connection to the past, every single time she'd started an expedition or been involved in an archaeological dig. It was the reason she'd pursued her chosen career—as an archaeologist, not as a television host—in the first place. To reach out and touch something from the past, to hold a piece of history in your hands and wonder about the person who'd last held that object hundreds, perhaps even thousands, of years before… Yes, archaeology had a way of getting down deep into a person's soul.

But in this case it was more than that.

It wasn't just the lure of history.

It was the legend of the Blood Countess.

The idea of standing on the same stones where the notorious serial killer had once lived held a kind of eerie fascination for many people. The fact that it all happened back in the 1600s didn't make any difference; as with Vlad Dracul, the Wallachian prince who was generally recognized as the inspiration for Bram Stoker's *Dracula*, the legend of Elizabeth Báthory had grown over the ages.

However, Annja wanted to expose the history behind it all. No doubt Doug would prefer her to ignore the high road and feature reenactments of the beautiful Báthory climbing naked out of a pool of blood. But that simply wasn't Annja's style.

If she was going to do a show about Báthory, she was going to tell the truth.

Or at least as much of the truth as anyone knew.

Annja stepped to the edge of the escarpment and looked out across the forested hills and rocky crags. The late-afternoon sun lit everything with a patina of gold as it sank toward the horizon. She imagined the countess had done the same thing many times, though with her own deeply tanned skin, long auburn hair and amber-green eyes, there was little chance of anyone mistaking Annja for the pale, dark-haired woman who had terrorized this land for nearly two decades.

Never mind my baseball cap, Annja thought with a laugh as she reached up and adjusted the brim to keep the sun out of her eyes. It was a nice day, warm and clear, and she could see for miles. It would get colder later that night, but for now she was perfectly comfortable in her long-sleeved shirt, shorts and hiking boots. It was her usual dig attire, and fans of the show expected to see her outfitted in the same. She didn't mind; it was what she would have worn anyway, show or not.

As she turned away from the overlook, she reviewed what she knew about the countess.

Báthory had been born in Hungary in 1560. Both an uncle on her father's side and her maternal grandfather had been princes of Transylvania. She was also cousin to Stefan Báthory, the king of Poland and duke of Transylvania. Elizabeth was raised on the family estate in Nyírbátor and taught to speak multiple languages, including Hungarian, Latin and Greek.

By all evidence an extremely intelligent woman.

Engaged to Ferenc Nádasdy, a Hungarian nobleman, at age twelve, Elizabeth became pregnant after an affair with one of the palace servants the following year. She gave birth in secret, but not before Nádasdy had the servant castrated and thrown to the dogs. The child, a daughter, was quickly disowned, and Ferenc and Elizabeth were married in May of 1575 when she was fourteen and a half years old. His wedding gift to his young bride was Csejte Castle and the territory surrounding it.

Fourteen and a half? Annja couldn't imagine getting married now, in her midtwenties, never mind a decade or so ago. She knew it was the custom of the time, but that didn't make it any easier to swallow. Especially given what happened next.

In 1578 Báthory's husband was appointed head of the Hungarian troops and led them to war against the

Ottomans. In his absence, Elizabeth was responsible for the care and upkeep of the castle and its environs, including the country house of the same name and the seventeen villages nearby.

Fertile hunting grounds for appetites that grew harsher as the years went by.

Annja knew the countess had gotten bored with castle life. She and her husband wrote letters back and forth, as any married couple might do, but Elizabeth and Ferenc talked about methods of torture to be used on the Turkish prisoners. She would suggest new techniques and her husband would report the results back to her; some of those letters were still stored among the Nádasdy family documents in the National Archives of Hungary.

Soon the countess was trying out techniques of her own on her staff, all peasants—and therefore of no consequence in her view—from the surrounding villages. Severe whippings and beatings were frequent, often for the slightest infractions.

As time went on, more girls were lured to the castle under pretense of working for the countess, and then those girls started to disappear. Unfortunately, there wasn't much the people could do about it. Báthory not only controlled the land they lived on but was related to the very authorities the villagers would've brought their concerns to.

What a terrible situation. Parents forced to watch as their daughters were taken from them with impunity. One of history's monsters, indeed.

Báthory had finally paid for her crimes. The countess was imprisoned inside this very castle. She'd lived alone for four long years before dying from some unknown illness. Even the date of her death was conjecture; several plates of food had sat untouched just inside her chambers, so there was no way of knowing if she'd been dead for a few minutes or a few days when she'd been found.

That's it! she thought. That's the opening!

Annja rushed over to the camera, snatched up the remote and got into position. She took a few deep breaths and then stared directly at the lens as she pressed Record.

"Four hundred years ago, a woman was walled up inside the castle that now stands behind me. Her crimes were so terrible she would earn a reputation as the world's foremost serial killer. Her name? Countess Elizabeth Báthory. Her rumored victims, six hundred and fifty in number, were all young women, and the savage way in which they were killed earned Báthory the nickname by which she is more commonly known—the Blood Countess. But was Elizabeth Báthory a monster? Or was she also a victim, caught between two sides of a titanic struggle for power that reverberates through this region today?

"Join me as we examine the reality and the myth surrounding the Blood Countess, Elizabeth Báthory, here on *Chasing History's Monsters.*"

3

Annja spent another hour shooting video of the castle ruins, footage she could splice in during the editing phase, and then packed up her gear. By the time she'd loaded the rented four-wheel-drive vehicle, the sun was just about down.

She drove through the small village of Čachtice, home to some three thousand residents, and headed for her hotel in nearby Nové Mesto nad Váhom, a town about five miles northeast of Čachtice.

Annja had been driving for less than five minutes when her headlights picked up a figure standing by the side of the road, frantically waving his or her arms. As she drew closer she could see it was a young woman of about twenty-five, dressed in hiker's boots and jeans and wearing a canvas jacket against the chilly evening. Behind her, Annja could see a backpack sitting on the ground.

Her first thought was *hitchhiker*, but then she caught sight of the young woman's face and realized something was terribly wrong. She pulled to the side of the road about ten yards away, turned off the engine and got out.

"Are you all right?" she called from her position by the driver's door.

The woman shouted something back at her. Annja recognized the language as Hungarian, or Magyar as it was known here, but it wasn't related to any of the half dozen languages she did speak, so there was no chance of her getting the gist of what was being said. The woman's frantic hand motions spoke a language of their own, however.

Come here! Quickly!

Most people would've been concerned at this point. A dark road with no one around made the perfect place for an ambush, and a woman driving alone in a foreign country would no doubt be an attractive target. Not only that, but she had just made it easier for any would-be bandits by getting out of her vehicle.

Annja wasn't concerned. If this was a setup, she'd deal with it. She'd been in tougher situations before and had managed to extricate herself just fine. It helped that she was the bearer of Joan of Arc's weapon, a broadsword she could pull out of where it waited for her—the otherwhere, she called it—with just a thought.

The sword had been shattered by the English commander who'd overseen Joan's execution, the pieces scattered into the mud like so much waste. In the wake of that sundering something miraculous had occurred; the lives of the two men who had been assigned to watch over Joan, a knight named Roux and his apprentice, Garin Braden, were extended indefinitely. Both were over five hundred years old and still as hearty as they had been the morning their charge had met her fate.

Roux had set out to retrieve the pieces of the sword, and one by one they'd been reunited. Annja had been present when the very last piece had been added to the puzzle and the sword had restored itself in a flash of power that bound her and the blade together in a stunning, and rather unexpected, fashion. The sword wasn't bound by the rules of time and space and so was available to her at any moment with just a thought. It made getting out of tight situations much easier.

The way the other woman was reacting, the obvious relief on her face that someone, anyone, had stopped to help, made Annja think that whatever this was, it wasn't a trap.

When Annja got closer, she realized the ground had given away on the side of the road. The woman was still talking nonstop, but now she was pointing frantically into the darkness.

Annja suddenly understood what the woman wanted. *Down there. He's fallen down there.*

Annja turned around, intending to go back for a light, and the woman shrieked and rushed forward, grabbing Annja's arm.

"Easy now, take it easy," Annja began, but the woman wasn't listening. She was clearly in panic mode, more than likely thinking Annja was leaving. The backpacker was talking a mile a minute, pointing into the darkness over the edge, and paying no attention to what Annja was saying.

Annja knew how to fix that, at least.

She dug in her heels, pulled her arm back sharply and yelled, "Wait!" as loudly as she could.

The sudden blast of sound broke through the woman's panic, and she snapped her head around to stare at Annja.

Annja held up her free hand in a "take it easy" gesture. "I'm not leaving," she said soothingly, hoping the woman understand a little English. "I'm going to get a light, so we can see."

She mimed shining a light over the edge and looking down after it.

Understanding blossomed on the other woman's face and she calmed down.

Annja turned and hurried over to her vehicle. Opening the rear doors, she pulled out one of the polymer cases containing the lights and carried it back to where the woman was waiting.

"I'm Annja," she said, pointing to herself. Then she pointed at her companion and raised her eyebrows.

That, at least, the woman understood. She smiled wanly and said, "Csilla."

"Okay, Csilla," Annja said, "show me what's got you so upset." She extended her hand palm up in a sweeping gesture, the universal "after you" sign, and then followed Csilla as she hurried over the edge of the drop and pointed downward at a spot a few feet to their left.

Annja nodded and then set the case on the ground next to her. She flipped open the catch and pulled out a handheld spotlight. The light used only a single thirty-five watt HID bulb, but it generated a fifteen million candlepower light beam that was twenty-eight hundred feet long. If there was something out there, this light would find it.

She hit the switch on the top of the rig and the beam of light leaped into existence, throwing back the darkness. The brush lining the edge of the drop jumped into view, seeming larger than life in the cold light of the spot.

Csilla nodded and pointed again, more emphatically this time.

"Siet! Siet!"

Annja didn't need to understand Hungarian to understand.

Hurry.

She did as she was told, pointing the spotlight in the direction Csilla was suggesting. Annja began to sweep the beam across the rocky slope below them.

At first she didn't see anything but the jagged shale for which the region was known, but then she caught sight of a flash of white against the harsh gray of the stone. Slowly, carefully, she swung the beam back and found the object a second time.

It was a human hand.

Female, judging by the size and shape.

It thrust up from the slope as if it were waving to them. The hand was attached to a forearm—*thank heavens!*—and the arm presumably to the rest of the body, though she couldn't see the latter. The woman was hidden by a depression in the slope.

"Hello? Can you hear me?" Annja shouted.

Silence.

She might be too injured to shout back.

"Hold on!" she called out. "I'm coming down after you!"

She thrust the spotlight into her companion's hand and ran over to the rear of her SUV. She grabbed her climbing bag and carried it over to Csilla, who was keeping the light on the hand.

"Were you traveling together?" Annja asked as she pulled several pieces of gear, including a nylon climbing rope, out of the bag. "Did she fall?"

Csilla shook her head, but Annja wasn't sure whether the woman didn't understand what Annja was saying or didn't know what had happened.

Annja pulled on a headlamp and switched it on, then grabbed the gear she'd pulled out. She looked around for a suitable spot to anchor her rope, finally selecting a tree that stood near the edge of the drop. Hurrying over, she pushed on it for a moment, testing its strength, before deciding it would do. Using a couple of slings and some carabiners, she quickly rigged an anchor and then fed the rope through it, tying the two loose ends together. She gave the rope—and the anchor—a good tug to double-check, then coiled the rope and tossed it over the edge.

She pulled on her climber's harness, secured a locking carabiner to the front and then clipped on to the rope.

"I'm going down. Keep that light on her," Annja said. Then she pointed at herself and down the slope in an effort to make her companion understand.

Csilla nodded.

Letting the rope play out between her hands, Annja

began backing down the incline. The footing was loose, and therefore treacherous. Annja wouldn't be able to get the other woman out of there if she cut herself on the shale while climbing down.

Slow and steady, Annja, she reminded herself. Slow and steady.

As she moved downward she began to edge sideways, angling toward the spot where the floodlight was shining. She called out several times, hoping for a reaction, but she didn't get anything in return. That wasn't a good sign; the woman was either too injured to respond or past the point of help. Annja hoped for the former.

An experienced climber, Annja was able to descend the hundred feet or so in less than ten minutes. She called out as she drew close.

"My name's Annja. Can you hear me?"

No response.

Annja carefully maneuvered herself over to the lip of the depression and looked down.

The woman lay facedown on the hard stone about two feet below Annja's present position, her long dark hair hiding her features. She was nude, which meant she probably hadn't been Csilla's traveling companion... and her injuries likely weren't accidental.

The woman lay unmoving and didn't respond to Annja's repeated calls. Her skin was extremely pale—blood loss?—and the woman didn't appear to be breathing.

The fall down the rocky slope had cut her body in several places, but there was very little blood around the wounds, leading Annja to believe the woman had been killed elsewhere and dumped here. Whoever was responsible must have expected the body to fall all the way to the bottom of the slope.

Fate, however, had intervened.

The woman's arm had become wedged in the cleft between two rocks, arresting her fall and holding her body in place against the slope. If her arm hadn't gotten stuck, her body would have been hidden from view and wild animals would've likely gotten to her remains long before anyone chanced upon them.

Someone would have gotten away with murder.

Getting the body out of there wasn't going to be easy, especially on her own, but Annja had to try. She could take the time to go back to Čachtice and look for some help, but the woman's weight might finally pull her arm free from the rocks while Annja was gone.

If that happened, the effort to recover the body would be considerably more difficult, never mind expensive.

No, if she was going to do something, now was the time to do it.

The question was, how?

The depression in which the woman's body rested was filled with loose rocks and debris. The footing was going to be treacherous, and it would be all too easy to step on the wrong piece of loose rock and send the body sliding free.

What she needed to do was get to a point below the body and work her way up toward it. That way, if the body slipped, she'd be in a position to do something about it.

Annja climbed back up the slope a few feet and then

moved a couple of yards to her right, far enough that her actions wouldn't have any impact on the body's position. She rappelled downslope about ten feet and then began searching for a suitable place to put an anchor. When she found it, a narrow cleft in the rock, she used a spring-loaded cam device attached to a sling to anchor the rope. She gave the anchor a tug to test it and then clipped the rope into it with another carabiner.

The wind had picked up since the sun had set, and the temperature was starting to drop. Annja could feel her hands tingle from the cold.

Get moving, she told herself. You don't have all night.

With the anchor in place, she moved confidently to her left, picking her way across the rock face until she was directly below the body. She could see it on the slope above her, just a few feet overhead.

Annja climbed upward.

She moved as carefully as possible until she could kneel next to the woman's body. She glanced around, hoping to find a spot where she could place another anchor, but all the debris made it difficult. Annja reached out and put her hand on the woman's forehead. Her skin was deathly pale and icy cold to the touch, but to Annja's astonishment she thought she felt some movement. The woman's arm was stretched out by her side, and when Annja glanced at it, she saw one of the fingers twitch.

The woman was still alive!

4

Annja's heart leaped. She reached out and felt for a pulse.

It was weak and erratic, but it was there.

In that instant, everything changed.

Time became the enemy, a crushing weight on Annja's shoulders. The woman probably had internal injuries, and exposure to the wind and rapidly falling temperatures wouldn't help. Every minute counted now. Annja needed to get the woman covered up, back to the top of the ledge, then off to a medical facility as fast as possible.

"I don't know if you can hear me, but I'm going to try to get you out of here. Don't struggle—just lie still and let me do all the work. Understand?"

She leaned in close but didn't hear anything. The woman's fingers might have twitched again in response.

"All right. Hang on. I'm going to free your arm, then roll you over."

Moving slowly and carefully, Annja put one hand beneath the woman's left armpit—the arm that wasn't trapped—and used her other to grasp the woman's wrist

just above the spot where it had become wedged between the rocks. She braced her feet as best she could
and then, before she had time to worry about it a second longer, hefted the woman upward just enough so
she could free her arm from the rocks.

No sooner had the arm come free than the woman's body began to slide downward. Annja had already
worked out what to do. She didn't hesitate, grabbing the
woman about the torso while pushing against the rock
beneath her to stop their slide.

For one heart-stopping moment Annja felt the two
of them sliding toward the drop below as the debris
shifted in response to the added weight. Annja held
the woman tightly against her chest. The anchor she'd
placed would stop their fall, but Annja might drop the
woman when the device jerked them to a halt. Thankfully the rocks were only settling into a new position,
and they stopped moving just a second or two later.
Annja sat with her back to the rock face and the injured
woman held securely in her arms.

Annja looked down at the woman she'd come to rescue. Her face was as pale as the rest of her, but even in
her present state Annja could see she was beautiful. Her
slim face, high cheekbones and full lips were framed
by long dark hair that was almost, but not quite, black.
It didn't take much to imagine what that face would be
like animated by even the slightest bit of personality.
Annja had no doubt the woman had been targeted for
that very reason.

Beauty, true beauty, always brings the predators out
of the shadows.

One of the woman's eyes was swollen shut but the other slipped open, and Annja found herself staring into her brilliant blue iris. It seemed to focus on her.

"Don't worry. I've got you. You're going to be all right," she told her. "I'm going to get you to the hospital."

The woman blinked—which Annja hoped was a sign she understood—then moved her mouth slightly.

Was she saying something?

Annja bent closer until her ear rested less than an inch above the woman's lips.

The woman tried again, her breath tickling Annja's face.

"Krv...Grófka."

Startled, Annja pulled back and stared down at the woman.

That was one Slovakian phrase she did understand. *Krv Grófka—Blood Countess.*

"What did you say?" Annja asked, not believing she'd heard correctly, but whatever it was would have to wait; the woman had slipped into unconsciousness.

If she didn't have hypothermia yet, she would soon unless Annja did something about it. Bracing the woman with her knees, Annja stripped off her coat, then gently lifted the woman and wrapped the jacket around her torso.

Now all she had to do was climb out of here while carrying the injured woman.

Get a move on, she told herself. Time's a'wasting.

It only took her a few seconds to figure out how she was going to manage the woman's weight while climbing. Taking a few slings from her belt, she fashioned a rudimentary harness and secured it around the woman's body. Keeping her cradled against her chest, like a mother carrying a child, Annja clipped the rigging into her harness.

If she slipped, at least they'd fall together.

Try not to slip.

Right. Gotcha.

Holding the woman against her chest with one arm, Annja got to her feet and began carefully moving back to the spot where she'd anchored the rope.

Csilla must have been watching what she was doing, for the light moved with Annja, lighting the way. It was full dark now so Annja was glad for its presence; it kept her from feeling alone. Once she reached the anchor, she swiftly unclipped it and stowed it back on her belt. With the rope now free she immediately began climbing upward.

Annja pulled on the rope while powering herself up the slope with her legs. Step by step, she made her way up the slope to where Csilla waited.

At the top, Csilla stepped forward and took the injured woman out of Annja's arms, allowing Annja to clamber over the edge and back on solid ground. Once there she unclipped from the rope, left it and the rest of her gear right where it fell and hurried over to her SUV, Csilla close at her heels. Between them they lay the injured woman across the backseat, and then Csilla climbed in back with her while Annja got behind the wheel.

"Hang on!" Annja cried as she started the vehicle,

threw it in gear and stomped on the accelerator, sending a stream of gravel flying out behind them as they shot down the road in the direction of Nové Mesto nad Váhom.

The village of Čachtice was closer, but it didn't have a hospital. Nové Mesto might be a few miles farther, but it had three separate hospitals, one of which wasn't all that far from her hotel. That was where Annja headed.

Knowing time was critical, Annja kept the accelerator mashed to the floor, rocketing down the narrow road as fast as she dared. She was betting they had two and a half, maybe three miles before they hit the town limits, and she let the SUV eat up the distance like a hungry beast, racing through the night.

A gentle melody broke into her train of thought, and when Annja glanced in the mirror, she found Csilla singing softly to the woman cradled in her arms. Annja didn't understand a word, but the tune and the tone of the lyrics was soothing, making her think it might be some kind of Hungarian lullaby. Csilla must have sensed she was watching, for she looked up and caught Annja's gaze with her own, then shrugged, as if to say, *What else can I do?*

Annja nodded back at her, understanding exactly how Csilla felt, and then focused on the road once more, demanding that the car go faster, as if by force of will alone they could beat the clock that was silently ticking down around them.

It wasn't long before they hit the town limits. Nové Mesto was nearly ten times the size of Čachtice and had the corresponding increase in traffic as well, but

Annja didn't slow down as Csilla leaned over the front seat and said, *"Siet!"*

Annja didn't need to be told twice. She leaned on the horn and began weaving in and out of traffic, shouting at people to get out of her way despite the obvious fact that they couldn't hear her. It didn't matter; the yelling helped release some of her stress, which, at the moment, was a welcome relief.

By the time they hit the town center they'd picked up a police escort. Annja barely heard the warbling of the siren—she was completely focused on keeping them alive long enough to reach the hospital. When the white multistory structure with a big red cross on the front appeared, she gave a shout of victory and roared into the parking lot, the police close behind.

Annja slammed the SUV into Park and jumped out, hands in the air, as the police car braked nearly on top of her. As soon as the officer managed to extricate himself from the car, he ran for the hospital doors. By then Annja had the door to the SUV open and was taking the still form of the injured woman from Csilla's arms. As she turned toward the hospital doors they burst open from the inside and the cop returned, this time with a doctor, an orderly and a rolling stretcher.

The doctor said something in his native tongue and she shook her head. "I don't speak Hungarian."

"What happened?" he asked, switching to English as he helped her lay the injured woman on the stretcher.

"I don't know. We found her halfway down a ridge by the side of the road a few miles north of Čachtice."

The doctor glanced at the cop, then bent over the patient. "Was she coherent when you found her?"

Annja remembered the comment she thought she'd heard. *Blood Countess*.

"No," she answered, brushing off the memory as a figment of her imagination. "She looked at me and seemed to understand what I was saying, but that's all."

The doctor nodded to show he'd heard her, but his attention was mainly on his patient. He began giving instructions to the orderly as they wheeled the stretcher toward the door. They were met by a pair of nurses and the little group quickly disappeared inside. To Annja's surprise, Csilla followed them.

As she watched them go, someone beside her said, "You should get that looked at."

Annja turned to find the police officer pointing at her leg. Looking down, she was surprised to find a nasty scrape across her right calf leaking blood into the top of her boot. She hadn't even been aware she'd cut herself, the adrenaline rush masking any pain she might have been feeling.

"Lovely," she said as the pain finally hit. It wasn't a serious injury, but it stung like a son of a gun. She glanced toward her SUV, then back at the police officer. He was a young guy, in his midtwenties or so.

"Don't worry, miss. I'll keep my eye on it while you get that taken care of," he said, standing a bit straighter under her scrutiny.

She gave him a smile. "Thanks. I appreciate it," she said, and then limped into the hospital after the others.

5

"Why don't you tell me your side of the story?"

Annja was sitting in an interview room at the police station with a fair-haired detective named Alexej Tamás. He was in his midthirties, and might have been attractive if he didn't have a permanent scowl plastered on his face. He'd found her at the hospital after she'd had the cut on her leg cleaned and bandaged, no doubt summoned by the officer outside. Tamás had asked her to accompany him to the station to give a statement, and she couldn't think of a good reason not to.

Now she was starting to question that decision.

Annja had been in more police stations than she liked to admit, had given more statements than she cared to recall, but still bristled at the insinuation that she was telling a "story." She might bend the truth occasionally, especially in situations that involved the sword, but this time around she was telling the whole story, and the detective's pessimism annoyed her. Still, she decided to give him the benefit of the doubt for the time being. Getting upset would only make her appear suspicious, and Detective Tamás already seemed predisposed to find the worst in people.

Better to be as cooperative as possible, Annja decided.

Smiling, she said, "Of course, Detective. I'd be happy to."

She told him about filming at Csejte Castle earlier that afternoon, being flagged down by the woman named Csilla and then climbing to help the other woman.

Tamás let her talk, making occasional notes on the legal pad in front of him, but didn't interrupt. Annja tried to read what he was writing, having gotten pretty good at reading upside down over the past few years, but the detective was writing in his native language, which might as well have been Egyptian hieroglyphics.

Then again, she probably could have translated the hieroglyphs.

Several long moments later she sat back and waited for Tamás's response. When it came, it was on a tangent she wasn't expecting.

"What were you filming at Csejte?"

She frowned. "I'm sorry?"

"I asked what you were filming at Csejte."

"Oh, just some filler for a piece we're doing on Elizabeth Báthory."

What else would someone be filming at Csejte?

"We? There are more of you?"

"Ah, no. I'm here alone. I meant 'we' in the sense of the television series I work for."

"Ah, I see. What television series would that be?"

"It's called *Chasing History's Monsters*. We look at historical figures and try to…"

He waved her explanation aside. "So you claim you didn't know the other woman—" he checked his notes "—Csilla Polgár, until she flagged you down."

This time Annja let her irritation show, but just a little. "Yes. I said that."

"So you didn't meet her here in town? She wasn't helping you with your television shoot?"

Meet her? Helping me?

"No, of course not. I told you, I'm here on my own."

"Is there someone who can vouch for what you're doing here? A producer, perhaps?"

Annja spoke without thinking. "Of course my producer can vouch for me, but what is this about? Why are you…?"

"His name?"

Annja stared at the detective. What was going on here? Did they honestly think she had anything to do with what happened to that poor woman?

She couldn't think of any other reason for the detective's questions.

"Doug. Doug Morrell," she told him flatly, showing her displeasure without actually saying anything.

Tamás was undeterred. He rose, stepped over to the door and opened it, speaking to someone in the hall outside. After a moment he came back to the table and took his seat. In his hand was Annja's cell phone, which she'd been asked to leave with the desk clerk when she'd arrived at the station.

"Let's call Mr. Doug, yes?"

She almost said, *Look, I'm not calling anyone until you tell me what on earth is...*

Annja smiled. "Of course."

She picked up the phone, started to dial Doug's office in New York and then stopped. It was close to 9:00 p.m. here in Nové Mesto. The six-hour time difference would make it 3:00 a.m. in New York. Even Doug wasn't that much of a workaholic.

One thing was for certain. He wasn't going to like being woken up at this hour.

Couldn't be helped.

Tamás was staring at her, so she stopped thinking and got to doing. She dialed Doug's cell phone and waited.

One ring. Two. Three.

"Do you have any idea what time it is, Annja?" Doug asked.

Annja couldn't tell if he was irritated or just half-asleep. With Doug, they were often the same.

"I know it's early, Doug, sorry about..."

Tamás stretched out his hand, waiting for her to give him the phone.

"Annja? What's going on? Why are you calling me at..."

"Got someone who needs to speak with you," she said, and then handed the phone to Tamás.

"Mr. Morrell? My name is Detective Tamás, Slovak Police. I wondered if you would be willing to answer a few questions about Ms. Creed?"

Annja sat there and fumed as Tamás asked Doug to confirm just about everything she'd told him, castigating herself the whole time for opening her mouth without thinking about the implications. She hadn't told Doug about the episode she was shooting; she'd intended on surprising him with it when she got back. If he told Tamás he didn't have any idea what she was doing in Hungary, that would set the detective's alarm bells ringing and he might want to keep her here for a lot longer than she intended.

Thankfully Doug had covered for her before. He must have answered the detective's questions to the man's satisfaction, because after several minutes Tamás handed the phone back to her.

"All I can say is that you'd better have a good explanation for being wherever the hell you are when I thought you were in Budapest."

There was no mistaking his tone; this time he was ticked.

"I do, Doug. And I guarantee you're going to like it. Let me finish up here and I'll call you later, okay?"

"Harrumph."

That was it—a grunt and then a dial tone. Sometimes Doug could be the worst kind of prima donna. Then again, she tended to be less than pleasant when woken up at 3:00 a.m.

She hung up the phone and slipped it back in her pocket, staring at Tamás the whole time, all but daring him to challenge her. She'd had enough of being treated like a criminal. Now she intended to get some answers.

"Satisfied?" she asked.

Tamás shrugged. "Just doing my job."

"I would think you'd be interviewing the victim, not harassing the Good Samaritan who saved her life."

The detective eyed her a moment and then sighed. "Trust me, if I could interview the injured woman, I would. Unfortunately, she passed away fifteen minutes ago, leaving you and Miss Polgár the last two people on earth to see her alive."

Annja didn't know what to say. She'd thought the woman was out of the woods when they'd gotten her to the hospital and turned her over to the medical staff.

Such a tragedy.

She wondered how Tamás had gotten word of the woman's death, as he'd been in here with her for the past half hour and hadn't taken any calls, but then she remembered his conversation with the guard outside the door when he'd retrieved her cell phone.

No wonder he'd wanted to verify her story. Annja and the woman who'd flagged her down were his only leads in what had suddenly become a murder investigation.

Annja looked up to find Tamás watching her, though this time with less hostility. She decided to risk a question.

"Have you been able to identify her?"

Tamás shook his head. "No, not yet. No one here recognizes her and there are no missing-persons reports that match her description, which probably means she isn't a local. We're searching for more information and processing her fingerprints now, but our access to the larger police databases is somewhat limited, so it will take a few days."

Her curiosity getting the better of her, she risked another. "Do they have a cause of death?"

The detective shrugged. "We won't have an official cause of death until the autopsy this afternoon, but I don't think we'll find anything surprising. She was thrown down a cliff and left to die in the cold."

Annja frowned. "But what about the blood loss?" she asked, almost to herself.

Tamás's softer expression suddenly sharpened. "Blood loss? What are you talking about?"

"Her skin was so pale, with a gray undertone to it," Annja told him. "I took that to mean she'd lost a lot of blood."

The detective relaxed. "Just a result of being exposed to the elements, I'm told. We'll know more after the autopsy."

The explanation didn't make sense to Annja—she'd seen the effects of exposure before and was convinced this was something else entirely—but she wasn't willing to raise Tamás's ire by continuing to pursue the issue. When he moved the conversation to another line of questioning, she let him do so without protest.

"What do you know about Miss Polgár?"

"No more than I've already told you," Annja said.

"To be clear, you've never spoken to her nor met her prior to tonight when she flagged you down to rescue the victim. Is that right?"

"Correct."

"What makes you think she had nothing to do with the victim's injuries?"

The question made Annja hesitate. "I'm sorry?"

"You said earlier you thought Miss Polgár had spotted the victim's upraised hand while hiking down the road and flagged down the first passing vehicle for assistance, which happened to be you."

"Yes, that's correct."

"So what made you believe Miss Polgár was traveling alone, instead of with the victim? Couldn't she have easily pushed the other woman over the edge?"

Annja distinctly remembered wondering if the two women had been traveling together, but she didn't mention that to the detective. There didn't seem to be much point, given that the injured woman was found nude. If it had been an accident, the woman would have been dressed in her hiking clothes. Annja said as much to Tamás.

"Not if Polgár knocked her unconscious and then stripped her before pushing her over the edge," the detective replied. "Polgár had several sets of clothing in her backpack, including another pair of hiking boots in a different size than those she was wearing."

Annja thought about it for a moment and then shook her head. "I didn't get that sense, Detective, sorry. She appeared genuinely concerned for the injured woman and was extremely helpful during the rescue."

"What better way to throw the authorities off her trail than to assist in the rescue of the woman she attacked and left for dead, no?"

The cynicism inherent in that line of thought made Annja happy she didn't have the detective's job. Still, she just couldn't see that young woman as the culprit.

"Thank you for your patience. We appreciate your

help with this investigation. Will you be staying in Nové Mesto much longer?"

"I have at least another day of shooting at Csejte Castle, and then some archival research at the state museum in Bratislava, so I'll be here for a few days yet."

Tamás nodded. "Please be sure to leave your contact information with the desk sergeant so I can get in touch if any more questions arise."

"Of course, Detective. I'm happy to help in any way I can."

"I appreciate that, Ms. Creed. Good day."

A uniformed officer escorted her down the hall, past another interview room where Polgár was being questioned by two plainclothes detectives. At the front desk a sergeant took down her cell phone number, the name and room number of her hotel, and asked her to keep them informed of when she intended to leave the country. Annja agreed to do so and five minutes later was standing on the steps of the police station, suddenly exhausted from her ordeal.

It had been a long day and night. It was time to get some sleep.

That, however, was easier said than done, as her rental car had been confiscated by the police as part of the murder investigation.

The rental car company was going to love this, she thought as she flagged down a cab for a ride back to her hotel.

6

Annja awoke the next morning with an uneasy feeling in her gut. The comments Detective Tamás had made during her interview lingered. She understood why he'd considered her and Csilla suspects—ninety percent of all violent crime was committed by someone known to the victim, and he'd thought she and Csilla knew each other or the woman they'd found. But once he'd learned the condition of the body and heard both of their statements, his attention should have shifted elsewhere. The idea that either of them had anything to do with the woman's death was ridiculous. The fact that he might actually think she and Csilla had brought the victim in for medical treatment in order to deflect suspicion was, well, crazy.

He hadn't seemed to be in a hurry to chase down the cause of death and that, too, set her nerves abuzz. She didn't need to be a *CSI* or *NCIS* fanatic to know that the best chance of catching a killer was in the first forty-eight hours after the crime had been committed. Leaving the crime scene, and whatever evidence it might contain, to the mercy of time and the elements while he waited for word from the medical examiner was asking for trouble. He should have had a crew out there last night.

Maybe he did, she thought. She didn't know what happened after her interview. Maybe they're still out there combing the rocky slope.

Easy enough to check, wasn't it?

She got up, made herself some coffee—wishing all the while it was hot chocolate instead—and picked up the phone. She needed to call Doug, and it was probably best if she got it over with now. Doug's mood didn't tend to improve with time.

The phone rang a couple of times, and then he picked it up.

"Doug Morrell."

"It's me," she said.

"Me? Me, who? This wouldn't be the infamous Annja Creed, would it? Wake-me-up-in-the-middle-of-the-night-without-even-an-apology Annja Creed? That one?"

Annja sighed, though she made sure to do it away from the phone where he couldn't hear. "I can explain, Doug."

"I'm waiting," he said.

Doug wasn't much younger than she was, but he knew next to nothing about history, or the state of the world, for that matter, which had a tendency to drive her nuts. He didn't care about the facts, he often said, but about the ratings. Always the ratings. He had no qualms about "enhancing" an episode with some creative special effects if he thought it would keep viewers from changing the channel. More than once Annja had been forced to threaten him with bodily harm—in a loving way, of course—if he mucked about with her carefully constructed on-screen performances. Over time they'd become friends, and Annja knew that, in the end, she could count on Doug.

She filled him in on what she was doing in Hungary and how she'd planned to surprise him with an episode on Elizabeth Báthory. Then she told him about getting caught up in a police investigation when she'd stopped to rescue the woman who'd been thrown over a cliff and…

"Wait, wait, wait!" he said, finally interrupting her stream of explanation. "Elizabeth who?"

Annja sighed again. "Báthory. Elizabeth Báthory, also known as the Blood Countess."

"Why's that?"

"Because she liked to bathe in the blood of virgins. Thought it would keep her from aging and give her immortality."

There was sudden silence on the other end of the line.

"Doug?"

Nothing.

"Doug?"

An intake of breath, and then his voice came thundering down the phone line.

"You're over there filming an episode about a woman who liked to bathe in the blood of virgins and you didn't tell me about it first? Are you insane?"

Annja wasn't sure what to say. Not that it mattered, since Doug wasn't finished.

"Not just blood, but the blood of virgins. Probably beautiful ones, at that! For heaven's sake, Annja, what were you thinking? We need to jump on this right away!"

"Ah, Doug, jump on what?"

"The reenactment, of course! We'll have to get someone good to play this Liz Batha-whatever woman and surround the bathtub with all the virgins and…"

Annja couldn't take it anymore. "The virgins were dead, Doug. How do you think she bathed in their blood?"

As usual, the facts didn't bother him in the slightest. "Well, of course they were, at some point. But not right away. And we can use that. We can most definitely use that. When will you be back with the footage?"

"I'm not sure this is such a good idea, Doug. Remember last time you tried…"

"Ancient history, Annja. We can't face today thinking about the mistakes of the past. If we're going to back you on the episode we need to be thinking about the audience. Now answer the question—how long?"

Figuring she could deal with any of Doug's so-called improvements to her episode once she was back in the States, Annja focused on getting the resources necessary to make it all work. "I need a few more days to get the right shots of Csejte Castle and then…"

"See-what?"

"Csejte Castle. The Báthory family estate here in Slovakia."

"Right, right. I knew that."

"So I should probably stick around for another three, maybe four days. I can get by on my own, no need to send anyone else, but it would help if the show kicked in some funding."

At the mention of funding, Doug's over-the-top enthusiasm was suddenly replaced with a miser's attention to details. "Funding? For what?"

"I need to eat and sleep, Doug."

"Okay, fine. I'll wire you some money tonight. Where are you staying?"

She told him.

"Three days. That's all you've got. After that I want you back here in New York with the footage so we can have the boys in the editing suite start putting it all together."

Three days. That should be good enough.

"Thanks, Doug. Got to go."

"Annja, I want…"

She hung up the phone before he could finish the sentence. The less she heard about what he wanted, the better. She could get back to the episode tomorrow; right now she needed to see what Detective Tamás was doing to solve the woman's murder.

Putting the phone back on the nightstand, she took a quick shower before getting dressed and headed out the door.

Annja was halfway across the parking lot before she remembered that her SUV had been confiscated. She went back into the hotel, asked to use the lobby phone and spent the next half hour explaining what had happened to the rental car, finally cajoling the clerk on the other end of the phone into sending another vehicle to her hotel until the first one was released by the police. When the car finally showed up it was a beat-up-looking sedan that spouted small clouds of gray exhaust at regular intervals like a mechanical whale spitting water through its blowhole. Annja didn't care; all she wanted was something to get her from one place to another.

She signed the paperwork, handed it to the clerk and settled behind the wheel. A crank of the key, a sputtering rasp of the engine until it caught and then she was wheeling the car around and dashing out of the hotel parking lot, retracing the route she'd driven so frantically last night.

Annja was fully expecting to come upon the police combing the cliff side, so she was surprised to make it almost all the way to Csejte Castle without coming upon the crime scene. Thinking that perhaps she'd gotten the distances mixed up in all the excitement of the rescue, she continued driving, only to find herself entering the village of Čachtice less than five minutes later. She hadn't seen a single police car or found anyone standing watch by the side of the road.

What on earth was going on?

She glanced at her watch, noting that it was almost 10:00 a.m.

Could they have come and gone already?

She didn't think that was possible. It should have taken them hours to search the surrounding area. Perhaps they've only done a cursory inspection and intend on coming back with a full crime scene unit?

Scowling, she pulled an abrupt U-turn. This time she drove slower, watching for the brightly colored climbing rope she'd left behind with the rest of her gear. It didn't take that long to find; the rope was still anchored to the tree, and its orange color stood out starkly against the dull gray of the tree trunk.

Annja drove well past the scene, not wanting to disturb any evidence, and then she parked by the side of the road. Getting out of the car, she stood by the driver's door for a moment, surveying the area.

There wasn't a police officer in sight.

Shaking her head, Annja hurried along the side of the road until she reached the tree she'd used to anchor her climbing gear. She looked over the edge, toward the spot where she'd rescued the injured woman.

It took a moment, things looking a bit different in daylight, but eventually she spotted the rocks that had trapped the woman's arm.

There wasn't any evidence that anyone besides her and Csilla had been here.

For a moment she considered undoing the anchor, coiling her rope and taking it and the rest of her gear, but then her good sense reasserted itself. Touching anything at this point would be interfering with a crime scene, and that was just as much a felony here as it was back in the States. While the gear was expensive, it wasn't *that* expensive, and it would be easy enough to replace. She had to believe the police would eventually take a look at the scene and they were bound to wonder how the heck she'd gotten down the slope without any gear. Best to leave it right where it was, she concluded.

Frustrated with how the morning was going, she headed back to Nové Mesto. Annja hoped she could see Detective Tamás and ask what was going on, but when she arrived back in town she found a small crowd gathered in front of the police station. She parked down the street and hurried back on foot to see what was going on.

As she drew closer, she discovered that a press conference had just gotten under way. Detective Tamás and a few others were standing on a small platform near the front door. A podium had been set up to his left, and an overweight man in a dark suit was standing behind it, speaking from a set of notes.

Four or five reporters, most likely from the local television affiliates, stood directly in front of the platform and held their microphones up. Behind the press were roughly twenty to thirty members of the general public.

Annja looked out over the small crowd, then stepped next to a young woman of about eighteen.

"Excuse me," she said, "can you tell me what he's saying?"

The girl glanced at her, then looked back at the speaker. "He's talking about that woman they brought in last night."

"I don't speak Magyar. Could you translate for me?"

She nodded. "The old guy is Sándor, the—how do you say—police inspector?"

Annja guessed she meant police chief but didn't bother to correct her.

"He's saying the case is important and that he has his best detective, Alexej Tamás, on the case. He's going to give the microphone to the detective, let him speak."

Sándor stepped away from the podium and Tamás took his place. The detective looked as if he'd had a good night's sleep, which irritated Annja.

He should've been up all night, combing that ridgeline for evidence, she thought sourly. She was starting to dislike Detective Tamás, and what he said next only served to irritate her further.

"The detective claims they are putting the proper resources into place to investigate this tragedy," the girl said. "He says they're still uncertain as to whether it was an accident, a crime or a suicide, but they hope to have more information in the next twenty-four hours."

"Accident?" Annja muttered, feeling her fury rising. "What on earth is he talking about? There's no way it could be either an accident or a suicide!"

The girl looked at her again, but this time her gaze lingered and Annja recognized the gleam of interest in her eyes.

"You know something, don't you?" she asked.

Annja grimaced, realizing she'd said more than she'd intended, but perhaps she could turn this to her advantage.

"Keep translating and I'll fill you in on what I know afterward."

"Promise?"

"Scout's honor," she said, holding up three fingers.

The fact that Annja had never even thought about being a Girl Scout was completely beside the point.

There wasn't much more after that, however. Tamás spoke for another minute—mostly platitudes about doing all they could to get to the bottom of things—and then took a few questions from the press. They still hadn't identified the woman and asked for the press's help; photographs of the woman's face were circulated through the crowd, and Annja took one for herself.

When the press conference wrapped up, she was more frustrated than when she'd arrived.

"I've seen you before, haven't I?"

Annja turned to find the girl staring at her, studying her features more closely this time.

"I don't think so," she told her, looking away.

But the girl would not be denied.

"Yes!" she exclaimed. "Yes, I have! You're that woman from the TV show, the one that was just filming in Prague."

Annja glanced around, afraid one of the journalists would overhear and take an interest in what was making the girl increasingly excited. She needed to get off the street.

"Not here," she said, grabbing the girl's hand and pulling her through the crowd. "Come on."

Annja led the girl to a café a short distance down the street. They settled into a table in back. Annja ordered coffee for both of them; she really didn't want any but knew the waitstaff would hover until they ordered.

When she turned back, she found the girl grinning at her, holding up her cell phone. A picture of Annja working with the film crew outside Faust House was displayed on the screen.

"You're Annja Creed, from *Chasing History's Monsters*," the girl said triumphantly. "My friend is a huge fan, so we went to watch you filming your show in Prague."

Annja couldn't deny it now, not with her own picture staring back at her, so she went with the flow, hoping to learn something useful from the situation. The girl *had* helped her after all.

"You're right. You've caught me. I'm Annja. Nice to meet you," she said, holding out her hand.

"Brigitta," the girl replied, shaking Annja's hand. "My friend is going to flip when I tell her I had coffee with you."

"Yes, well, about that…" Annja began. "Perhaps you can wait a few days before doing so?"

Brigitta was watching her closely. "You're not here on vacation, are you? You're working, and whatever you're working on has to do with the woman from the press conference, doesn't it? That's why you know what happened!"

Brigitta was no slouch, Annja had to give her that.

"Yes, I'm working. And it *might* have to do with the woman they were just talking about. I'm not sure yet, though, and that's why you can't tell your friend about meeting me. If word gets out that I'm here, I'll have a difficult time finding the information I need."

The girl's eyes had gotten wider as Annja spoke, and now she leaned forward.

"It's the Blood Countess, isn't it?" she asked quietly. "She's come back, just as legend claimed."

Annja was shocked. That was twice in less than twenty-four hours that she'd heard Báthory's nickname floated about. Granted she was in Báthory country, but still…

"What legend is that?"

Brigitta laughed. "Right. Like the host of *Chasing History's Monsters* doesn't know the legend of the Blood Countess's return?"

"Humor me," Annja said with a smile.

"After she was tried and convicted of bathing in the blood of all those women, the king had her walled up inside her own bedroom suite as punishment for her crimes. You know about that, right?"

Báthory hadn't gone to trial, was never convicted and was walled up inside her bedroom at the request of her own family, but that was beside the point, apparently. Annja just clenched her teeth and nodded, seeing no need to correct her companion.

"She lived for four years—four years, can you imagine that!—before they found her dead on her bedroom floor."

"Yes, that's true," Annja said. "But that's nothing new. Most people who know anything about Elizabeth Báthory's history know that."

"Yes, but what they don't know is that Báthory wrote a message in blood on her bedroom wall before she died."

Uh-huh, Annja thought. Aloud she said, "And that would be…?"

The girl's eyes gleamed. *"I'll be back,"* she said, in what was quite possibly the worst Austrian accent Annja had ever heard.

As Annja sat there, staring at her without expression, Brigitta burst into laughter. "I had you! I totally had you!"

Annja wasn't amused. "Right. Well, it was good meeting you, but now I've…"

"Wait! Wait!" the girl said between giggles, reaching out and grabbing Annja's arm to keep her from leaving. "I'm sorry. I was just joking around. I'll tell you the real story. Honest."

Grudgingly Annja let herself be persuaded. Something about the girl called to her, and she had learned to trust such instincts since possessing the sword. There was information to be learned here; she was certain of it.

"I wasn't kidding. The countess did write on the wall of her bedroom before dying. She used candle wax to do it, though, not blood. They even found the candle in her hand."

"I see." Annja eyed her skeptically.

"No, seriously," Brigitta protested. "The family tried to cover it up but word leaked out. Some say it was through the countess's lover, though how anyone could love a woman like that, I don't know."

Growing tired of all the chitchat, Annja said, "Can you please get to the point?"

"Oh, right. Sorry. The countess wrote *amikor vissza* on the wall above her bed."

"Which means?"

"*When I return.* How creepy is that? Maybe she's come back. Maybe it was the countess that killed those girls after all."

Annja was about to thank her for her time and get the heck out of there when the word Brigitta had used hit her like a shovel over the head.

Girls.

Plural.

Annja settled back into her seat and stared at the teenager sitting across from her.

"What girls?" she asked.

7

The phone rang seven times before it was answered. That wasn't a good sign; it meant she'd considered not even taking his call. She only did that when she was annoyed with him, and her annoyance would make the news he'd called to deliver that much more dangerous. He was going to have to be careful.

When she finally answered the phone, all she said was, "Yes?"

"We may have a problem."

"I pay you to handle the problems. Why are you bothering me?" she asked.

"This one's a little different."

"I'm listening."

"Something went wrong with the latest disposal. The subject was recovered by two women and brought to the hospital in Nové Mesto. The police were notified."

There was a pause and then, "And?"

"The subject was neutralized as per our usual containment plan. Arrangements have been made and the investigation will take its usual course."

"So what's the problem?"

"One of the women who recovered the subject is an American media personality. The host of a popular television show."

"Who is she?"

He checked his notes. "Her name is Annja Creed. She's the host of a program called *Chasing History's Monsters*."

There was a chuckle from the other end of the line. "How interesting. Was she alone with the...subject?"

"For a brief time, yes."

There was another pause, a much longer one this time.

"Did they speak?"

He sighed quietly. "It's hard to say. I don't believe the subject was able to do so, but I could be wrong."

Then he held his breath. This was the moment. If she told him to deal with it, he was all right. He would do as required and that would be that. But if she said she needed time to consider the issue or that she was sending someone else to handle the problem, then he would need to cut and run as swiftly as possible. The cleanup crew would have orders to eliminate any potential threat or loose end and, given what he knew, he would be priority number one for both.

The silence stretched and he was starting to think about putting down the phone and getting out while he still could when she finally spoke.

"Send me what you can dig up on this Creed person. Keep an eye on her but do not take any other measures until I tell you to do so. This may actually play to our advantage."

He let out the breath he didn't know he'd been hold-ing, cleared his throat and said, "Of course."

She hung up the phone without another word, the dial tone suddenly loud in his ear.

He didn't mind.

Escaping her wrath for another day was good enough.

8

"What do you mean, 'girls'?" Annja asked. "Has there been more than one?"

Brigitta nodded. "Of course. The Blood Countess needs many victims to fill her bath, doesn't she?"

She seemed to think Annja was crazy for asking the question. But Detective Tamás had made no mention of any other woman murdered in such a fashion. Could it be that he didn't know? Or had he been playing his cards close to his vest, not wanting to tip his hand when Annja was still a suspect?

"Tell me about them."

But this time Brigitta wasn't as forthcoming.

"Oh, no," she said. "We had a deal. I translate for you and you tell me what you know about the woman from the press conference. Spill it. Then I'll tell you about the others."

Not the type to back out on a deal, Annja reluctantly did as she was asked. She told Brigitta about her visit to Csejte Castle and about how she'd helped rescue the now-deceased woman on the road back to Nové Mesto. She left out the details, giving a broad overview of what had happened, but the teenager sat spellbound throughout, reminding Annja that not everyone would have climbed down the rocky slope to rescue the poor woman.

When she was finished, Annja said, "Now your turn."

Brigitta launched into her tale with enthusiasm.

"Okay, so my friend's cousin knew a girl who heard that the police found a woman murdered in Kočocve, which is about an hour from here. All the blood had been drained from her body."

"Your cousin's friend?"

"No, my friend's cousin," Brigitta corrected her, not even noticing the look of disbelief on Annja's face.

She went on, "And there was this other killing, about four months ago, I think, that I heard about from this girl on Facebook. I don't know her or anything, but we're friends on Facebook, you know? She told me that hikers found a woman's body totally drained of blood and left in the middle of the woods outside of Trenčín. Can you believe that?"

No, Annja couldn't. Rumors weren't going to help her. She tried to get some concrete facts.

"Do you know the names of the victims?"

Brigitta shook her head.

"Do you know the names of the people who told you about them?"

"Well, no. They're just people I know, you know?"

Uh-huh.

"So how do you know they're telling the truth?"

"What do you mean?"

"How do you know the bodies were really found?"

"Why would they lie about something like that?" Brigitta asked.

Annja could think of at least a dozen reasons, including trying to impress the naive and rather good-looking teen who was sitting across from her waiting for an answer. Not that saying so would do any good.

She wasn't going to get anywhere with this, she decided. She should cut her losses and get back to work. At least she now knew what was said in the press conference.

"Perhaps you're right," she said, smiling to take any unintentional sting out of her remarks. "I think the information you've given me is going to be helpful. I appreciate it."

"You're going to keep looking into it, aren't you?" the girl asked eagerly.

Annja could see where this was going from a mile away. She needed to nip things in the bud before they got out of hand.

"That's for the police to handle, not me. I've got to head back to the States soon to finish the episode we were filming in Prague." She got up from the table, still smiling. "Tell your friend I said hello, and thanks for the translation help."

Brigitta asked if they could take a picture together and Annja obliged, then got out of there as quickly as she could. For a moment she'd thought the girl had been on to something, but it was nothing more than the usual rumors that followed a legend like Báthory's. When you've got a figure that epitomizes evil like the Blood

Countess did, there was plenty of room for stories to grow and change over the years. Rumors of women killed the same way were almost to be expected, even hundreds of years later.

But what about the woman she'd tried to save? Hadn't she suffered extreme blood loss? That was just it. Annja wasn't sure. She'd thought loss of blood had been a major factor in the woman's death, but Annja didn't know that for a fact.

She was tempted to do exactly what she'd told Brigitta she would—walk away and let the police handle it. Just head home to New York, focus on the show and leave whatever this was behind her.

But something wouldn't let her. There was an injustice here that needed rectifying—that was clear—and she'd been unable to walk away from such things since the day she'd accepted the sword and become its bearer.

The dead woman had no one to speak for her, and Annja knew she would have to become her voice.

But where to begin?

That was one answer Annja did have.

Start where it all began.

At the end.

The cause of death.

HALF AN HOUR later Annja was standing in the hall outside the hospital morgue, waiting for the opportunity to see the man in charge, one Dr. Petrova.

She'd already tried to speak to Detective Tamás, figuring he was her easiest avenue to the information she needed, but she had ultimately been turned away by the desk sergeant. He'd told her the detective was too busy to see her at the moment but she was, of course, welcome to wait. Annja knew where that would lead. She had better things to do than sit around waiting for the detective to deign to see her.

Like waiting for the pathologist to do the same.

No sooner had the thought occurred to her than the doors to the morgue opened and a tall man wearing a white lab coat over a dark suit stepped out. He was in his late sixties, Annja guessed, with a craggy face, arms that appeared too long for his torso and an air of superiority.

He glanced up, noticed her standing there and said something in what she thought was Slovakian.

She shook her head. "I'm sorry, I don't understand. Do you speak English?"

He glared at her but answered nonetheless. "Yes, of course. Can I help you?"

"I certainly hope so. Are you Dr. Petrova?"

He eyed her warily. "Yes."

"My name is Annja Creed. I was the one who…"

"I know who you are," he said. "What do you want?"

Annja was taken aback at the sudden hostility but plowed forward nonetheless. "I understand the woman I brought in to the emergency room last night never recovered. I was interested in knowing how she died."

"Why?"

Annja shrugged. "Personal closure, I guess. Knowing there wasn't anything more I could have done will help me get past this."

"No."

"No, what? There wasn't anything I could have done?"

"No, I'm not going to discuss the issue with you. Good day."

Petrova walked past and continued down the hall without a backward glance.

Annja stood there, stunned by his reaction. She hadn't expected him to say much—it was, after all, an active investigation—but she didn't think her knowing the cause of death would impede that investigation. His overt hostility had seemed…unusual.

As though he had something to hide.

She watched Petrova turn the corner at the end of the hall and then glanced back at the doors to the morgue.

Before she could talk herself out of it, she pushed them open and stepped inside.

9

Annja discovered there wasn't much difference between a Slovakian morgue and an American one. She saw the same stark lighting, the same white tiles, the same row of flat metal tables with the floor drains positioned underneath. The refrigeration drawers were situated along the back wall, and a darkened office loomed to her right. Two of the tables contained sheet-covered bodies, but otherwise the room was empty.

Annja breathed a sigh of relief.

There was no telling when Petrova, or anyone else for that matter, might be back. The smart thing would have been to turn around and get the heck out of there before she was discovered; she didn't think Petrova would take kindly to her trespassing. But if she'd intended to do the smart thing she wouldn't be here in the first place.

She crossed the room to stand next to the examination tables. A white sheet covered the form on the first table, but by its sheer size Annja suspected it wasn't the woman she was looking for.

Still, best not to leave anything to chance, she told

herself as she reached up and lifted the edge of the sheet, revealing the thickly jowled face of a man in his early fifties with a bullet hole just above his left eye.

She put the sheet neatly back in place and moved to the next table. This time, when she pulled the covering back, she found herself staring into the face of the woman she'd worked so hard to rescue the night before.

She pulled the sheet a little lower, revealing a large Y-shaped incision that started at the top of each shoulder and descended along the center of the woman's chest, indicating that the body had already undergone an autopsy. Now all she needed to do was find the results.

She checked the end of the table, hoping she'd find the file hanging there waiting for review, but struck out. She was going to have to look around, and the office was the obvious starting place.

When she tried the door, however, she discovered it locked.

Good thing I've got a key, she told herself with a grin.

With just a thought she summoned her sword from the otherwhere. It sprang into existence, ready for action, a broadsword with a hilt that felt as if it were made to fit her hand alone. She was overcome by the sense that she'd been born to wield this blade. Not for the first time, she found herself wondering if Joan of Arc had felt that way when the weapon was in her hands.

The clock is ticking, she reminded herself.

Placing the tip of the blade in the crack between the door and the jamb, Annja bore down on the weapon with as much force as she could muster, driving it between the two, and then she gave it a hearty twist.

The old lock gave with an audible crack.

She paused, waiting to see if the sound had attracted any attention. When no one came to investigate, she stepped into the room and turned on the lights, releasing her sword back into the otherwhere at the same time.

There wasn't much to see. A battle-scarred desk and high-back swivel chair sat in the center of the small room. Behind them, against the far well, was a row of dark green filing cabinets.

The top of Petrova's desk looked like a cyclone had hit it. Papers and files were lying in haphazard piles amid half-empty coffee cups and an ashtray full of cigarette butts. A phone must have been buried under there somewhere, because Annja could see the cord running to the wall.

She stepped over to the filing cabinets and pulled open the closest drawer. A quick glance showed that all the files inside were arranged alphabetically by last name. She checked for a "Doe, Jane," but came up empty. She had no idea what the Magyar equivalent would be.

Maybe this wasn't going to be as easy as she thought.

Checking the other cabinets revealed that they, too, were arranged alphabetically, and with that information she was able to deduce that each drawer held the cases for a particular year, with the most recent being at the far end. Unfortunately, she didn't find what she was looking for there, either.

Almost five minutes had gone by since she'd first

stepped foot in the morgue, and Annja was starting to get anxious. The longer she stayed here, the greater her chances of being caught.

Turning her back on the filing cabinets, she moved to the desk. She sat in Petrova's chair and began riffling through the folders on top. One of them caught her eye, and when she pulled it from the stack, nearly knocking over a cup of moldy coffee in the process, she saw that instead of a name this file had a number written on its tab. Curious, she opened it.

Inside she found a report on a twenty-eight-year-old male who had been discovered dead of a drug overdose. Or, at least, that was what she thought it said; she knew a few words in Czech, and Slovakian was quite similar. She looked for the section of the report where the individual's name would be listed and found the spaces blank.

That was when it clicked.

The number was for those cases where the subject was unidentified.

She searched through the stack and quickly checked the handful of files that were identified by number only, glancing at the photograph stapled to the inside left of each folder. They were split roughly between men and women, but none of them were the woman she was looking for.

She sat back, flummoxed and irritated, wondering where Petrova had put the file. She tried to remember if he'd had anything in his hands; perhaps he'd taken the file with him.

No, his hands had been empty. She was certain of it.

Which meant it had to be here somewhere.

She leaned forward, deep in thought, and only realized the doors to the morgue had opened when they banged against the interior wall. With seconds to avoid being seen, if she hadn't been already, Annja did the only thing she could think of.

She slipped underneath the desk.

A male voice called out in Slovakian. Annja only recognized one word—*Petrova*—but it wasn't too hard to figure out what was being said given the tone and inflection. "Dr. Petrova, are you in there?" or something similar was her guess.

She'd left the door to the office partially closed. Now she heard it squeak as someone pushed it fully open and footfalls sounded close by.

"Petrova?"

Annja held her breath, praying that whoever was standing on the other side of the desk didn't notice the damage to the doorjamb or find anything irregular about the fact that the lights had been left on in Petrova's absence. Something thumped onto the desktop, making her jump slightly, but she didn't give herself away.

Seconds passed and Annja didn't hear anything more. Had Petrova's visitor left the room?

She let her breath out slowly and waited a few more seconds before climbing quietly out from beneath the desk.

No one was in sight.

As she got to her feet, her gaze fell on the manila

envelope in the center of Petrova's desk. Picking it up, she opened it and slid out the file it contained.

The dead woman's face stared back at her from a picture inside the file.

Annja pulled out her cell phone and quickly took pictures of each page. When she was finished, she returned the file to the envelope and put the envelope back on the desk.

Five minutes later she was exiting the hospital and heading for her hotel, wondering how she was going to get the pages translated.

TELLING HERSELF SHE didn't really have a choice, Annja gritted her teeth and dialed the number. The phone rang twice and then a smooth male voice said, "Annja. What a pleasant surprise."

"Hello, Garin."

"Things must be quite amok for you to be calling me. To what do I owe the pleasure?"

Like Annja, Garin was tied to the sword. He'd been there the day Joan of Arc was executed, a fact Annja had once found hard to accept. That any man should be allowed to live over five hundred years was a miracle; that this gift had been given to this man, rogue and scoundrel that he was, often had her shaking her head at the unfathomable nature of the universe.

She and Garin had always had a volatile relationship. He was good-looking, in an alpha-male kind of way, with black hair, dark eyes and a neatly trimmed goatee that gave him a slightly villainous air. He was not only extremely rich but extremely arrogant, as well. When she'd first met him, Garin had tried to take the sword from her by any means possible, believing its existence made him vulnerable, but recently they'd settled into a kind of uneasy truce. Thankfully he'd also stopped trying to kill his former master, Roux, the other "old man" in her life.

She didn't trust Garin as far as she could throw him, but she had, from time to time, relied on his help when no other options were available. Like now.

Annja needed to have the file translated, and she couldn't go to her usual sources. Doug would wonder what she was doing messing about with the investigation around the dead woman instead of working on the episode he was now funding. Her friend Bart in the Brooklyn police department would ask how she'd gotten her hands on an autopsy file that was only twenty-four hours old and what, exactly, she needed it for. She wasn't ready to answer either question just yet.

She had even, momentarily, considered trying to track down Brigitta, but that seemed like more trouble that it was worth.

She'd phoned Roux first. His "gray areas" were less rigid than her own, and she knew he wouldn't hesitate to help her, but his majordomo, Henshaw, had said that Roux was playing poker in Monte Carlo for the next few days, and Annja knew that nothing could drag him away from the table when the going was hot.

That left Annja with very little choice.

It was Garin or Brigitta.

She'd almost—*almost!*—gone with the girl.

But in the end she'd sensed that this was too important to spend all that time tracking her down. Something had pulled her into this mess and she was determined to get to the bottom of it.

She gritted her teeth and said, "I need your help, Garin."

"Ah, such sweet music to my ears. I'm at your service. Give the word and I'll have the chopper pick you up and whisk you away from all your troubles."

"Totally not going to happen," she told him sharply. "Can you be serious now?"

He laughed, and Annja found herself turning red at the sound. That son of a…

"What can I do for you, Ms. Creed?" he asked while working to stifle his laughter.

"Do you know someone who can read Slovakian?"

"For the right price, I can find someone who reads ancient Sumerian. Slovakian certainly won't be a problem."

Annja had hoped as much, but it was good to hear her hunch confirmed. "All right. I'm sending you an email with some documents I need to have translated."

She had already sent the images from her phone to her laptop and had the email ready to go. All she had to do was hit Send.

Garin's joviality disappeared as he turned his attention to business. "It's coming through now." A pause. "Okay, I've got it."

"If you can have your people take a look…" Annja began, but didn't get any further.

"This is an autopsy report."

"How do you…?"

"Twenty-three years old. Good physical shape. Dark hair and eyes. Name unknown. What have you gotten yourself into, Annja?"

The way he asked the question made her certain it was rhetorical, but she answered nonetheless.

"I stopped to help an injured woman the other night and she died from her injuries. I want to know what happened. How did you get the information translated so fast?"

"Hmm, what's this now? A toxicology report?"

What on earth?

Then, suddenly, she understood. Garin could read Slovakian.

"What does it say?" she asked.

"The toxicology report? Completely inconclusive."

"Inconclusive for what?"

"Anything. The blood they drew was apparently contaminated with a foreign substance they couldn't identify. There's also a note that the sample available was of such a small size they couldn't run the screening test more than once."

Annja frowned. "Why didn't they just request another sample?"

She could hear Garin tapping the keys on his computer. "Doesn't say."

"Okay, forget that," she said, waving it off for the time being. "The main autopsy report should say the cause of death."

"It does."

Annja waited, but Garin didn't say anything more.

"Well, what is it?" she asked.

"What do I get out of it?"

For a moment, Annja was taken aback. What does he get out of it?

Then she remembered she was dealing with Garin. She'd never met a more selfish individual. He didn't do anything unless there was a percentage in it for him.

This included, apparently.

"Have you no shame, Garin? A woman was murdered."

"Happens every day, dear Annja, more times than you can count. That's irrelevant to me. You want to know what this report says. I want to know what I get if I give you that information."

The problem was that Annja didn't really have anything to trade. Garin was richer than most developing countries and could buy almost anything that caught his eye. If he couldn't buy it, he could usually charm someone into providing it for him. He quite literally wanted for nothing when it came to material possessions. Yes, on occasion Annja had been able to entice him with a particularly interesting artifact or with information on a lost culture or an intriguing historical puzzle; but this time around she had nothing to trade.

"I'm asking you nicely, Garin."

"And what? I'm just supposed to give you what you need because of that?"

She knew he was pushing her buttons, goading her into losing her temper, but she could feel her control slipping away despite the knowing.

"You know what? Never mind. I'll figure it out myself!" She pulled the phone away from her ear and hit the end call button.

Sitting down in front of her laptop, she called up an online translation service and set the software to convert her English words to Slovak. Then she typed "cause of death" into the box on the left. In the box on the right, the words *príčina úmrtia* appeared.

"Ha!" she said, as if Garin could hear her back in Munich.

Annja then called up the photos she'd taken in the morgue office and searched them for the phrase. She found it on page four, and in the box next to it were the words *strata krvi*.

Another query into the online translator and she sat back, staring at the words blinking at her from her computer screen.

Blood loss.

There were several lines of notes directly beneath, no doubt giving more details, but try as she might she couldn't get the translation to make any sense. The words weren't all that clear in the photograph and without any real knowledge of the Slovak language all she was doing was guessing at what some of the words and letters might be. The translation software was kicking back nonsense as a result.

She sat there, tapping her fingers on the tabletop. Then, with a sigh, she turned and picked up her phone once more. She hit the redial button and waited for Garin to answer.

He picked up before it finished ringing the first time. Of course.

"A weekend of skiing with me at my chalet in Switzerland," he said.

"Lunch at the Mall of the Americas in Bloomington, Minnesota."

She couldn't think of a more innocuous place. It would drive Garin completely nuts.

He was far from finished with his bargaining, however.

"An overnight visit at my home here in Munich. Pajamas optional."

Right.

"Dinner in Paris at Roux's, with Henshaw as chaperone."

Garin sputtered indignantly. "Roux's? Henshaw? Are you mad, woman? I've already spent more years than I care to count under that senile old man's thumb, and his *manservant*—" Garin said the word the way someone else might say *the plague* or *hemorrhagic fever* "—is even worse than he is."

Annja had him and she knew it.

"Fine. Last offer, take it or leave it. Dinner in New York at a restaurant of my choosing."

"And a nightcap at that charming little flat of yours in Brooklyn?"

"Dinner. That's it," she said.

"Fine."

Garin's tone was one of annoyance, but Annja had learned to detect the subtleties in his voice, and she thought he was secretly pleased.

She had to admit she was, too. A little. At least she'd get a first-class meal out of it.

"The woman died of blood loss."

"I already know that! What do the notes beneath the cause of death say?"

Garin was silent for a few moments as he puzzled it out. "Whoever wrote this has the handwriting of a child," he said at last.

And you've got the disposition of one, Annja thought.

"A few of the words are hard to make out, but for the most part the notes appear to deal with the excessive blood loss the victim had undergone prior to dying."

"Excessive?"

"That's what it says. Apparently he didn't have to drain the fluid from the body before beginning the autopsy. He found two large puncture wounds in the thigh close to the femoral artery and surmises that the blood loss was a result of these injuries."

Annja knew the human animal was tenacious, that it would fight for its life with tooth and nail if necessary, and that sometimes—not often, but sometimes—people could cling to this world by the narrowest of margins, refusing to give in to that creeping darkness that waited to swallow them whole. But to remain alive with only the barest amount of blood left in the body? That went beyond tenaciousness, verging instead on the miraculous.

So says the woman carrying the mystical sword of a long-dead saint, Annja thought with a wry shake of her head.

One thing was clear: this had been no accident.

"Is that it?" she asked.

"Yes. So where shall we dine? I'm thinking perhaps…"

"Thanks, Garin, you've been really helpful. I'll call you about dinner. Bye for now."

She hung up the phone before he could say anything more. Annja knew he wouldn't call her back; his pride wouldn't let him. She would have to deal with him sooner or later, but for now, later was just fine.

She stood there, pondering what she'd just learned. It seemed clear that the woman had been the victim of a vicious attack. Maybe the killer was trying to tie his activities to the legend of the Blood Countess to earn greater notoriety. All hell was going to break loose when the press learned that the victim had been drained of most of her blood. If Annja was going to find justice for this woman, she needed to stay ahead of all that.

The first priority was finding out just who the victim was. Hopefully the woman's identity would lead to the killer.

The police hadn't been able to identify the victim through fingerprints or dental records, so she must not have been in trouble with the law. Nor had she applied for work with any government agency or any major corporate firm. Given that Nové Mesto was one of the larger communities in the area, it seemed likely that the woman had not come from the city but from one of the smaller, rural towns nearby.

Like Čachtice.

Best to start there, Annja thought as she headed for her car.

10

Annja had learned that crimes were not usually solved by brilliant deductions or leaps of logic in the style of Sherlock Holmes but by the slow and steady accumulation of information. Like archaeologists at a dig site, sifting through layers of dirt to get to the artifacts buried by the passage of time, so, too, do detectives sift through the evidence to find out who committed the crime and why.

She knew the police were hoping someone would see the press conference, recognize the woman's picture and call to tell them who she was. But that could take days, maybe even weeks, and Annja was convinced the killer would strike again, and soon. Better to act now than to wait for information to come in on its own timetable.

When Annja arrived in the village of Čachtice, she parked in the town square. Taking the photograph of the dead woman with her, she began knocking on doors, asking those who answered if they knew the woman in the picture.

She had spent some time with her English-Slovak

phrasebook and memorized a few key phrases, such as "Do you speak English?" and "Have you seen this woman?" Combined with the words for "yes" and "no"—*ano* and *nie*, respectively—Annja had all the Slovakian she needed to make a little headway into the subject of the murdered woman should anyone be willing to talk with her.

Unfortunately, she soon discovered that they weren't.

Time and time again Annja would knock on the door and be greeted pleasantly enough by the home owner, only to have that same individual shake their head and withdraw the moment she pulled out the victim's photograph. Several times those of the older generation took one look at the picture and gave her the sign of the horns to ward off evil—a hand gesture formed by extending the index and little fingers while holding the ring and middle fingers down with the thumb—before slamming the door in her face.

Annja put their reactions down to their not wanting to talk about the dead with a stranger, but she had to admit to a certain amount of unease each time it happened. She knew it was crazy, but it still made her wonder just what these people knew that she didn't. The hairs on the back of her neck would stand at attention every time they forked their fingers at her.

She wandered down street after street, knocking on every door she found but getting nowhere. It was long past dark by the time she decided to call it quits. Tired from being on her feet all day and frustrated at the lack of results, Annja headed back to her car. She glanced over her shoulder and thought she saw something duck out of sight behind one of the buildings about thirty yards away.

Probably just a dog, she thought, and kept walking.

But after a few more minutes an itch began to form between her shoulder blades. She'd had the feeling often enough to know what it meant. Someone was watching her.

She stopped, turned and scanned the road behind her.

It was empty.

Or, at least, it appeared so, but Annja knew it wasn't. She might not be able to see whoever was back there watching her, but she could feel the weight of their stare.

Nothing about it felt friendly, either.

Annja turned back and continued on her way, her thoughts churning along at a furious pace as she analyzed the situation.

The streets were deserted at this hour, since the rural residents of this community synchronized their lives with the rise and fall of the sun. The road she was on was lit only by dim lamps spaced about a hundred yards apart, creating large stretches of shadow that were dark enough to hide anything.

To get to her car, which was still at least half a mile away, she was going to have to brave that gauntlet and hope whoever was behind her didn't catch up before she reached the safety of the rental.

A head start would be nice...

And she knew just how to create one.

She looked back over her shoulder, betting that whoever was following her would duck out of sight, just as they had before. Her guess proved correct; she caught the barest flash of movement as her tail slipped behind a parked car.

It was the break she was looking for.

The moment her tail went to ground, Annja took off running, the hard rubber soles of her boots pounding out a rhythm against the blacktop. She pumped her arms as she ran, wanting to put as much distance between herself and whoever was behind her as she could before they discovered she'd played them.

Five yards.

Ten yards.

Twenty yards.

She was starting to think her imagination had been running wild when there came a shout from behind her, followed quickly by one—no, two—sets of footfalls pounding the pavement in her wake.

Apparently whoever was back there wasn't alone.

Things were about to get interesting.

Annja thought about running to the nearest door and pounding on it while yelling for help, but she decided against it. Who knew how long it would take for someone to answer. Given the reception she'd received earlier, she wasn't confident anyone *would* answer her pleas.

She had no idea what those chasing her wanted, but if they were willing to go through this much trouble to catch up to her, then it probably wasn't good.

Better to try to increase the distance between them while looking for other options.

So move it, girl! she told herself.

She tucked her head down and ran.

The street she was on was entirely residential, but she remembered some shops and a restaurant or bar about four blocks away. If she could reach that area ahead of her pursuers, she could slip inside one of the stores and ask for help. The men following her might be happy to chase her down under the cover of darkness, but she doubted they'd do the same once she was in the light.

She passed beneath one of the streetlamps and kept going, counting silently. When she reached ten she chanced a look back and was just in time to see two large figures sprinting through the glow of the lamp.

The two men were gaining on her.

Annja was a good runner, and her strength and speed had seemed to be slightly enhanced when she'd taken possession of Joan's sword, but even that extra edge wasn't going to be enough, she realized. She'd been walking the streets for hours and was already tired before this chase began. She wouldn't be able to maintain her short head start for very long, not if those behind her were fresh and in reasonably good shape. If she was going to escape, she needed to outwit them rather than outrun them.

With this in mind, Annja cut right, down the next street she came to, raced ahead and then turned left at the next corner. She was still headed in the same direction, but she hoped that by breaking their line of sight she might encourage them to give up the chase. If they were just random thugs, they might decide the rewards weren't worth the effort now that she was on to them.

On the other hand, if they persisted, she'd know she probably wasn't just some random target.

A dog barked suddenly and lunged at her from behind a fence nearby, but she ignored it and raced on. Moments later she heard the dog do the same thing at the men tracking her.

She could hear her boots striking the pavement as she ran, no doubt alerting her pursuers to where she was, and wished she could stop and kick them off. But if she did, they'd catch her.

Another street, another change of direction, her heart pounding in her chest and her breath coming out in short gasps. The initial adrenaline rush was starting to wear off and she was feeling the effects of spending all day on her feet. Thankfully she was closing in on her destination, and she began to think she might make it. She could only hear one pair of footsteps behind her now and hoped the second man had dropped out of the race. One person would be much easier to deal with.

A group of parked cars loomed to one side and she desperately wanted to stop and see if any of them might be unlocked but she didn't dare. Stick with the plan, she told herself. Almost there.

As she passed the final two cars she saw movement out of the corner of her eye. Annja looked that way just in time to see a dark figure rise up from between the vehicles and lunge toward her.

Annja reacted instantly, her actions honed by years of practice with and without the sword. She swung her arm out beside her in a classic martial arts blocking maneuver, fist clenched and forearm tight, knocking her assailant's arms away from her before he could grab hold. The move exposed the side of her attacker's head as his body was pushed in a semicircle by the force of her blow.

The voice of her first martial arts instructor suddenly echoed in Annja's head. *The best defense is a good offense. Strike and then strike again.*

Annja took that advice.

She could smell oil and grease—mechanic, maybe?—as she continued her spin, lashing out with the elbow of her other arm, slamming it into the side of her assailant's head with all the force she could muster.

The man grunted in pain and doubled over, only to have his face collide with Annja's right knee as she brought it up toward him.

There was a dull crack as his nose, or perhaps his cheek, broke with the impact.

That was enough; the would-be attacker dropped between the cars like a wet sack of laundry.

Annja's breath was heavy in her ears as adrenaline flooded her system, but that didn't prevent her from hearing the sound of running feet coming from the darkness behind her.

Now the odds were in her favor, however, and she was tired of running. It was time to take a stand.

She reached into the otherwhere and drew forth her sword, the blade gleaming in the darkness as the moonlight reflected off its surface. She swung the sword in front of her, making it clear that she knew how to use it.

"Come on!" she shouted into the darkness. "Let's see what you've got!"

The running footsteps slowed and then stopped.

Annja turned directly toward the sound and thought she could see a figure standing in the shadows about ten yards away. She took a few steps in that direction, sword held high, and that was enough to convince whoever was out there that discretion was the better part of valor.

Her assailant turned tail and ran off without a word.

Annja watched him go until he was out of sight.

Then, and only then, did she release her sword back into the otherwhere.

Her first assailant was still unconscious, which was good since Annja wasn't all that delicate when she dragged him a few yards up the street and into the circle of light from the nearest streetlamp.

He wasn't much to look at—just a bullnecked thug dressed in oil-stained coveralls and a pair of work boots. Annja quickly searched him, hoping to find some ID, but came up empty-handed. That alone didn't mean anything—people left their wallets behind all the time—but given that the duo seemed to have been following her, Annja took it as a sign the entire encounter had been planned ahead, right down to the lack of identification should one of them be waylaid in the process.

That suggested something larger at play than a simple robbery or sexual assault.

So now what? She didn't relish the thought of sitting in the police station all night while filing assault charges, especially when it was going to come down to a "he said, she said" situation. The cops would see that her assailant had come down on the wrong side of the situation, and they might even try to press charges against her if the "victim" came to and started spinning a story about getting attacked by a crazy woman who knew karate.

That, she didn't need.

In the end she decided an anonymous phone call to the police about two drunk men fighting in the street would be best. When they arrived, they'd find her assailant unconscious, assume he'd gotten the short end of the stick and throw him in the drunk tank overnight for good measure.

Annja propped the unconscious man against the lamppost, made the call to the authorities and then continued down the street.

Five minutes later she reached the restaurant/bar—perhaps *tavern* would be a better word—she'd been running toward and decided that after the day she'd had, she deserved a drink.

She pushed open the door and stepped inside.

11

The tavern consisted of one long rectangular room with a bar on the left and a dozen or so round-topped tables and chairs on the right. Two customers were sitting at the near end of the bar and a handful of others at the tables. There didn't appear to be a waitress; if you wanted something you walked over to the bar and asked the barkeep.

That was fine with Annja; she didn't want to deal with any more people than necessary.

She crossed the room and took a stool at the far end of the bar, away from the other customers and with a good view of the entrance. As she sat down a door to her right opened and a woman came out carrying two plates of food. She set them down at the end of the bar and called out to the barkeep before disappearing into the other room once more. As she did so, Annja got a good look into the kitchen just beyond and noted the open door at the far end of the room leading outside.

At least there's another way out, she thought.

A metal clip at the edge of the bar held a couple of laminated menus, and she grabbed one when she saw the barkeep eyeing her. She turned slightly so she could pretend to study the menu while keeping her eye on the entrance. She wanted a good look at whoever came in next, just in case assailant number two had decided to double back and follow her again.

When five minutes had passed and no one entered, Annja figured she was safe and focused on the menu. The smell of food wafting out of the kitchen reminded her that she hadn't eaten since morning; she was famished.

The barkeep wandered over when she put the menu down, drying his hands on his apron as he came. He said something to her in Slovak, but then switched to English when Annja shook her head to indicate that she didn't understand.

"Dinner or just drinks?"

"Both. I'll have the steak and whatever dark beer you recommend, please."

The barkeep nodded. "Be a few minutes for the steak, but I can get you the beer right away."

"That's fine."

The barkeep shouted something into the kitchen, got her the beer and then left her alone until the food was ready. Annja kept her eye on the door while she waited but no one came in after her and gradually she relaxed.

Ten minutes later the kitchen doors banged open and a hard-looking woman with a hairnet and an apron deposited her plate in front of her without a word. When the hot smell of freshly cooked meat hit the air Annja forgot all about her mysterious follower and dug in with gusto.

She was halfway through her dinner when the bell above the door announced a new customer. Annja glanced in that direction, her concerns about being followed still fresh in her mind. She relaxed when she saw that the man entering the room was in his midsixties and walked with a limp. The man who'd been following her had moved much too fast to have been hampered by an injury. So she ignored him and went back to her meal.

Until he pulled out a chair and sat down next to her at the bar.

Annja glanced over and found herself staring into the bluest eyes she'd ever seen. She might have been taken in by those eyes if they weren't filled with a flatness that instantly put her back on guard and had her hand twitching for want of her sword.

He held her gaze for a moment and then smoothed a hand over his craggy face and white beard before he looked away, glancing about the room as if checking to be sure no one was watching them. Apparently satisfied that they weren't being observed, he picked up the menu and held it in front of him, pretending to study it.

"People around here don't like it when strangers start asking questions," he said in English.

Annja felt a chill run up her spine. This man hadn't been following her, but he could've been working with those individuals. Why else come in here after her?

Annja turned her body slightly in his direction, leaning away from the bar and giving herself more room to maneuver. "Is that a threat?"

"Don't look at me!" he said sharply, but beneath his breath. "Keep eating."

Annja did as she was told, her thoughts whirling. It seemed she might have misjudged the situation.

"It's not a threat. At least, not from me."

Keeping her voice low and her attention on her plate, she said, "That's a bit contradictory, wouldn't you say?"

He grunted but didn't say anything more. The barkeep stepped over and asked what he wanted. The man ordered a lager and was quiet until his drink was set in front of him. Once the barkeep had gone back to his place at the other end of the bar, the newcomer said, "You've been asking questions about the killing the other night, flashing that girl's picture about. That can be dangerous, Ms. Creed."

The fact that he knew who she was didn't surprise her. He had sought her out after all. But Annja had no intention of acknowledging his comments, at least not until she knew who she was talking to and maybe not even then. Instead, she asked him a question.

"Who are you?"

He considered his response for a moment and then said, "A friend."

Annja shook her head as she stabbed a piece of meat with her fork. "Not good enough," she said, taking a bite.

"It's going to have to be."

Annja wiped her face with her napkin and made to get up from her chair. "Nice chatting with you."

The stranger's arm shot out and pinned her wrist to

the bar, the bulk of his body hiding his action from the barkeep and the other customers.

"You can't leave," he said.

Annja's free hand twitched and she almost called her sword, but she managed to resist the impulse at the last moment. Her anger, however, was less controllable. "Get your hand off me before I cut it off," she said in an icy tone.

"There is a man waiting across the street. I believe he's looking for you. It isn't safe for you to leave," he said. "Not yet."

He took his hand off her arm as requested.

For a moment she considered marching over to the front door and going outside, just to see what would happen, but then her good sense asserted itself. She'd already had one confrontation tonight—she didn't need another. Annja settled back into her chair and waited for her companion to make the next move.

She watched from the corner of her eye as he casually looked around the room, checking to see if anyone had noticed their interaction. Then he glanced at her and went back to staring at the bar top.

"I'm sorry. I didn't mean to be harsh."

Annja accepted his apology with the slightest of nods.

"My name is Novack. I didn't come here to harm you. On the contrary, I came to warn you that you've chosen a dangerous path. If you persist in asking questions, you're only going to draw attention."

"Attention from whom?" Annja wanted to know.

"The wrong kind of people."

Annja leaned closer, her emotions flaring. "A woman was murdered. If my questions bring those responsible out of hiding, then so be it."

"They've already killed once. Who's to say they won't make you their next target?"

Annja smiled but there was no warmth in it. "They're welcome to try," she told him.

Novack—first name or last name?—glanced around and then reached inside his coat. Annja stiffened, expecting him to pull a weapon, and was relieved when it turned out to be a small manila envelope.

He slid it across the bar toward her hand.

"I was hoping you might say that. Meet me in the Church of the Holy Savior in Čachtice tomorrow evening at seven if you want to know more."

Annja frowned. "I'm not going to meet you anywhere," she said, even as she picked up the envelope and opened it. "Why would I meet with someone who won't even tell me their full name?"

She glanced inside the envelope and her breath caught in her throat. Staring up at her was a color photograph of a naked woman lying dead on the ground somewhere. The front of the photo was stamped with the word *Doklad* in bright red.

That was a Slovak word she knew.

Evidence.

"What on earth...?" she began, looking up, only to find Novack halfway across the tavern headed for the exit.

She opened her mouth to shout after him, but then remembered how careful he'd been to avoid being seen speaking with her, and cursed under her breath instead. She jumped off her bar stool, threw some money on the bar to cover her bill—and then some, she thought—before hurrying to catch up.

By the time she reached the street, however, she was too late.

Novack was nowhere to be seen.

12

With Novack's words of warning echoing in her head, Annja kept a sharp eye out as she made her way the last few blocks to her car. She didn't see anyone following her, but that didn't mean they weren't out there somewhere, watching her. When she reached her car she got in, locked the doors and drove straight to her hotel.

Inside her room, she pulled the photograph out of the envelope and sat down to have a closer look.

When she'd first seen the photo she'd thought it might show the woman she'd tried to rescue, but now she realized that wasn't the case. This woman was not only blonde where the other was brunette, but she was also taller with a slimmer build. She was lying on her side, her eyes open and staring at the camera, and Annja could feel the accusation frozen forever in that gaze.

Find them. Find whoever did this and make them pay.

As with the woman Annja had found, there were no major wounds or other visible injuries to suggest a cause of death. Annja looked for the puncture wounds that had been described in Jane Doe's autopsy report, but the woman's position prevented her from seeing if they were present.

She didn't want to jump to conclusions. She had no idea where or when this photo was taken. It might not be related to the other case at all. He might be using it to lure her in for some reason.

But the more she looked at the photo, the more she stared into the dead woman's unseeing eyes, the more convinced she became that whoever killed this woman had also killed the other.

That made at least two. Were there more?

She didn't know, but she intended to find out.

Grabbing her laptop, Annja fired it up and spent some time searching for new reports of murdered women in the Trenčín region of Slovakia. While she was able to pull up a few incidents, she didn't find much beyond articles about the press conference from earlier that morning.

If she wanted to get to the bottom of this, it looked like she'd have to meet Novack at the appointed time and place after all.

Both excited and frustrated by the day's events, Annja decided to call it a night. She took a quick shower to rid herself of the dust kicked up from the day's canvassing efforts and climbed beneath the sheets, thoughts of the dead women dancing about in her mind as she drifted off to sleep.

THE FOLLOWING MORNING had its own share of surprises. While enjoying a coffee and croissant in the hotel dining room, Annja glanced at the TV and saw Detective

Tamás stepping up to the podium for another press conference. English subtitles were running along the bottom of the screen, allowing her to read along.

Tamás looked somber in a dark suit and tie, but he seemed to give off an air of smug satisfaction as he addressed the small group of reporters.

"Ladies and gentlemen, thank you for being here. We have two pieces of news to share with you this morning.

"The first is that we've identified the victim as Marta Vass, a twenty-three-year-old student from Budapest who was here on a sightseeing expedition."

Reporters began shouting questions, but Tamás held up his hands and waited for them to quiet down before continuing.

"The second is that as of 8:45 a.m., we have charged Csilla Polgár with the crime of murder in the first degree."

Pandemonium broke out as all the reporters began shouting questions. Annja sat there, staring at the television in shock.

On screen, Tamás waited for the clamor to die down and then said, "I can answer a few brief questions."

A reporter in the front row raised his hand and Tamás indicated that he should go ahead.

"Can you tell us what happened, Detective?"

"Both Miss Vass and Miss Polgár are students in Budapest. We believe they were traveling together when an argument broke out and Miss Polgár killed her companion in a fit of rage with a vicious blow to the head. At that point she stripped the body and pushed it over the side of a ridge to try to hide it. Unfortunately for her, another individual came along at that moment and Polgár was forced to improvise, pretending to assist with recovering the dying woman in order to throw law enforcement off her tracks.

"The victim received medical treatment upon arrival at the hospital here in Nové Mesto, but the doctor's efforts were ultimately unsuccessful."

"Is there an official cause of death yet, Detective?" a reporter asked.

"Yes. According to the medical examiner, the victim was struck in the back of the head with a blunt object. This caused massive internal hemorrhaging, which eventually led to her demise."

Annja shook her head in disbelief. She'd held that woman in her arms and hadn't noticed any such injury. Nor had the autopsy report mentioned anything even remotely similar.

What was going on here?

"Can you tell us who the third party is?" a reporter shouted, while another asked, "How do you know this other individual isn't involved, as well?"

"I am not at liberty to reveal her identity at the moment. Her story checks out and we're confident that she was being a Good Samaritan when she stopped to assist Miss Polgár and Miss Vass. If you want to speak to her, you'll have to track her down yourselves."

Gee, thanks, Detective, Annja thought. Now every journalist in Slovakia would be looking for her!

Hopefully, they would assume the so-called third party was a local and start there, giving her some time before she had to start dodging reporters. If not, she'd deal with it. Right now she needed to talk to Tamás. She *knew* Csilla was innocent, and now that Tamás had followed through with his half-witted theory, she felt an obligation to help the woman.

On screen, Tamás answered a few more questions and then ended the press conference, disappearing back into the police station. Annja thought about calling him, but every reporter in the country would be doing the same thing right about now, trying to get the inside scoop on the charges against the alleged killer. If she were Tamás, she'd have some of the rank and file taking the calls until things quieted down. She thought she could get through to him without too much trouble—she was, after all, a material witness in the investigation—but something told her she should do this in person. She wanted to see his face and gauge his reactions.

The question was how to get in a room with him without bringing the press down on her head. Going to the station didn't seem like the smartest choice, as she had little doubt the media would be scrutinizing anyone who entered for the next several days. It wouldn't be hard for an enterprising reporter to match her photograph with one of the publicity stills from the show and wind up wondering what the star of *Chasing History's Monsters* was doing here. That would bring its own media frenzy and simply exacerbate the problem.

A meeting at her hotel—either in the restaurant or her room—was out of the question for the same reason. There were too many staff members milling about.

No, she needed somewhere that was easily accessible but a little more private.

After a few minutes of thought, she came up with the perfect place.

"DETECTIVE!"

Annja had been waiting in the underground garage beneath the police station for the past half hour. The entrance was guarded by a uniformed officer, but when an overzealous news team tried to park their truck too close to the barrier, the officer had dutifully walked over to direct them elsewhere and Annja had taken the opportunity to slip past.

She'd lingered in the shadows, avoiding anyone who entered the garage while she waited for Tamás. Annja had anticipated that he might try to slip out of the office while all the media hubbub was going on, and was finally gratified to see him step off the elevator and walk toward his car, an older-model black BMW parked not too far from where she was hiding.

Tamás turned at the sound of her voice and waited for her to catch up with him. He didn't seem surprised to see her.

"What can I do for you, Ms. Creed?"

While waiting, Annja had decided that a full-frontal assault was the best chance she had of eliciting a reaction. She summoned up an air of aggravation and said, "You can tell me what the heck is going on, for starters."

Tamás frowned. "I'm sorry?"

"I saw the press conference this morning."

"And?"

"And there's no way Csilla Polgár murdered that woman! You know it and I know it. I told you as much when you questioned me earlier."

Tamás, however, didn't take the bait. He remained calm and unflustered as he said, "I understand how disturbing it must be for you to know that the woman you were working side by side with is, in fact, a cold-blooded killer. I'm sure that is unsettling to say the least. But that doesn't change the facts."

"Facts?" Annja replied. "What facts? All you've got is a theory, and frankly, it sounds like a rather crazy one at that."

"Crazy as it may be, it *is* what happened. Perhaps you've heard the expression truth is stranger than fiction. This is clearly one of those occasions. If you hadn't come along, I have little doubt that Miss Polgár would have left the scene far behind."

"But that's the thing, Detective. If she hadn't flagged me down, I probably wouldn't have even seen her standing there. All she had to do was back up a couple of steps and I would have driven right past. Why would she expose herself that way?"

Tamás shrugged. "I couldn't possibly tell you. Criminals do stupid things all the time."

Annja decided to try a different tack. "You keep calling her a criminal, but I'm at a loss to understand how you arrived at that conclusion. What evidence do you have tying her to the crime?"

"You mean besides that fact that she was there at the crime scene?"

"That's not enough and you know it. If it were, you would have arrested me, as well."

If his expression was any indication, he was starting to get annoyed with her, but his reply, when it came, was civil enough.

"If you remember, I came close to doing that very thing. Lucky for you we have witnesses putting the other two women together at Csejte Castle earlier that afternoon. I have little doubt that we'll locate Miss Vass's belongings in the very near future, and when we do, we will find Miss Polgár's fingerprints all over them."

"But what about the—" she almost said *autopsy report* but realized her mistake at the last moment and switched to "—cause of death?"

"What about it?"

"You said Vass was killed by a blow to the back of the head, but I held that woman in my arms. There was no sign of an injury like that."

Not to mention the fact that the autopsy report said the cause of death was massive blood loss.

Tamás looked at her closely, and for a moment Annja thought she'd gone too far. But then he seemed to shake off whatever suspicions her comment had prompted and smiled at her.

"I admire your passion, I truly do. But in this case I think it is misplaced. You didn't see any sign of the injury because, as far as I understand, the damage was primarily internal. The victim's thick hair seems to have cushioned the blow to some extent, preventing the skull from being crushed outright, but it did nothing to assuage the cerebral hemorrhaging that followed. Now if you'll excuse me, I have a meeting to attend."

He nodded, then opened the door to his vehicle and slipped inside. Annja watched as he started the engine and backed out of the parking space. Instead of driving off, however, he rolled down his window.

"Go home, Ms. Creed. There's nothing more you can do, and it will be months before the case goes to trial. When we need you, I'm sure the embassy will be in touch."

With that, he drove out of the garage, leaving her alone in the shadows with her thoughts.

13

Annja was more frustrated than ever. She knew Tamás was lying about the cause of death, and that made her wonder if he was lying about the relationship between Vass and Polgár, as well. It was certainly a convenient solution—claiming that the two women not only knew each other but had been traveling together and had gotten into an argument that had turned deadly. That explanation no doubt appealed to the detective's need to tie up all the loose ends. The question was, what was the truth?

Annja wasn't sure.

Tamás had claimed that witnesses had seen the two women together near the ruins of Csejte Castle. Talking to them might help her decide if Tamás was acting in good faith or if he really was at the heart of what was starting to look like a conspiracy to cover up more than just one murder.

She was suspicious, to say the least. She'd been at the castle all afternoon and hadn't seen either of the two women, but she had to admit that didn't necessarily mean they hadn't been there. Annja had been pretty absorbed in her work at the time and might simply have missed them.

But if Vass and Polgár had been there, and Tamás had found someone who'd seen them, then Annja should be able to find them, as well. What she needed to do was think like the detective.

So where to begin?

Yesterday she'd spent time knocking on doors in the village, but perhaps that had been the wrong approach. The locals had lived in the shadow of Csejte Castle for so long that very few probably visited the ruins. Those who did were likely involved in a business that catered to the tourists. According to Tamás, Vass and Polgár were on a sightseeing trip, so perhaps the best starting point would be with those who regularly interacted with such visitors. Annja could start with the locals who set up carts along the road leading to the castle and then move into town to check with the hotel staff and restaurant owners. If the women had been there—and in her mind it was a big if—someone must have seen them.

Novack's warning about stirring up the wrong kind of people came to mind, but she brushed it aside. She'd gotten pretty good at causing trouble for the wrong kind of people, and there was no way last night's threat would deter her from what she knew was right. She'd just pay more attention to her surroundings and make certain she wasn't caught out alone after dark.

Satisfied that she had a plan of action, Annja crossed the underground lot and started up the ramp to the gate beyond. The detective must have said something to the guard on his way out because the man did little more than glare at her as she passed by and headed down the street to her car.

She sat in the driver's seat for a moment, taking stock of it all. It was clear now that her instincts had been right—there was something fishy going on. From the lies about the cause of death to the rush to point the finger at Csilla Polgár, never mind the photograph of what seemed to be another victim, there were way too many loose ends. It was as if everyone around her was operating under the directions of some hidden third party; she could almost see the pattern… Almost, but not quite.

It *was* there. She had no doubt about that.

Annja made a brief stop at her hotel, where she took the time to hunt around online for a couple of decent headshots for both Csilla Polgár and Marta Vass—a feat made easier by the news broadcasts that morning. Then she printed up a dozen copies to use while canvassing the streets of Čachtice.

Before long, Annja was parking her car at the bottom of the road leading up to the castle ruins. She started working her way through the various vendor stalls set up in the parking lot, asking if any of the attendants had seen the two women.

After striking out, Annja returned to the town square, parked in the same spot she'd used the day before and resumed her canvassing. Rather than focusing on residential properties, however, Annja made straight for the tourist destinations—the restaurants, shops and bars, few though there were, that catered to those who'd come to see the Blood Countess's ruined castle. Most of the employees she questioned spoke

English and she had a much easier go of it than the day before, but unfortunately, she came up with pretty much the same results. One or two people thought they might have seen the women, but they readily admitted they might have recognized Csilla and Marta from the news reports. They couldn't describe what the women had been wearing or what they'd been doing, so Annja wrote down their names and contact information but didn't put much stock in their testimony.

Given that the Belák Kamil hotel was the only major establishment of its kind in Čachtice, Annja sat in the lobby for almost an hour, asking everyone who came through the door if they'd seen the two women, but she struck out. To top it all off, someone must have complained about her, for it wasn't long before the manager wandered over, asked her to stop bothering his guests and had a bellman escort her from the property.

The bellman hadn't seen the two women together, either.

He left her on the sidewalk outside the hotel with a friendly smile and a suggestion to come back later that night for a drink.

Or, at least, that was what she thought he was saying. His English was almost as bad as her Slovakian.

Annja was standing there, considering her options, when she noticed several small groups of women all going in the same direction. Curious, she followed.

The women led her down the street, around the corner and into the small park just beyond. There she found a few dozen more local women standing in front of a mobile command center, like those used for blood drives by the American Red Cross. Portable canopies had been set up to shade the women from the sunlight as they stood in line.

A registration table had been set up in front of the vehicle. A man and a woman were manning the table, and from the cut of their two-thousand-dollar suits they certainly weren't from the local health clinic.

Annja moved closer, trying to get a sense of what was going on. The women in line would go to the table, answer a few questions and then receive a clipboard full of paperwork to fill out. When they were finished the clipboard was returned to the table where it was reviewed by one of the attendants and then passed to someone waiting inside the vehicle. One by one the women were called inside, only to emerge a short time later. Those wearing short sleeves like Annja had fresh gauze taped on the inside of their forearms just below the elbow.

Maybe it was a bloodmobile after all.

But if so, where were all the men? And why weren't the women inside longer? They were coming out after just a few minutes, rather than the fifteen to twenty minutes it usually took to donate blood.

None of the volunteers looked particularly worried— just the opposite, in fact—so Annja didn't think it was related to a local health scare. Maybe it was some kind of routine test, like that peptide study she'd been reading about recently that used a blood test to uncover breast cancer in its earliest stages.

Annja shifted to her right a few feet, and when the door opened she was able to get a quick glance of a white-smocked attendant drawing blood from a young woman sitting in a plastic chair, a cup of what looked like orange juice in her other hand. On the pocket of the attendant's lab coat was a stylized logo containing the letters *TGI*.

Then the door closed, cutting off her view. Perhaps if she…

"Can I help you?"

Annja jumped; she hadn't heard the woman come up behind her.

She turned, an excuse already on her lips, only to find herself struck momentarily dumb.

Standing before her was one of the most beautiful women she'd ever seen. Piercing eyes of crystal blue framed by long brown hair, red lips and skin so smooth it practically begged to be touched. She was taller than Annja by a good two inches even without her heels, and her custom-tailored suit showed off her athletic frame almost to perfection. And if her physical good looks weren't enough, the newcomer practically oozed confidence, as if she should be chairing the board of a multibillion-dollar corporation instead of handling, well, whatever this was.

Annja disliked her immediately.

It wasn't the annoyance she felt at being startled; Annja brushed that off with barely a thought. This was something at the gut level, some buried instinct that was telling her to step carefully around this woman, the way you might move cautiously but expeditiously when the big dog next to you starts growling and foaming at the mouth.

Something must have shown on Annja's face, for the woman smiled suddenly, breaking the tension and banishing the strange vibe she'd been giving off. When Annja smiled back, she found herself wondering how she could have ever felt suspicious about this woman.

"I'm sorry if I startled you," the woman said, extending her hand. "Diane Stone."

She and Annja shook hands. "Annja Creed."

"You seem rather interested in our operation. Is there anything I can answer for you?" Stone asked.

Annja glanced over at the mobile lab. "I didn't mean to intrude. I was just down the street, saw the crowd and wondered what was going on."

Stone smiled again. "It's nothing all that exciting actually. We're here with the University of Budapest, doing a genealogical study on several ancient Hungarian bloodlines. The women are providing a blood sample. We'll extract the DNA and use that for sequencing the various genomes to try to trace those bloodlines back through the centuries."

Annja digested that for a moment, trying to match the cut of Stone's suit with the salary a university professor typically made. The two didn't quite gel. Not by a long shot.

Not wanting to be rude, but still curious, Annja said, "You work for the university, then?"

The other woman laughed. "God, no. I work for the firm that was hired to handle the sample collection. I'm a glorified technician, nothing more."

Right. And I'm the Queen of England, Annja thought. But why lie about it?

That initial feeling of unease returned, and Stone seemed to be watching Annja's reactions a bit too closely. Annja didn't know what she was looking for, but the glint of calculation in the other woman's eyes was enough to put her guard up. Perhaps it was time to be on her way.

Annja glanced at her watch and feigned surprise. "Oh, my gosh! I didn't realize it was so late," she exclaimed. "Thanks for your time and good luck on your project!"

She shook Stone's hand, said goodbye and headed quickly across the park in the direction from which she'd come. When she glanced back a few moments later, Stone was still standing in the same spot. Annja couldn't say for certain, but it felt as if the woman was watching her.

It was odd enough to send a chill racing up Annja's back.

When she got a few blocks away, Annja stopped in the shade of a large oak and pulled out her cell phone. She dug around in her contacts until she located the number she wanted and then dialed. The phone rang twice before a male voice answered.

"Ahoj?"

"Hi, Henry, it's Annja."

Annja's first love was archaeology and she'd spent a good deal of time over the past several years elbow-deep in dirt at one dig site or another. As a result, she had contacts all over the world, and Henry Vlahović was one of them. A professor of medieval history at the University of Budapest, he and Annja had met at a conference a few years ago. They'd struck up a friendship based on a mutual love of history and their fascination with medieval culture.

Vlahović switched from his native language, Czech, to English. "Annja! So good to hear from you. Where in the world is the ravishing Ms. Creed right now, may I ask?"

Henry was twice her age but always flirted shamelessly, which Annja found endearing. When they'd first met he was fascinated with all of her exploits, particularly with her travel for her work on *Chasing History's Monsters* and the digs she assisted on. As a practical joke he'd once sent her a Where's Waldo? calendar with all the images of Waldo replaced with tiny pictures of Annja. It was corny as heck but had made her laugh, and as a result he'd gotten into the habit of asking where she was whenever they had a chance to reconnect.

"Funny you should ask," she said with a smile. "I'm right around the corner from you in Čachtice, Slovakia."

"Čachtice? What on earth are you doing… Oh. Báthory's castle. I should have guessed."

"Got it in one, Henry," Annja said. "Listen, sorry to call you out of the blue like this…"

"You're welcome to call anytime, you know that."

"Thanks. I was hoping you could check into something for me."

"What do you need?"

"I ran into a group in Čachtice this morning who said they were doing some work on behalf of the university.

Something to do with tracing Hungarian bloodlines. Do you know anything about that?"

"Not a thing," he replied. "You're sure it's through us?"

"Absolutely. The contact on-site, a Diane Stone, confirmed it."

"Well, I don't know anything about it. And I would, too—a project like that would have to be approved by my office. What was the name again?"

"Stone. Diane Stone." Annja could hear Henry rustling through the papers on his desk. She'd been in his office once and remembered a massive steel affair almost completely covered with piles of loose papers and file folders. How he found anything was beyond her.

"I'm looking at the list of projects we have under way right now and I don't see anything about Hungarian genealogy. Are you sure she said the U of B?"

"I thought so…"

"I'd check with Weigel at the University of Bonn. I seem to remember him mentioning something about bloodlines at the conference last month. Maybe you simply misheard her."

"I'm sure you're right, Henry. Thanks for the help."

"You're very welcome, Annja. When you're done you should swing on over if you have any free time. Do this old man good to take a young lass like you out for dinner. I know a great restaurant right on the Danube that you'll love."

Annja laughed. Henry loved good food almost as much as he loved history, which was another thing they had in common, and she had no doubt the restaurant he had in mind would be superb. "I'm due back in New York in a few days to edit our latest shoot, but if we finish early I'll give you a call."

"Sounds like a plan, my dear. Take care!"

Annja said goodbye and hung up the phone.

Curiouser and curiouser.

14

After her conversation with Tamás earlier that morning and her complete lack of progress in finding anyone who would talk to her that afternoon, Annja knew she had no choice but to make the rendezvous with Novack. The photograph he'd given her hinted at the possibility that Vass's death wasn't an isolated killing. If that was true, as horrible as that reality might be, it was potentially good news for Csilla. If Annja could establish a link between the killings and show that Csilla was back in her native Hungary at the time of at least one, if not more, of the other murders, then Tamás would have no choice but to let her go.

Unless he claimed she had accomplices.

Annja shook off the thought.

Even *he* wouldn't be that ridiculous, would he?

At the moment it didn't matter. First, she needed to determine if there had been any other killings. She'd worry about linking them together, as well as proving Csilla's innocence, after that.

She grabbed some dinner in a restaurant catering to tourists who'd come to see the castle and asked again about Vass and Polgár. While the staff spoke excellent English and were happy enough to chat with her, the answer was still the same. Not only had no one seen them together, but they hadn't seen either woman at any time. It was as if the two women had never reached Čachtice at all.

Annja paid the bill, including a decent tip, and lingered over coffee, her thoughts churning.

After a moment she borrowed a pen from a passing waiter and drew a rough sketch of the company logo she'd seen on the technician's lab coat earlier that afternoon. When she was satisfied, she took out her phone, snapped a photo and emailed it to Doug in New York.

Once she confirmed that the file had been sent properly, she dialed his number. It was 6:00 p.m. in Čachtice, which made it around noon in New York City, but she got his voice mail anyway.

She didn't waste time with pleasantries. "Just sent you an image, Doug. I need you to put the research staff to work. Ask them to figure out which company it belongs to and send me everything they can find on the company itself. I think that company is connected to what's going on over here. Call me when you have something."

The "research staff" was nothing more than a pair of interns, but they were eager to please and would hunt down that logo faster than she could. She'd been stretching the truth when she'd told Doug the company was connected to her investigation into Vass's death. Right now it was nothing more than an anomaly—if she could even call it that—but her instincts were telling her something fishy was going on with that so-called study. Henry had confirmed that the university wasn't involved, which meant Stone, if that was even her name, had been lying.

It wasn't a crime to stretch the truth, Annja thought with a wry smile. She'd just done the very same thing, but taking blood samples under false pretenses was another matter entirely. And Annja had lied to Doug for a good reason; he wouldn't have asked the interns to dig up the information if Annja had simply said she was curious. But Stone had no valid reason—at least none that Annja could think of—to lie about what the medical team was doing.

Annja didn't like being lied to. It made her sink her teeth in like a bulldog and she wouldn't let go until she had the answers she was looking for. Stone's operation might not have anything to do with the weirdness surrounding the investigation into Vass's death, but given her limited number of leads, anything unusual was fair game at the moment.

A glance at her watch told her it was time to head to her rendezvous with Novack. She'd passed the church where they planned to meet during her canvassing that afternoon, so it was a simple matter to drive over and park around the corner. She sat in the car watching the road behind her for a few moments to be certain she wasn't being followed. Then she got out, locked the vehicle and walked down the street at a leisurely pace.

The church was an old stone affair half-covered in creeping ivy. A small rectory stood at the back of the property, just visible from the street. A dim light burned over the front door, as if welcoming her with reluctance.

Annja strode up the walk, pushed open the heavy wooden door and slipped inside.

Candles burned at strategic locations throughout the interior, casting a soft light over the simple wooden pews and stone altar. She looked around but didn't see anyone.

Had she beaten him here?

Rather than stand around in the entrance and look conspicuous should a priest or parishioner come in after her, Annja strode down the center aisle and took a seat a third of the way toward the front. She had barely settled into place before Novack slipped out of the shadows off to one side of the nave and slid into the pew behind her.

"Did anyone see you come in?" he asked.

Annja shook her head. "Not that I'm aware of."

"Good." Novack was silent for a moment and then asked, "What did you think of the photograph?"

Annja was decidedly curious about where it had come from and why he'd given it to her, but she wasn't going to admit it. Not yet.

Instead of answering, she asked a question of her own. "I asked this before and I'll ask again—who are you? Why are you bringing this information to me?"

Novack glanced around just as he had in the bar, though who he thought would be spying on them in an empty church Annja didn't know. Apparently satisfied, he faced her, took a deep breath and said, "My name is Havel Novack and I'm a former senior sergeant in the Criminal Police."

That explained how he'd gotten the photograph.

"Former?"

His jaw tightened, but his voice was calm and steady as he gestured at his leg and said, "I was asked to retire after my injury."

There was some bitterness there, but nothing to cause concern. She could rule out vindictiveness against his former comrades as a reason he might be meeting with her.

Novack went on, "Before leaving the department I took certain…precautions. Doing so has allowed me to continue my investigation despite the attempts to cut me off."

This was starting to sound like one of those bizarre conspiracy theories. With just the hint of a rueful smile cresting her lips, Annja asked, "And what investigation is that?"

"The systematic deaths of twenty-three young women over the past five years."

Annja's smirk disappeared.

Twenty-three?

"Do you see now why I asked you to be careful?" Novack said.

Annja barely heard the question. She was still trying to get her head around twenty-three murders. In five years? They were talking about a murder every two to three months.

"So many? Tell me you're exaggerating."

"I assure you I am not. There may even be more."

Annja had suspected something was going on, but

this was way beyond anything she'd imagined. Twenty-three.

"Why bring this to me?" she asked. "I'm not a cop or a private investigator."

"No, you're one better. You're a seeker of the truth. I can see it in you. You won't rest until the answers are laid out before you."

She didn't know about Novack's claim that he could "see" her drive to find the truth, but she had to agree with his assessment. Now that she was involved in this whole mess, she would see it through to the end.

"All right, I'm listening," she told him.

"Twenty-three murders. All of them young, good-looking women in their twenties and thirties. In the beginning there were months between them. Sometimes as many as six to eight. Lately, however, they are coming more steadily. The last three have only been a month apart."

Annja knew that serial killers often fell victim to their own need, murdering victims more frequently until, in their own haste, they made a mistake and wound up caught by the authorities. Some psychologists theorized that the killers' own subconscious guilt drove them to such frenzied lengths, but Annja wasn't convinced. She thought it was a much simpler emotion than guilt—good old-fashioned greed.

One could argue that Báthory had brought about her own downfall by taking one too many victims. It made sense that a killer using Báthory's legend as a basis for his—or her—crimes would do the same.

And yet…something wasn't right. Twenty-three murders in the same area should have raised a huge outcry. The police should have been all over this, with a multidisciplinary task force assigned to handle the investigation. When Annja had brought the latest victim into the hospital, they should have immediately put two and two together. They hadn't. Just the opposite, in fact.

"If there have been twenty-three murders in the past five years, why are the police acting as if this latest one is an isolated incident?" she asked.

"Because this is the first time the victim was someone who actually mattered. At least to the authorities."

Annja stared at him, not understanding. "Come again?"

Novack handed Annja a file filled with case summaries for each of the twenty-three alleged victims, including color photographs. She began leafing through the documents, and it didn't take long for her to understand what her companion was talking about.

The "murders" were actually a collection of suicides, accidental deaths and missing persons. Many of the women were noted as being on the fringes of society—prostitutes, known drug users, runaways and the like—and their absence had either been reluctantly reported to the police weeks after they'd dropped out of sight or hadn't been officially reported at all. Many of the disappearances had been uncovered by Novack while talking to others on the street. The handful that weren't from the fringes were loners by nature and could just as easily have packed up and moved on without telling anyone where they were going.

She looked up, confused. "These aren't murders. Why are you wasting my time with this?" she asked.

Novack didn't bat an eye. "Ignore the reports. They're worthless. Look at the photographs instead."

Annja pulled several of them out of the file. "What do you expect me to…?"

The file contained two sets of images. The first were crime scene photos, like the one Novack had given her the night before. The second set was a haphazard collection of images—most likely cobbled together by Novack himself from arrest records, CCTV cameras and photos supplied by relatives—that showed the victims as they'd been before they'd died. It was these images that caused Annja's comment to die in her throat. The hair on the back of her neck stood at attention.

All the women looked remarkably similar.

They could have been cousins, Annja thought. In some cases even sisters.

They had narrow faces and expressive eyes, with clear skin and healthy-looking hair. The hairstyles themselves were all different—some wore their hair long, as Annja did, while others had cut theirs considerably shorter, and one even had a crew cut—but their features were remarkably similar.

Annja knew it was a long shot, but she asked the obvious question anyway.

"Are they related?"

"No."

She looked up from the photos. "You're sure?"

"Absolutely. I did the research myself."

"They all look far too similar for this to be a coincidence," Annja told him.

Novack nodded. "I agree."

"What do the police say?"

"They disagree with me."

"Then you need to go back and try again. Get them to listen to you."

"I tried. Several times, in fact. Shortly after my last attempt I was brought into the captain's office and told that I was, without argument, going to announce my retirement for medical reasons."

That must have been both humiliating and painful.

"But honestly, my forced retirement isn't what's got me worried."

The conversation was starting to feel surreal. "Twenty-three possible killings aren't enough?"

"No. It's what the killer's doing afterward. At least three of the bodies—maybe more—were drained of their blood."

Annja looked up slowly. "You mean the victims bled out, don't you?" she asked, just to be sure.

Novack shook his head. "No, I mean drained. As in all of it. If I was the superstitious type I'd say that Báthory had come back from the dead."

The image of those two unusual wounds on Marta's leg flashed through Annja's mind.

"The medical examiner's report noted that the latest victim had several deep cuts along her torso, from which she could have bled extensively, but she also had two puncture wounds on her inner thigh near the femoral artery."

The former senior sergeant watched her closely as he asked, "How do you know what the autopsy report says?"

This time it was Annja's turn to shake her head. "That's not important right now. Just tell me if any of the other bodies had the same kind of injuries."

He nodded. "Two that I know of."

That was all?

"You're sure there aren't others? Were the injuries noted in the autopsy reports?"

"I didn't see those reports—I was already retired by the time these two victims turned up. But I know the injuries were there."

Annja was skeptical. "How could you if you didn't see the reports?"

He hesitated, as if reluctant to answer, but finally said, "I sneaked into the morgue and examined the bodies before they were sent off to the undertaker."

Annja laughed; she couldn't help it. Apparently she'd found a kindred spirit.

Novack frowned, misunderstanding. "I have a man on the inside who's been helping me, but he couldn't get to the reports without being discovered, so I did what I had to do."

She shook her head. "I'm not criticizing," she told him. "Far from it. I was laughing because I would have done the exact same thing in your position."

He didn't look all that mollified, but at least he let it go.

"Did you see any of the earlier bodies?"

"A few. On the cases I was assigned to, at least.

I don't remember seeing anything like what you described, however. If there had been injuries like that, the medical examiner, Petrova, would have discovered them."

"Unless he's part of the cover-up."

Even as she said it, she knew it couldn't be that simple. Too many people would have seen those reports. Petrova wouldn't have been foolish enough to hide the presence of such wounds in the other twenty-two alleged victims only to list them so blatantly on the autopsy report for the twenty-third.

Then a thought occurred to her: perhaps this time he didn't have a choice.

"Were any of the other victims still alive when they were found?" she asked Novack.

"No."

Annja felt her pulse quicken. Thanks to her "interference," the latest victim had been brought to the local hospital before she succumbed to her injuries. Those involved wouldn't have been able to tuck the situation away under a rug somewhere; too many people were involved at that point, from the doctors and nurses at the hospital to Annja herself.

The autopsy report hadn't been made public and probably wouldn't be, not with an active murder investigation under way. Nor had there been any mention of the cause of death at the press conference. Annja only knew about the blood loss and the puncture wounds because she'd broken into Petrova's office and seen his notes. By naming Csilla as the alleged killer, those involved, be it Petrova or someone else, could keep the facts from coming to light long enough for it not to matter.

Besides being clever, it made a weird, twisted kind of sense.

If everything Novack had said was true.

But Annja wasn't convinced yet. It was still possible that he'd fabricated all of this as part of some delusional need to remain in the spotlight. Novack might have deliberately picked the so-called "victims" because of how similar they looked to one another. In fact, the idea that Novack might be suffering from his own fabricated delusion actually made more sense than the widespread conspiracy to cover up the murders of twenty-some-odd people.

But something in his story rang true, enough that she wouldn't be able to walk away without checking it out for herself.

It was only when Novack asked, "What are you thinking?" that Annja realized she'd been silent for a while.

"I'm thinking that you've convinced me of the importance of doing some more digging."

Novack breathed a sigh of relief. "Thank God," he muttered underneath his breath.

"Who else knows about this?" Annja asked, gesturing to the folders.

"Once I was fairly certain there was a pattern, I brought the first ten cases I'd located to my direct superior. He dismissed it out of hand and, as you know, took me off active duty. After that I didn't see the point in sharing it with anyone except Radecki and, of course, now you."

"Radecki?"

"Martin Radecki," Novack qualified. "He's a junior officer from my old squad. He came to me a few months ago, asked if he could help. He'd heard rumors I was working on something big when I'd been sacked. The other guys laughed at him, but he was willing to dig in and get his hands dirty. He's the one who's been getting me some of the information from the crime files. He's gonna go far, that one."

Just a handful of people, then.

It wasn't as bad as Annja had thought.

"I'm going to take a closer look at these files. Where can I reach you when I'm done?"

Novack shook his head. "I've been moving around lately. Why don't I just reach out to you?"

Annja didn't understand his reluctance, but she decided not to push the issue. "All right," she said. "Give me a few days and then get in touch."

His expression was grave as he said, "Don't take too long. A young woman sits in a jail cell wrongly accused while the real killer still roams free."

15

This time she answered the phone almost immediately.

"Yes?"

"Sorry to disturb you, but there's been a development I think you should be aware of."

"Let me guess. Ms. Creed is continuing to make a nuisance of herself."

"Yes. She's been in touch with Novack."

"So?"

"Novack can still hurt us."

"Unlikely. No one listens to him, not after what we did to his reputation."

He gritted his teeth, not liking the direction the call was going. Why couldn't she see the danger here?

"I believe this Creed woman will listen. If you review the material I sent over, you'll see that she has the tenacity of an irritated mastiff and..."

"I've read it."

The flat tone of her voice let him know he was on dangerous ground, and he quickly backpedaled.

"My apologies. I didn't mean to imply that you had not. I was merely concerned for our enterprise."

"*My* enterprise," she corrected, to which he wisely said nothing. At least her tone was less angry.

She was quiet for a moment and then, "What would you suggest?"

He didn't hesitate. "Eliminate Novack. Cut the head off the snake before it grows any bigger."

"Do you think that's necessary?"

"I do. He hasn't stopped his investigation—we know that. I suspect he isn't sharing all that he's uncovered. There's no telling how much information he's gathered since leaving the force. At least when he was inside we could control him."

He winced the moment the comment left his mouth—he'd argued pretty vehemently about leaving Novack as an active duty officer where they could keep an eye on him. His argument hadn't gone over well, and calling her attention to his stance after all this time wasn't so smart. Thankfully her mind was on other things.

"I met her today, you know."

He froze. That was, perhaps, the last thing he'd expected to hear. Had Creed gotten that close already?

"What happened?"

He must have let some of his anxiety creep into his tone because she laughed and said, "Relax. She was in the village, showing those pictures around again, and stumbled upon the collection team. I was on-site at the time and decided to say hello, see what the fuss was about."

"Do you think she suspects?"

"No. She thinks it's a genealogical study and nothing

more." She paused, and then said, "She's quite beautiful, you know."

Her beauty, or lack thereof, didn't make a difference to him. It was his job to make certain their operation continued without disruption, and all Creed represented to him was a potential chink in their armor.

"I know you ordered Creed left alone," he said, "but now there's been direct contact between them. She has a reputation for uncovering the things others would prefer to keep hidden, and leaving her to continue her investigation could be damaging to us in the long run."

She was quiet a moment, considering. At last she said, "No, I want Creed left alone. She has some powerful friends who could be a problem for us should they come looking for her."

"I can make it look like an accident."

"Yes, I know. You've gotten quite good at that over the years."

He said nothing; those very skills were the reason she paid him so handsomely. No need to brag.

"If and when the time comes, I'll have you deal with her, but not until I give the word. And don't think your little stunt the other night went unnoticed. She might not have ended up with Novack if you hadn't pushed her in that direction."

He took the rebuke silently, for he knew as well as she did that she was correct. It had been a clumsy operation and he was embarrassed by how it had turned out, but at least next time his people would know not to underestimate Creed. For a cable television host, she had more than a few tricks up her sleeve.

His boss wasn't quite finished yet, however.

"Besides, after seeing her, I'm wondering if she might be a good fit for our program. I don't want her harmed until we can determine if that's the case."

"I understand."

"If you think it's time to deal with Novack once and for all, then go ahead. Just make it clean."

He smiled. It's about time...

"Don't worry," he said. "I'll handle Novack."

He knew just how to do it, too.

16

Back at the hotel, Annja began going through the information Novack had provided, looking for connections between the victims, similarities in methods of death and the like. She needed something the police couldn't just brush off. Novack had gone through the file numerous times doing exactly what she was doing now, but she did it anyway, because a fresh pair of eyes could sometimes find details that had been previously overlooked.

Annja read each file in turn, taking several pages of notes in the process. Novack had said that Vass was the first victim "the police couldn't ignore," and after spending time with the documents he'd provided, she understood why he'd used that phrase. The vast majority of the women had been drifters, runaways, prostitutes—"the dregs of society," they might have been called in another place and time. Annja preferred to think of them as the less fortunate. "There but for the grace of God go I" came to mind. She became even more determined to get to the bottom of the whole mess.

These women were no less deserving of justice than anyone else.

She was going through the causes of death, looking for a pattern of any kind, when her phone rang.

"Hello?"

"What time is it over there anyway?" Doug asked.

Annja glanced at the clock. "One o'clock in the morning."

"Did I wake you?"

"No."

Annja heard muttered grumbling on the other end and couldn't resist a smile. She'd apparently spoiled his attempt at payback.

"Got something for me, Doug?" she asked sweetly, pretending not to have heard his disappointment. Might as well let him save face.

"I've had the interns slaving away all day on that task you gave them."

"Any luck?"

"Yes, though I don't understand how it plays into your story about the crazy woman who bathed in the blood of virgins. I think…"

"Let me do the thinking, Doug," Annja said. "Just tell me what you found out."

He huffed but did as she asked. "The logo is for a company known as Transgenome Industries."

Annja dragged her laptop over to her and typed in the name. "What do they do?"

"Damned if I know. Way too much science for me to make sense of. Something about DNA sequencing and replication, whatever the heck that is."

Doug's forte was marketing, especially to the millennial audience. Anything beyond that was definitely hit or miss. But he'd gotten her what she needed, and she began scanning the news articles that mentioned Transgenome Industries.

"It's all kinda weird, if you ask me."

She hadn't, but she asked anyway, just to keep him happy. "What's that?"

"TGI's parent company is Giovanni Industries."

That made Annja sit up and pay attention. "The cosmetics giant? That Giovanni Industries?"

"The very same. They're hidden behind a couple dozen shell companies but one of the interns—Denise? Donna? I forget—used to be a finance major and she tore through them like a bull in a china shop. She assures me that at the end of the road is Giovanni Industries."

Interesting. What the heck did a cosmetics company want with DNA samples from random Slovakian women?

Annja had no idea.

"Anything on Stone?" Annja asked.

"Nada. Nothing. Zilch."

Annja knew that didn't necessarily mean anything. Some people were pretty protective of their privacy, and Stone might be one of those types. She could have taken care to keep most information about her off the internet.

If Stone were a US citizen, Annja could check a variety of public records databases for information about her, from the Social Security Administration to the Department of Motor Vehicles. She could call her friend

Bart in the Brooklyn Police Department and ask him to find out whether she had a criminal record. Bart could even use his contacts with the IRS to determine whether she was filing federal taxes and from where she was doing so. There was no way a US citizen could avoid that kind of scrutiny.

On the other hand, if the woman had lied about her identity, Annja could search the web for days on end without finding anything useful.

Given that the rest of the information Stone provided proved suspect, to say the least, Annja expected she'd lied about her identity, too, and Doug's inability to find anything appeared to bear that out.

"All right. Thanks, Doug. I'll take it from here."

"You're kidding, right?"

Annja's brow furrowed. "Kidding about what?"

"You're supposed to be working on a story about the vampire chick who bathes with virgins!" Doug said, exasperated. "What's all this stuff about a cosmetics company?"

Annja sighed. She should have seen this one coming.

"Báthory wasn't a vampire, nor did she bathe with virgins."

"But you said…"

"I said she bathed in the blood of virgins," Annja told him firmly, trying to cut him off before he got too far down that road. "And I don't know what the genetics firm—note I said 'the genetics firm,' not 'the cosmetics company'—has to do with the killings. I'm working on that."

Doug was silent a moment.

"The killings?" he asked finally, tentatively.

"Yes, the killings. Why do you think…?"

"Wait. What killings?"

As Doug's question rang in her ears, Annja realized she'd been so caught up in the events surrounding Csilla's arrest and the information Novack had given her that she'd forgotten to fill Doug in on everything that had happened.

She did so as quickly and as succinctly as possible.

"So let me get this straight," Doug said when she was finished. "Someone's snatching women off the street, killing them and then draining their blood in the very place where the crazy vampire chick did the same thing five hundred years ago *and you didn't tell me about it!*"

Annja pulled the phone away from her ear as Doug continued to rant and shout. She waited until he paused to take a breath and then cut in.

"Look, I'm still putting all this together, Doug. I don't know if there really is a killer out there or if this cop has simply lost his marbles. I just don't know."

"Well, figure it out, then! This could be the episode of the year. Think of the headlines. *Chasing History's Monsters* Producer and Host Uncover Real Modern-Day Monster and Bring It to Justice."

Annja knew there was no way in creation any news editor—in print, video or online—would use such a long and clunky header, but arguing about it with Doug was a lost cause.

"Trust me, Doug, as soon as I do, you'll be the first to know."

"I'm serious, Annja! We could really push the envelope on this one. Do a reenactment of the whole bath scene with virgins lying about right before the vampire chick kills them…"

"Doug?"

"Casting could come up with some innocent-looking models, I'm sure, and…"

"Doug?"

"Hmm, maybe not. Okay, I'll settle for seductive looking—I'm sure they can manage *that*, at least— and then we'll have you rise up out of the bath covered with blood and looking right into the camera as you tell the story…"

"Doug!"

Her shout finally shut down his long rambling discourse. "Jeez, you don't have to yell. What's the problem?"

"I'm not coming out of a bath."

He jumped in again. "You don't have to be naked, but how about a bikini? You know, a small one? We could just…"

Annja closed her eyes and counted to ten.

Doug must have sensed something was amiss, for his talking trailed off after a minute or two.

"Annja? Are you still there?"

Through clenched teeth, Annja said, "Let's get something straight, Doug. I'm not wearing a bikini on television. I most definitely am not climbing out of a bathtub with blood on me, fake or otherwise. And if you think I'm going to let an important historical subject like Countess Elizabeth Báthory be portrayed as a blood-sucking vampire chick, then you've got another think coming!"

Her producer was silent for a moment, and then he asked, tentatively, "Báthory? She's the vampire chick, right?"

"Argh!" Annja cried, and stabbed the end call button on her phone.

Then, just to be safe, she pulled the battery out.

She settled onto the bed and tried to get back into studying the files, but her concentration had been broken and the hectic day had finally caught up with her.

She packed up the files and took a quick shower. Tomorrow she'd finish her research, and hopefully that would help her form a plan of action.

In the meantime, though, sleep was calling.

17

"Good morning. Can you help me?"

Annja was standing in the local library, where she'd gone soon after waking up. She wanted to independently verify the information Novack had supplied to her by going through back issues of the local newspaper for any and all reports relating to the various tragedies that had been contained in the files.

The woman Annja was speaking to was in her midfifties, with a bright smile and a pair of tortoiseshell glasses with thick lenses that gave her features an owlish cast.

"I'll certainly try," the librarian said in excellent English. "What are you looking for?"

When Annja explained that she wanted to go through every issue of the local paper for the past five years, the librarian smiled politely and said, "That's a lot of issues."

"I'm sure it is," Annja replied, "which is why I need your help."

She could imagine what was going on inside the woman's head—"are you nuts?" likely being the most prominent refrain—and she was thankful for the librarian's professionalism. The woman led Annja through the stacks and down two flights of stairs to a room in the basement where the bookshelves were lined with thick binders containing print copies of all the newspaper issues for the past two years.

"Anything older than this gets shipped off to the media center, where it's digitized and stored on the library's network. You can access those files at any of the terminals on the second floor. If you need anything, press twenty-eight on that phone over there," she said, pointing at a white telephone hanging on the wall in the corner, "and that will connect you to the circulation desk."

Annja waited until the librarian had left the room, and then she checked her notes to find the date when the most recent "victim" from Novack's files was found. Once she had that, she pulled down the binders containing the issues from that month and began to leaf through them, page by page.

It was time-consuming work, made more difficult by the fact that many of those involved were on the fringes of society and often not mentioned by name, if at all. People died every day under a variety of circumstances, and often they got no more than a line or two of commentary in the press. Annja's job was to sort through all of these, trying to match the details of the deaths she had in the files with those listed in the newspaper. Her goal was twofold, to verify that the report was accurate—that someone had died in the manner specified—and then to see if the press reports on the victims had anything to add to Novack's reports.

She took a break for lunch, grabbing something to eat in a small outdoor café not far from the library, and then she returned to continue her search. This time, however, she took her work back up to the main floor, tired of feeling as though she was hiding away in the basement.

She'd been back at it for almost an hour when she realized someone was standing in front of her table, waiting. Annja looked up from the newsprint she was studying to find Detective Tamás. He still had his coat on, which meant, given the warm temperatures in the room, that he'd just come in from outside. In his right hand he was carrying a slim briefcase.

"Hello, Ms. Creed," Tamás said.

If he'd come here directly from being outside, this visit was no accident. He was looking for her.

"Good afternoon, Detective."

Tamás pointed at the chair on the other side of the table from her. "Do you mind if I sit down?"

"It's a public building."

Tamás hesitated, and Annja regretted her remark. There was no need for rudeness.

"I'm sorry, Detective, it's been a long day. Yes, of course, join me."

Tamás took off his coat, draping it over the back of the chair, and then sat, placing his briefcase on the table next to him, within easy reach. He glanced at the pile of ledgers holding the newspaper's back issues.

"I don't think you're going to find much information on the countess in the local paper," he said, smiling.

Annja smiled back at him as she said, "No, you're probably right. But the paper does have some fascinating things to say about several recent murder cases."

Tamás cocked his head to one side, seemingly uncertain how to take her comment. "I'm sorry. Did you say murder cases? Why on earth are you interested in something like that?"

"Oh, I don't know," she replied, her gaze never leaving his own. "Maybe because several of them are quite similar to the Vass killing. Was Csilla Polgár traveling with all of them?"

Tamás scowled at her and opened his mouth to say something sharp, but then understanding flooded his features and he sat back in his chair, rebuke unspoken. He watched her closely and then, with a faint smile on his face, said, "You've been talking to Novack, haven't you?"

Annja kept her face impassive. "Who?"

"Havel Novack?"

Play dumb.

"I don't know who that is."

Tamás laughed. "Right. And you just happened to come across information on the Cynthia Bardecki case on your own?"

Annja glanced down and saw she'd written Bardecki's name on the pad of paper in front of her at some point earlier that morning.

Watch it, she told herself. He was not only smart, he

was observant, too. He'd read that upside down with just a glance.

She shifted position, sliding her arm casually over the top of her pad as she said, "I'm afraid you have me at a loss, again, Detective. Who?"

"I suppose the names Lenka Burget, Kate Cérna, Liv Frank and Adriana Moravec mean nothing to you, as well?"

Annja stared at him. Novack had given her a file last night for each and every one of the names Tamás had just mentioned. There were quite a few others, of course, and Annja suspected that Tamás could have named them all had he chosen to do so.

What was going on here? she wondered. Novack had said only a few people knew about his theory; was Tamás in on the cover-up? Was that why he had come here?

Tamás must have sensed her anxiety because he said, "You are perfectly within your rights to access public information in any way you see fit. Please understand that I'm not trying to interfere with your research."

She sensed a "but" coming…

"But before you continue and get yourself involved even deeper in what is already a mess, I'd ask that you read this."

He reached into his briefcase, pulled out a thick file folder and pushed it across the table toward her.

Annja glanced at it but made no move to touch it.

"What is this?" she asked.

"Havel Novack's personnel file. He reported to me for several years before he retired."

"Isn't that confidential?"

"Normally, yes. But I'm bending the rules in this situation." His smile was both ironic and a bit sad. "You seem to think I'm doing everything I can to railroad Miss Polgár, but I assure you that I'm just following the evidence as I see it. I think you'd do the same in my case, which is why I brought you the file. You might want to have a look at it before wasting any more of your time. I trust that you'll return it when you're finished?"

Annja stared at the file for a moment, not touching it, and then she nodded, not sure what to say. He sounded so believable, and yet...

"Good day to you, then, Ms. Creed."

Tamás got up, retrieved his jacket and case, nodded to her once and then left.

Annja waited until he was out of sight before reaching for the file. It felt as though it weighed ten pounds as she dragged it across the tabletop.

Just my imagination, she told herself.

Inside was a written testament to Havel Novack's life on the force. Evaluations. Commendations. Records of the cases he'd worked and the collars he'd made. Firearms qualifications. Public service projects. You name it, it was in there. Annja read through the file with fascination, learning that Novack was a dedicated officer who took his job seriously and worked hard to live up to his role as a figure of truth and justice.

Everything supported her own conclusions about the man and his behavior until she got about three-quarters of the way through the file.

That was when things started to go downhill.

According to the documentation, Novack had suffered through a long and bitter divorce, like so many police officers before him. Following the divorce, he'd started drinking, a little here and there, until the pressure got to be too much, it seemed, and he began to do it more regularly.

Annja read on with increasing dismay, through reports of botched arrests and compromised investigations. Novack's downward spiral was all documented there in black-and-white.

Then came the final straw.

Novack had begun poking into cases that were not his own. He had been reprimanded twice for interfering in the work of other officers and had been placed on two weeks' leave to try to sort himself out. According to the paperwork, Novack had come back from his time off with the paranoid idea that a serial killer was loose in Nové Mesto and the surrounding communities. The killer was had supposedly targeting young women and draining the blood from their bodies in the manner of the Blood Countess.

The more Annja read, the more dismayed she became.

Novack had finally confronted the divisional captain, demanding that someone pay attention to the killings he'd uncovered and threatening to go to the press if they did not. At that point Novack was declared unfit for duty and retired on a medical pension.

There was no mention of a knee injury, which was

the reason Novack had given her for his being drummed off the force.

Annja finished reading the file, closed the folder and sat back in her chair, wondering what the heck she was going to do next.

Had all this been for nothing?

She tried to consider the situation dispassionately, just as she did when evaluating an artifact or a dig site. What did she really know? Not think or believe or suspect, but know.

Marta Vass was dead, killed by person or persons unknown. Her body had been drained of blood before being dumped on that ridgeline. Csilla Polgár had been arrested for the crime. Both Annja and Havel Novack believed Csilla to be innocent. Novack also believed a serial killer was preying on vulnerable members of the local community.

Those were all facts.

Now Annja believed that Csilla was innocent, but she couldn't say for sure. Not 100 percent. After all, what did she really know about the woman anyway?

Very little.

Maybe Tamás was right; maybe Polgár and Vass were traveling together and got into an argument that ended in tragedy. She didn't think it was true, but that didn't mean it wasn't. Fact was, she really didn't know.

All she had to go on was her gut feeling.

And her gut told her that Csilla hadn't done it.

But that was where her problem arose. Her gut was also telling her that the information Novack had supplied her with was on the up-and-up—that women were being targeted by a smart killer who had managed, either with the police's help or without it, to keep his or her activities under the radar.

And yet Novack's personnel file was pretty damning. Both to Novack and his theory. The former officer had made no mention of his drinking problem when they'd met last night. In fact, if Tamás was to be believed, Novack had not only left out that little detail but had actively lied about the reason he'd been drummed off the force. Given all the documentation Tamás had provided on the man's mental state, it was getting harder to believe that Novack's entire narrative wasn't just some fantastical story. After all, what real proof did he have?

That wasn't fair, she said to herself. What proof did she have that her sword could appear and disappear at will?

She almost brushed off the question as ridiculous—her subconscious could be a real pain at times—but then she realized it wasn't so ridiculous after all.

Annja was going to have to make a choice.

18

Annja needed time to relax and get her thoughts in order, so she had a leisurely dinner in a nice little Italian place a few blocks from her hotel. She even had a piece of tiramisu and a cup of hot chocolate for dessert.

In the end, she decided to give Novack a chance to explain himself. She owed him that much. If he'd had a drinking problem but was clean now—which he'd appeared to be when she'd seen him the past two times—then perhaps he was simply too embarrassed to bring it up. He'd readily admitted that he'd been all but drummed off the force, so she couldn't fault him too badly for not wanting to talk about the details. Especially if he'd been hoping to convince her of a rather outlandish story to begin with.

If he came clean and admitted the lie, she'd continue working with him on the investigation. Her gut was still telling her something was wrong here.

If she walked away and it turned out he was correct, she'd have condemned Csilla to imprisonment for a crime she didn't commit, and the killer might go on to destroy the lives of others.

That was something for which she wouldn't be able to forgive herself.

But she needed to know she could trust him to uphold his end of the partnership and that he wouldn't crack under pressure.

Pleased that she'd made a decision, Annja finished off her hot chocolate with one last gulp, paid the check and headed back to her hotel. She said hello to the doorman as she passed inside. After waiting for the elevator with a pair of elderly men who smelled of cigarettes and mouthwash, she rode up with them in silence. They got off on the floor below hers.

As Annja came down the hall toward her room, she noticed that her door was slightly ajar. No more than an inch, but even an inch was problematic, because she was certain that she'd not only pulled it firmly shut but locked it behind her when she'd left.

She stopped a few feet away from the door and listened.

She didn't hear anything.

Annja glanced up and down the hall, checking to be sure that it was empty. Confident that she wouldn't be observed, she reached into the otherwhere for her sword.

Feeling more confident now that she had a weapon in hand, Annja stepped to the side of the hallway and slowly advanced until she stood just outside her room with her back to the wall.

She listened again, but aside from the drone of a voice somewhere on the floor above, she didn't hear anyone moving about inside her room.

Still, it paid to be careful.

She reached out with the tip of her sword and nudged the door open the rest of the way.

Armed assailants didn't come charging out of the room, nor did a hail of withering gunfire chew the door into smithereens.

You've been watching too many movies, Creed.

Annja gave it a moment, and then peeked around the corner quickly before pulling her head back.

Her room was in shambles. Drawers were hanging out of the dresser, clothes were everywhere and it looked like someone had torn apart the mattress.

The files.

She wanted to rush in, to see if they were still there, but prudence reared its head and she took her time, slowly moving around the doorway and into the room just in case someone was still inside. She found the bedroom and the bath empty. A quick check of the closest confirmed no one was hiding in there, either.

Satisfied that she was alone, Annja released the sword back into the otherwhere and stared at the destruction around her.

They'd been thorough, whoever they were. Every drawer had been pulled out, their contents dumped on the floor. The television had been smashed open, the interior no doubt searched for heaven knows what. The mattress and box spring had been pulled off the frame, but not before the sheets had been stripped off and the interior torn open with a knife. Clumps of mattress stuffing were everywhere.

Of course her backpack, her laptop and the thick

stack of files Novack had given her the night before were nowhere in sight.

The first two items she understood, but the files? They weren't worth anything on the street. Who would want those?

She turned and examined the door, noting splinters in the wood of the jamb right next to the lock. It looked like someone had jammed a screwdriver or crowbar into the space and leveraged the door open. It wouldn't have been quiet, but it would have been fast, and if they'd closed the door behind them no one would have realized what they were doing. If there had been someone watching her at the restaurant, they could have searched the place pretty thoroughly without fear that she'd walk in on them.

All her doubts about the validity of Novack's theory were now gone. The destruction of the room and the theft of her backpack and laptop were just a cover for what the thieves had really been after.

The files themselves.

And the only reason someone would want those was if they contained damaging information…something that might point to those responsible for all the deaths.

Someone wanted to interrupt, possibly even stop, the investigation.

Annja had no intention of letting that happen.

Novack was on to something. He had to be. If he wasn't, they never would have come for the files.

She was about to summon the manager and have him file a police report when her phone rang. She dug it out of her pocket…only to find it wasn't her cell phone ringing after all.

Hotel phone.

Annja glanced at the desk where the phone had been; it was little more than a splintered ruin.

But the phone cord was still plugged into the wall.

Annja picked it up and began following it, hunting for the phone.

The ringing went on, and something in the sound spoke of a deep urgency. Whoever was on the other end was in trouble. Annja began digging through the detritus, following the cord.

"Keep ringing, keep ringing," she ordered it as she threw clothing and clumps of mattress stuffing and bits and pieces of the television out of the way in her frantic search until at last she found what she was looking for.

Annja snatched up the receiver.

"Hello?"

Silence.

"Hello? Anyone there?"

For a moment she thought it was a dead line, that she'd been too late, but then a man's voice whispered in her ear.

"Annja?"

"Yes. Who is this?"

"They're here, Annja. At least one, maybe more. I don't think I can get out."

"Who's there? Where are you?"

The voice was familiar, but she couldn't put her finger on who it was.

"Keep the files safe. They're all we have."

Novack.

Annja glanced at the wreckage of her hotel room and suddenly understood where her intruders had gone.

"Where are you?"

"My home." He rattled off an address on the northeast side of the city. "I don't think you're going to make it in time. Take the files to Radecki. He'll know what to do."

"Novack, wait! I…"

She heard a crash over the line, followed by several shouts, and then the dial tone began pulsing in her ear.

Novack had hung up.

Or someone had hung up for him.

Annja turned and sprinted down the hall, headed for the stairs at the far end. She didn't have time to wait for the elevator.

She raced down three flights of stairs, threw open the door at the bottom—almost colliding with a room service waiter—and dashed across the lobby followed by the staffer's shouts. Annja didn't care. She only had one thought, and that was to get to Novack as quickly as she could.

She unlocked the car door, flung herself behind the wheel and raced out of the parking lot, headed north. At the first traffic light she took a moment to punch the address Novack had given her into her cell phone and waited for the maps function to tell her where to go.

With a route in hand, Annja rushed through the city, cutting corners and racing through lights whenever the opportunity presented itself, and she still felt as if she was moving too slowly. She barely knew Novack—had only met with him twice—but she had seen in him a kindred spirit, someone else who wanted to see justice triumph. Allies like Novack were few and far between, and there was no way she'd allow him to face whoever was behind all this on his own.

She had to get there in time!

The GPS told her to turn right and so Annja did, bouncing over the curb and nearly taking out a row of newspaper kiosks in the process before accelerating back into traffic. She weaved in and out around the slower-moving cars and leaned on her horn when they weren't fast enough to get out of her way.

After what felt like hours, she left the busier part of the city behind and entered a residential area. The GPS took her through a series of turns down some side streets, and she could see from the map on the screen that she was getting close.

Hang on, Havel, almost there.

She came to a stop sign and was about to roll through it when a fire truck came roaring up behind her, lights flashing and sirens blaring. Annja caught the faint smell of smoke. The smell grew considerably stronger when she lowered the car window.

As she watched the fire truck drive on, she realized it was headed in same direction as she was.

Oh, no.

19

Annja was still a block away when she saw the flames. Their lurid brilliance lit the night sky ahead of her, outlining the trees and houses like some kind of macabre stage show.

Her heart dropped.

She turned into the cul-de-sac where Novack lived and stopped the car right in the middle of the road, staring at the conflagration.

There were four houses on the street—two on her right, one on her left, plus the one dead ahead that was engulfed in flames. She could hear the crackling of the fire as it ran rampant across the building, like some malevolent creature.

The fire truck she'd been following joined one that was already on the scene. Both of them were pulled to the curb right in front of the house. Firefighters from the new arrival scrambled to add their hoses to the mix, while those who'd arrived earlier poured a steady stream of water onto the flames.

It didn't seem to be doing much good.

The flames rose hungrily into the night.

Annja found a place to park and hurried toward the house.

A small crowd had gathered on the lawn of Novack's neighbor, watching the fire silently. Annja ran over to them, calling Novack's name, hoping she would find him standing there, unharmed. She grabbed one person after another, turning them around so she could see their faces, quickly moving to the next when she saw it wasn't him. It took only a few seconds to realize he wasn't there. When she didn't find him, Annja turned and headed for the house.

She didn't make it very far. The fire was consuming the entire structure, and the flames roared as the heat beat against her face, preventing her from getting too close. She shouted Novack's name, barely able to hear herself.

Firemen appeared on either side of her. One draped a wet blanket over her shoulders while the other took her arm and began to pull her away from the fire, shouting in her ear that she needed to move back, that it wasn't safe where she was.

"There's someone inside!" she shouted, fighting against them. "You've got to get in there! You've got to get him out!"

But her pleas fell on deaf ears as they dragged her away from the blaze. She struggled at first but then gave in so they wouldn't have to carry her. The truth was there wasn't anything she could do anyway; if Novack was inside, he was already dead.

A paramedic appeared at her elbow. "What's your name, miss?"

"Annja," she replied, still staring at the flames.

"Come with me, Annja."

She tore her gaze away and did as she was told. The paramedic was a few years younger than she was, but his voice was calm as he led her over to the back of an ambulance and helped her sit down. Now that they were away from the fire, he exchanged the wet blanket for a dry one and examined the exposed skin of her face and hands before handing her a bottle of cool water. "You don't look like you suffered any flash burns. Drink this, though, or your throat is going to be scorched from the heat."

He watched her as she drank, waiting until she'd finished half the bottle—and calmed down—before asking his next question.

"Do you know if there was anyone inside?"

Annja nodded. Her throat rasped as she said, "Novack. Havel Novack. It's his house."

The name didn't seem to mean anything to the paramedic. His expression was the same as he asked, "How do you know he was home?"

"We spoke on the phone not ten minutes ago. He sounded anxious, as if there was a problem, so I drove over to see if I could help."

There was a loud crash, and Annja looked over the paramedic's shoulder to see a section of the roof collapse into the house's interior, allowing fresh flames to leap skyward. Firemen were working frantically to contain the blaze, using multiple hoses on the burning house as well as soaking the structures on either side in an effort to keep the fire from spreading. Additional emergency vehicles were arriving even as she watched, but it was looking like a lost cause.

She realized the paramedic was speaking to her again.

"…if that's all right."

She shook her head, focusing her attention back on him.

"I'm sorry, I missed that."

He watched her carefully as he repeated himself, saying, "I'm sure the police will want to hear what you have to say. Why don't you just wait here for a few minutes, if that's all right with you?"

Annja nodded. "Sure. Sure, I'll wait."

The paramedic moved off to tend to some firefighters who had gotten too close to the flames, leaving Annja to watch the scene from the back of the ambulance. She looked on, still shocked by the sudden turn of events.

There was no longer any question of backing down. They—whoever *they* were—had killed a cop to keep their secret safe, and that meant they would stop at nothing to prevent the information Novack had collected from coming to light. It must be obvious that Annja was working with Novack—the files had been in her hotel room after all—which meant the killers would be gunning for her next.

To prevent that, she needed to go on the offensive.

It wasn't going to be easy, though, since she had no idea who she was looking for.

The cops had arrived and were forcing the spectators back, away from the property and out of reach of the flames and heat. As Annja watched them, movement caught her eye, and she turned to see a dark sedan park a short distance away.

Something about the car was familiar, but she didn't recognize it until the driver got out.

It was Tamás.

At the sight of him, Annja's breath caught in her throat.

Her thoughts whirled.

Who had been involved in this investigation from the very start?

Tamás.

Who had known she was talking to Novack?

Tamás.

Who had tried to discredit the former detective in her eyes, to gently nudge her away from partnering with the man?

Yep, that's right. Tamás.

She felt a cold chill run up her spine, and she turned away so he wouldn't see her face.

Tamás had been Novack's superior officer. Tamás had been one of those recommending Novack's retirement. And Tamás had been assigned to the Vass case when she'd been brought into the hospital.

Metaphorically speaking, Tamás's fingerprints were all over this mess.

Could he be the one? Could he be the killer?

Annja didn't know.

But one thing, at least, was clear. She didn't want to be anywhere near the man until she had an answer.

She pulled the blanket closer around herself to help

hide her features as she watched him hustle over to the scene commander and begin asking questions. Annja waited until Tamás's back was to her, and then quickly glanced around.

No one seemed to be looking in her direction.

Easy now, nice and slow. Don't call attention to yourself.

The ambulance was parked next to a large tree, and Annja used that to her advantage, slipping around the side of the vehicle and into the shadows cast by the branches. As soon as she was out of sight, the truck now between her and Tamás, she began walking at a brisk pace away from the scene. She was tense, expecting to hear a shout and find someone chasing after her, but she kept walking, and when she reached the end of the cul-de-sac and pursuit hadn't materialized, she began to breathe easier. Annja took the first turn she came to, headed deeper into the neighborhood and away from the main thoroughfare where there were sure to be additional police vehicles on the way.

Novack's voice echoed in her head as she walked.

Get the files to Radecki.

She didn't have the files anymore, but she had a lot of the material in her head, and she was confident she could recreate enough of a timeline to tell Novack's associate what was going on, if he wasn't up to speed already.

She made a few more turns until she found herself alone on a side street without a car in sight. Good enough, she thought.

She pulled out her cell phone and called the police

station where she'd been interviewed a few days earlier. When she reached the desk sergeant, she asked to be transferred to Officer Radecki's line.

The phone rang a few times, and then a recorded message played in her ear. She had no idea what was being said as the message was in Slovakian, but with little other help available she took a chance and left a vague message that wouldn't mean much to anyone but Radecki himself.

"Hi, it's Havel's friend. We've got a lot to talk about so I thought we might get together—the sooner, the better. Call me at this number."

She didn't bother leaving her cell number; the station's automatic caller ID would give Radecki what he needed to reach her.

Now there was nothing to do but wait.

And walk.

20

An elderly man in a pickup truck gave Annja a ride, letting her off a few blocks away from her hotel. She thanked him with a wave and waited for him to drive out of sight before she turned and headed toward the hotel. She'd only gone a few yards, however, before her steps faltered, and then she stopped.

She couldn't go back to her room.

If someone wanted to eliminate her, just as they'd done with Novack, the hotel would be the first place they would look. They'd already been in her room.

The hotel was a trap.

She needed somewhere new.

Simply switching to one of the nearby hotels wouldn't work. That was the most obvious option and those pursuing her were likely to think of it, as well.

No, she needed something farther afield.

Annja pulled her phone out of her pocket and hunted down a small, isolated hotel in one of the less picturesque sides of town. She saved the address and then, after flagging down a cab, showed it to the driver.

The first cabbie refused to take her there, which told her she had just the right kind of place.

So did the second.

The third, however, was more than happy to take her money. He drove her to the requested destination without a word and hurried off as soon as she got out of the car.

Annja took one look around and thought, You're not in Kansas anymore, Toto.

The hotel, a four-story affair with a blinking neon sign that was missing three letters, was sandwiched between a run-down tenement building and a deserted gas station. A few hard-looking men loitering on the steps of the tenement next door perked up at the sight of her, but she stood her ground and stared back, like a lioness protecting her kill, and the hyenas looking to scavenge the scraps got the message very quickly.

Annja went inside and got herself a room on the third floor. The elevator didn't look all that sturdy, so she chose to take the stairs.

Her room contained only what she'd expected—a bed, a sink and a hardback chair. Nothing more and nothing less. Austere chic, she thought with a wry grin.

But good enough for now.

She chained the door behind her, then took the chair and wedged it under the doorknob. It wouldn't keep a determined person out for very long, but even a few moments could be a precious resource in certain situations.

Satisfied with her preparations—as feeble as they were—Annja collapsed onto the bed and was asleep in moments.

A RINGING PHONE jarred her awake.

She sat up abruptly, her heart pounding, and glanced at the screen on her phone.

It was 2:00 a.m.

"Hello?"

There was silence and then a male voice spoke. "This is Havel's friend. Do you understand?"

Annja swung her legs over the side of the bed, instantly alert.

"Yes."

"You've heard?"

He could only be talking about the fire, she realized. A mixture of sorrow and anger swam through her at the thought. She pushed it aside, focusing on what was being said. "Yes, I've heard," she replied.

"We should talk."

"I agree."

"Meet me where you first met Havel in an hour. Can you do that?"

Annja frowned. The tavern in Čachtice would have closed hours ago. "It's two in the morning. It isn't going to be open."

"I'll take care of that. Just be sure you're there on time. If you're late, I'll be gone." He hung up the phone without saying anything more.

An hour.

She'd have to move quickly. Čachtice wasn't very far away—she could make the trip in less than fifteen minutes—but finding a cab in this neighborhood at this hour was going to be tricky.

She was already dressed, so all she had to do was

pull on her shoes. It occurred to her that all she had
left were a few bucks, her phone and the clothes on
her back. Everything else—including her camera
equipment—was either locked in the safe at her first
hotel or stored in the trunk of the car she'd abandoned
at the scene of the fire.

It was a depressing thought, but she shrugged it off
with a reminder that Radecki, the man she was going
to meet, was also a cop. If anyone could get the police
off her back and help her collect her belongings, never
mind the rental car itself, he was the one.

She took the stairs to the lobby and banged on the
bell sitting on the check-in counter until the pimply-
faced kid who worked the night shift sauntered in from
the back room. He looked her up and down, as if he
was evaluating a piece of meat, and then licked his lips.

"You might want to ring that again," he said in English, indicating the bell with a nod of his head. "I'm
not sure I heard you the first fifty times."

Annja ignored both his stare and his attitude.

"I need a cab. With a driver who speaks English."

He nodded. "You need a cab. Huh. Well, good for
you."

Then he just stood there, making no move to help
her.

Annja counted to five—no way she was getting to
ten—and then said calmly, "Perhaps you misunder-
stood. I need a cab and I need you to call one for me."

He gave her the head-to-toe look again and said,
"What's in it for me?"

It was two o'clock in the morning on a day when

her hotel room had been invaded, her belongings stolen and her partner in a serial killer investigation horribly murdered for what he knew about the case. And now this punk was leering at her.

Maybe she was overtired. Maybe she was stressed over the day's events. Maybe she'd just reached her limit when it came to idiots trying to make the world more miserable for the rest of us.

Whatever the trigger, she'd had enough.

With a cold smile, Annja stepped closer to the front desk. When her hands were hidden behind the counter, she reached into the otherwhere and drew forth her sword. Then she walked around the front desk, keeping the man in her sights. Before the desk clerk could say another word, she had him backed up against the wall, the point of the weapon pressed tightly against his bare throat.

Calmly, Annja, calmly, she reminded herself.

"I've had a really long day and it's going to be even longer before it's done. I would like you to call a cab for me. I've asked nicely, but you've chosen not to respond in the proper fashion, leaving me no choice but to be more forceful in my request."

She pressed down ever so slightly on the hilt of the sword.

The clerk went very still, his eyes wide and locked on Annja's face.

"Do we understand each other?" she asked, turning the blade one way and then the other.

He winced and very carefully nodded his head.

"Good. Call the cab, please."

Annja stepped back and lowered her sword, freeing the clerk to do as she'd asked.

He turned his back to Annja and reached for the phone.

Annja released the sword back into the otherwhere.

The clerk dialed a number and spoke rapidly in Slovak when someone answered. Then he hung up.

"Done," he said. "Ten minutes."

"You know what's going to happen if you called the police instead of a cab company, right?"

The clerk nodded vigorously as he reached up to rub the spot where the sword had pressed against his throat. Then he looked around frantically.

"Where did the sword go?"

Annja smiled sweetly at him. "What sword?"

"The one you were just…"

Seeing the expression in Annja's eyes, he stopped talking.

"Ten minutes, then," Annja said, and made a show of checking her phone for the time.

The clerk grew paler and kept a worried eye on the clock while they waited.

The cabbie was true to his word, arriving nine minutes after the call had been made. The clerk had such a look of relief on his face as the cab pulled to the curb outside that Annja couldn't resist one final jab as she stepped out the door.

Looking back over her shoulder, she said, "Tell anyone what you've seen or heard today and I'll be back to pay you a little visit. And this time I won't be so easy on you."

The clerk went paler still and looked as if he were about to pass out.

He won't tell a soul, Annja thought, and left him to his own devices.

Annja got into the cab, told the driver where she wanted to go and then settled back as he pulled away from the curb and headed out of Nové Mesto.

21

The tavern was shuttered and dark when she arrived. She had the cabbie drive past the building and let her out up the block. Once he'd driven off, she walked back.

The street was quiet.

Deserted.

As Annja strode toward her destination, it occurred to her that she didn't have any way of knowing if the person she'd spoken to on the phone had actually been Radecki. After all, he'd never identified himself directly; he'd just mentioned that he was Novack's friend. He could have been anyone, really. He didn't even have to disguise his voice, as she'd never spoken to Radecki before and wouldn't know what he sounded like.

In short, she might be walking into a trap.

At least she wouldn't be going in there unarmed.

Annja crossed the parking lot and walked over to the front door. She tensed, expecting security lights to come on, but the area remained dark. Reaching out, she tried the door.

Locked.

She checked her phone and saw that she was five minutes early.

Rather than standing at the front entrance, where anyone driving by could see her, Annja decided to wander around and see if the back door was unlocked.

Out back she found a large Dumpster that hadn't been emptied in a while, a stack of cardboard boxes that were waiting to be broken down and added to the trash and the aforementioned door, standing unadorned beneath a dim lightbulb. When she tried the knob, she found it unlocked.

She glanced around, didn't see anyone and decided to go inside.

Annja found herself inside the kitchen, just as she'd expected. The door leading into the main dining area was propped open and a few lights were on over the bar. Her attention was still focused in that direction when the barrel of a gun was pressed against her head from the shadows next to her.

"Don't move," a male voice said.

For a split second Annja thought about doing the very thing she'd just been ordered not to. The guy was standing too close, the gun pressed directly against her head, and as a result she felt she stood a fair chance of getting out from under the muzzle before he could pull the trigger. But she'd come here to learn something, so she decided she might as well see it through. If he was going to shoot, he would have done it already.

She did as she was told.

A hand came out of the shadows and quickly frisked

her. It was neatly and professionally done, and when it was over the gun was withdrawn.

"Sorry, had to be sure," the voice said, and then the lights over the cooking ranges came on, pushing back the darkness.

Annja blinked, letting her eyes adjust, and she then turned to look at the man standing a few feet away.

He was tall and dark haired. His face was all hard planes and angles, with scars that told of a childhood bout with chicken pox or something similar. He had intelligent eyes and a warm smile, which took away some of the harshness of his appearance. He was dressed in a dark jacket over a T-shirt and jeans, with thick-soled boots on his feet.

He holstered his pistol and then put out his hand. "Martin Radecki."

Annja smiled. "Annja Creed," she said as she reached to take his hand in her own.

The moment their palms touched Annja sprang into action, twisting his hand around and down while grabbing his elbow and leveraging it up with her other hand. She knew from personal experience that the pain at his wrist was excruciating in that position. To escape it, he had no choice but to drop to his knees and turn in whatever direction she wanted him to turn, which put him in her complete control. She held his wrist with one hand and removed the pistol from the holster on his belt with the other.

"I don't take kindly to having guns held against my head," she said in his ear.

"Aaagh! Okay, okay."

Annja knew her point had been made, so she released him and stepped back, holding the pistol down at her side. She watched him closely as he climbed to his feet, rubbing his wrist as he did so, but he made no move to advance on her.

He was clearly ticked that she'd gotten the drop on him, but he was also wise enough to know that he'd had it coming. He muttered something, took a deep breath and put his hands up in surrender.

"Look, I'm sorry. Didn't mean to get us off on the wrong foot. Just needed to be careful given all that's going on."

Annja could understand that; she needed to be careful, too. She held the gun loosely in her hand as she asked, "Do you have some identification?"

Radecki nodded. "In the left breast pocket of my coat."

"Take it out. Slowly, please."

He did as he was told, pulling a billfold from inside his coat and opening it to show her his badge and ID card.

Satisfied, Annja waved at him to put it away. She nodded her head toward the other room. "Why don't we go sit down and talk?"

Radecki led the way.

He motioned for her to take a seat at the bar while he slipped behind it. "My cousin owns the place," he said. "No one will bother us here. Get you a drink?"

Annja saw that the light on the coffee machine was on and there was a fresh pot sitting on the burner. "Coffee's fine," she said. She would have preferred a hot chocolate, but she needed the caffeine to make up for the sleep she'd lost. She had a feeling this was going to be another long day.

"Cream? Sugar?"

"Both, please."

He turned his back to her for a few moments while he set about making them both a cup of coffee. Annja put the pistol on the bar next to her where Radecki could see it. She wasn't ready to give it back yet, but he might be less anxious if it was in plain sight. She was going to need his help moving forward and didn't want to antagonize him more than she already had.

If Radecki noticed it when he turned around and put their coffee cups on the bar, he didn't say anything.

"Here you go." He put the cream and sugar on the bar, as well. "Just in case you like it lighter or sweeter than I made it."

For someone who had just stuck a gun against her head, he was trying awfully hard to clear the air.

She could appreciate a man who admitted when he was wrong.

The coffee was stronger than she liked, with a slightly bitter aftertaste, but she drank it anyway, knowing it would help kick-start her system.

She must have made a face because Radecki said, "It's Arabica coffee, from the Sidikalang region of Indonesia. My cousin discovered it while traveling a number of years ago and it's the only coffee he serves now. It's definitely an acquired taste—sorry about that."

"It's fine," she said as she added another spoonful of sugar to diminish the aftertaste.

They were silent a moment, and then Radecki said, "They found Novack's body in the ruins of his house this morning. They'll do an autopsy, of course, but right now they're saying he got drunk and fell asleep with a cigarette in hand."

Annja glanced at him. "Did he smoke?"

"No."

She thought about that one for a moment. "And yet that's the official story?"

"Yeah. They're saying his drinking got worse after he left the force and he probably took up smoking as a result."

"Who's the primary?" Annja asked.

"Alexej Tamás."

That wasn't surprising, she thought.

"How much do you know about what Novack's been working on?"

"Pretty much everything. I've been trying to help him from the inside where I can, but it's hard to know who to trust."

That she could understand. She was certainly feeling the same way.

"I'm afraid I have some more bad news," she said.

She told him about the thieves breaking into her room last night and stealing Novack's files. "Did he have other copies?"

Radecki shrugged. "I don't know. If he did, I would think they would have been in his home, and if they were…"

He didn't really need to say anything more.

"I have a pretty good memory," Annja said. "I think I can…"

She didn't get any further. A wave of dizziness suddenly washed over her, so unexpected that it cut her off in midsentence.

She sat there, head down, until it passed.

"Are you all right?" Radecki asked.

"Yeah, I'm fine," she answered, but when she looked up at him the room seemed to tilt and shift a second time. She grabbed the edge of the bar to steady herself.

"You don't look so good," the cop said, but his voice sounded as if it was coming from across the room instead of across the bar.

Something wasn't right.

She shook her head, waiting for her sight to clear.

What the heck was going on?

She looked up and saw Radecki watching her closely. He didn't appear all that concerned. He just calmly took another sip of his coffee and glanced at the clock.

The coffee…

She looked down at her drink as a third wave of dizziness tried to drown her. Her head was spinning wildly now. The cup seemed to lurch to the left and then to the right. She was starting to have trouble putting her thoughts together.

"What…"

She tried to move the coffee away from her and ended up pushing it right across the bar and over the edge. The sound of the cup shattering seemed to echo in her ears.

"…did you…"

Annja looked to where the gun had been seconds before only to find it wasn't there. A glance in Radecki's direction showed it sitting on the bar directly in front of him.

"…do?"

Radecki didn't answer.

Her vision was starting to tunnel, a dark gray haze creeping in on all sides, and Annja knew she was in trouble. She pushed away from the bar, wobbling a few steps on unsteady legs before crashing to the floor.

The sound of her heart hammering in her ears was almost overwhelming. She knew she had to get away, but she was finding it difficult to remember what she was running away from. Her instinct for self-preservation took over in the absence of logical thought, and she managed to force herself to her hands and knees.

As her head lolled about, she caught one dizzying glimpse of Radecki as he came out from behind the bar, walking toward her, pistol in hand.

Move! her mind screamed.

Annja began clawing her way forward, pulling with her arms and kicking with her legs, fighting for every inch.

She barely got a third of the way across the floor before she ran out of strength, the haze having all but overwhelmed her. She knew she had only seconds before she succumbed to unconsciousness.

Too late, the notion of her sword occurred to her.

She rolled over, staring up at Radecki looming above her, gun in hand.

With a supreme effort of will, Annja reached into the otherwhere for her sword.

As her fingers closed around the hilt, she finally lost the struggle, the blade vanishing into darkness along with her consciousness.

RADECKI STOOD OVER the woman, staring down at her unconscious form. He didn't see her beauty; all he saw was a threat to the enterprise he'd worked so hard and so long to build.

A threat to his future prosperity.

His finger itched on his weapon's trigger.

He wanted nothing more than to raise his gun and put a bullet through the woman's skull. End it, here and now.

The muzzle began drifting upward, an inch at a time.

It would be so easy...

His finger slipped around the trigger guard.

He could say it was an accident. That she had discovered the truth and tried to kill him. Just a few pounds of pressure...

Abruptly he turned away, lowering the gun to his side.

She wanted Creed taken alive. She'd been quite clear in that. If he disobeyed her now, she was sure to exact some kind of retribution. The last thing he wanted at this stage of the game was to face punishment at her hands; she was the most merciless woman he'd ever met, and woe to the one who found himself helpless in her control.

This time, he would do as he was told.

Even if it went against his every instinct.

Holstering his gun, he took a few deep breaths. When he was in control of himself once more, he stepped back over to the now-unconscious Creed and nudged her with his foot. When she didn't respond, he drew his boot back and kicked her, hard, in the ribs.

Still no response.

Good.

He bent down beside her and checked her pulse.

It was steady and strong.

Even better.

He rose to his feet and took his cell phone out of his pocket. He hit a quick-dial key and listened to the phone ringing on the other end.

In only a moment she answered.

"Yes?"

"Our problem is taken care of."

"And the other package?"

"Right here at my feet."

There was a pause. "Intact, I take it?"

"Of course."

"Good. Bring it to me."

"On my way."

22

Deep in her drugged sleep, Annja dreamed.

They were not pretty dreams.

She ran through stone hallways lit only by torches burning in sconces on the walls, her bare feet slapping the cold flagstones and her breath coming in ragged gasps.

In the shadows behind her something kept pace, slowing when she slowed and speeding up when she tried to force more effort out of her already tiring limbs. She didn't know what it looked like, or if it was even human, but there was one thing she knew for certain.

She couldn't let it catch her.

So she pushed on, running as quickly as her bare and bloodied feet would carry her, frantically searching for a way out.

Doors would occasionally appear on one side of the hallway or the other, set at irregular intervals, but every one that she tried was locked. Most of the time there was only silence when she yanked on the door handle, but at other times she heard screams and cries for help coming from behind the barrier. There was nothing she could do for them, however, so she was forced to continue on.

Step after step, corridor after corridor, in a seemingly endless maze with pursuit never far behind…

When the door appeared at the end of the hall, Annja almost didn't believe it was real. She glanced back as she reached it, caught a glimpse of a hulking shadow and knew she had only one chance to get this right.

She grabbed the door handle.

Please, please, please…

She pulled, and to her utter surprise the door opened.

A room lay just beyond.

Annja quickly stepped inside and pulled the door closed behind her.

The smell hit her first, the thick coppery scent of fresh-spilled blood. As her eyes adjusted to the dim light, she could make out a bath set into the floor a few yards in front of her. The thick fluid that filled the bath looked almost black in the low light.

Oh, no…

She realized what she was looking at even as the surface of the bath was disturbed and the figure of a woman began to emerge from the depths, blood flowing down over her head and upper body.

Annja could feel fear welling up inside her like a tide as she stared in disbelief at the figure ahead of her.

This can't be happening…

She didn't realize she was backing up until her shoulder blades struck the door.

Ahead of her, the woman stepped from the bath,

arms raised in supplication and longing, a silent invitation for Annja to join her.

It was only when the woman's eyes snapped open that Annja realized she was looking at herself…

ANNJA AWOKE WITH a start, leaving one nightmare behind only to discover she was trapped in another.

Her head was pounding, and it was making her vision shimmy and dance. She blinked several times, waiting for her eyes to be able to focus. When they did she found that she was lying on the cold tiled floor of a room somewhere, her hands tied together in front of her with thick nylon rope. Her feet were likewise bound; she didn't need to see them to feel the rope wrapped securely around her ankles.

A drain sat in the middle of the floor, about six inches in front of her face. Seeing it made her realize the side of her body that was resting against the floor was chilled and damp. The floor had obviously been wet when they'd dumped her here.

She raised her head slightly, taking in the wall in front of her. It was hewn out of solid rock and looked ages old, but the twisted tangle of pipes high on the wall were shiny and new.

Where on earth was she?

She flexed her wrists, hoping that whoever had tied them had done a poor job, but no such luck. She was trussed up better than a Thanksgiving turkey and completely at her captor's mercy.

Needless to say, that concerned her more than a little.

It was clear now why Novack had been getting nowhere with his investigation; Radecki had been sabotaging it the whole time. Whether he was the killer or just part of the cover-up remained to be seen, but given her current situation, Annja was leaning toward the former.

Which meant she needed to get out of here as soon as possible!

She brought her knees up toward her chest as best she could, tucking herself into a ball, and then rolled over so she could see the rest of the room. It was pretty much like the first half, with the exception of the steel door set into the wall in front of her. The door had a reinforced window that was about a foot square.

More telling was the fact that there was no handle on the interior of the door. That suggested this wasn't a temporary holding cell; it had been built specifically for that purpose.

Suddenly the drain in the floor took on much darker connotations.

I have to get out of here!

Her first order of business was cutting free of her bonds. Thankfully she had the means to do so right at hand.

She rolled across the room until she fetched up against the nearest wall, then maneuvered herself around so she was sitting with her back against it. She drew her legs up in front of her until she could put her feet flat on the floor, and then braced her hands on her knees, palms inward.

Calling her sword to hand, Annja put the hilt of the weapon between her knees with the blade sticking up. Holding her legs tightly together so the weapon wouldn't fall, Annja placed the knotted rope binding her wrists against the edge of the blade and began to saw back and forth.

She hadn't even managed two passes when she heard voices right outside her door.

Knowing she couldn't be caught with her sword in hand, she dismissed the weapon back into the otherwhere with a thought and tipped herself over so she was lying flat on the floor once more.

Closing her eyes, she worked on steadying her breathing and pretended to be unconscious.

The door swung open with a screech, evidence of either poor maintenance or lack of use. Several sets of footsteps sounded in her ears.

"I know you're awake," a male voice she recognized said, "so there's no use in pretending. The dose of the drug was adjusted to your body weight."

Radecki.

Annja opened her eyes.

The traitor stood before her. Beside him were two men who had the look of enforcers—hired thugs brought in to do the heavy lifting so Radecki didn't get his hands dirty. They were dressed identically in dark jeans, dark T-shirts and leather boots, the classic uniform of muscle heads the world over. They stared at Annja with all the emotion of a pair of mannequins.

"Get her hooked up," Radecki said, quickly confirming who was in charge.

Annja didn't know what he was talking about, but

the amused smirk on the officer's face let her know she wasn't going to like it, whatever it was.

As the two thugs moved toward her, Annja wished she could call forth her sword, but the pistol holstered on Radecki's belt would've made any such move a losing proposition. She might keep the men at bay for a time, but in the end, Radecki would still hold all the cards.

For now, she'd wait and see.

She could still feel the sword waiting in the otherwhere, and as soon as her hands were untied, she'd be able to access it again.

The thugs moved in, one on either side, and, grabbing her under the arms, lifted her to her feet. They brought her over to Radecki, who was now standing in the middle of the room holding a small black box that reminded Annja of a remote control.

Still smiling, Radecki tapped the button on the remote.

A whirling noise sounded from above her head, and Annja looked up just in time to see a cable drop from the darkness above. Her head was still pounding so it took her a moment to understand just what it was, and by that time one of the thugs had caught the hook that was set on one end, hooked it through the bindings circling her wrists and nodded to Radecki.

The winch was already reversing itself as Annja began to struggle, and within seconds she found her arms being dragged up over her head toward the ceiling.

Too late, she realized what was happening and tried to twist her arms free, kicking her feet, but all she managed to do was set her body swaying back and forth like a pendulum as she hung by her wrists a few inches above the floor.

The bindings tightened, but not so much that they cut off her circulation. Still, she knew she would lose strength the longer she hung like this, and soon she wouldn't be able to feel her hands at all, not to mention how completely vulnerable the position left her.

"Much better," Radecki said with a wide smile. He came over and put one hand on her hip to steady her. "It seems I have you right where I want you."

Annja answered with her usual defiance. Hanging a good foot or so above him, she was in the perfect position to look down, smile and then spit in his face.

"For a woman in your circumstances, that wasn't the smartest thing to do," Radecki said as he wiped the spittle from his face. His voice had lost its jovial tone and was now flat and hard. "Gentlemen, if you wouldn't mind…"

Annja had expected Radecki to react with violence, but she wasn't prepared for the hammering blows that came from either side as the two thugs began to work her over, haymakers falling like rain with frightening regularly. Her body twisted about with each blow so Annja had no way of predicting where the next punch would land. Within seconds she was doing all she could to hold on to consciousness against the overwhelming pain that enveloped her.

"Enough!"

The order was spoken with absolute authority, and

the blows instantly stopped. It took Annja a moment to realize that the order hadn't come from Radecki.

Annja glanced up to see who'd given the command. Diane Stone stood in the doorway.

23

"What's going on here?" Stone demanded, her hands on her hips and a hard look in her eye.

With the biggest threat to their operation—Novack—now taken care of, Radecki no longer felt as vulnerable and decided it was time to show more steel around his associate.

"Nothing to concern yourself with," he replied. "Just teaching our guest to show some respect."

A month ago he never would have responded in such a fashion, but Stone didn't show a hint of surprise. Her face remained impassive, but Radecki thought he saw her nostrils flare.

Get used to it, he thought. He was done lying down and letting her walk all over him. She didn't scare him anymore.

"I'll be the judge of what should or shouldn't concern me," Stone told him, but she left it at that and turned her attention to their prisoner.

"We meet again, Ms. Creed. How unfortunate for you."

That, at least, was a sentiment he could agree with.

Creed had been nothing but a pain in the neck since she'd stuck her nose into this whole mess, and he was more than pleased to finally be able to remedy the issue.

Creed didn't say anything, but her eyes watched them like a hawk. Radecki would bet that even now she was trying to plan her escape. She was in for a rude surprise either way; like those women five hundred years before, no one with any hint of beauty ever left this place alive. Not while the "Blood Countess" was in charge.

"What's the matter?" Stone asked the prisoner as she took a closer look at her. The guards Radecki had brought with him stepped back, away from Stone, as if afraid of the woman. Truth be told, Radecki really didn't blame them.

"Cat got your tongue?"

Creed stared at Stone with a disdainful look on her face. Radecki had to give her credit; she had some stones, that was for sure.

"Where am I and what am I doing here?" Creed asked.

The woman's words were forceful, but she was still twisting about in the air, her feet a few inches above the floor.

Stone must have found it amusing as well, for she laughed in response. "Really, Annja—may I call you Annja?—you aren't in any position to be demanding anything."

Radecki watched as Stone stepped forward and grabbed Annja's chin in her bare hand. The prisoner tried to twist free, but Radecki knew from personal experience that Stone was much stronger than she looked, thanks to the treatment.

If he had his way, he'd just take her out back and put a bullet through her brain, but apparently Stone had seen something that had captured her interest. As Radecki looked on, Stone turned Creed's face back and forth, examining her closely. Radecki had seen Stone behave this way before and wasn't surprised when she asked, "Has she been tested for the marker?"

He shook his head, then answered aloud when he realized Stone hadn't even bothered to glance in his direction. "Not yet. I was busy dealing with our other recent acquisition."

Stone turned. "Any trouble?"

"No."

The drugs Petrova had cooked up to simulate a heart attack had worked beautifully. Once the "body" had been moved down to the morgue, it had been a simple matter for Petrova to fake an autopsy, fill out the required paperwork and order the remains to be taken to the crematorium for disposal, as there was no known next of kin. No one but Radecki, who had been driving the disposal unit, would ever know that the individual would never reach the crematorium, never mind that the deceased was actually very far from being dead.

Why waste raw materials like that when you didn't need to? he thought to himself.

Stone must have been thinking along similar lines, for she asked, "When will the harvesting procedure begin?"

"Probably already has," Radecki replied. "I turned

her over to the techs about fifteen minutes before coming down here. It doesn't take very long to do the prep work, so they should have her hooked up to the extractor by now."

"Good. We need to ramp up our output. Demand for the product is increasing exponentially."

Radecki shook his head. "I keep telling you, we can't sustain such an increase. The raw materials simply aren't there. We need to raise the price. Fewer customers at a higher rate of return will make this far more sustainable."

Stone glared at him. "Let me worry about the raw materials. You just do your part and keep the police off our backs. I want her tested and the results on my desk by morning, is that clear?"

"Crystal," Radecki answered sourly as he watched Stone walk away without a backward glance.

One of these days…

He turned his attention back to their prisoner, spinning her around so he could see her face. "Be a good girl and don't give the nurse any trouble, huh, Creed? I'd hate to have to come back here and teach you a lesson about discipline." He paused, pretending to think it over.

"Actually, go ahead and misbehave," he said, patting her condescendingly on the cheek. "Teaching you a lesson is exactly the kind of thing I'd be happy to do right now."

To his chagrin, Creed chose not to fight.

"Maybe some other time, then," he said cheerfully. He was about to order his men to take her down, but then thought better of it. The nurse would probably have an easier time of it if Creed was exhausted from hanging there a while. He'd send his men back for her later.

"Let's go," he told the other two. "We've got work to do."

They left the cell, making certain to lock it securely behind them, and then headed for the elevator, taking it one floor above. Radecki's two companions turned left while he went right, heading for the large conference room that served as the nurses' duty room.

Most of the crew was still on shift down in the medical facility, but he found two of the senior staff sitting around enjoying their cups of coffee. He grabbed the closest, a plain-faced woman in her midfifties. He vaguely remembered vetting her for the project nearly two years before and he knew she could be relied on to do the job properly. A glance at her name tag reminded him of her identity—Phillips.

"Got a job for you," he told her as she turned to greet him. "There's a new test subject down in the containment area. Stone wants a full panel done right away. Bring the samples to my office once you're done so I can get the results to her as quickly as possible, understood?"

"Yes, sir."

He waited for her to gather a specimen kit, and then headed for his office on the next floor above while she went to deal with the prisoner.

ONCE THEY LEFT her alone in the cell, Annja got right to work. She didn't know how much time she had before the nurse would show up to take the sample. She had to be free before her company arrived or she'd miss her best opportunity to get out of here.

She'd been hanging from her arms for more than five minutes and had lost a good deal of sensation. Her escape plan depended on her hands and arms, however, so she hoped she had enough left in the tank to manage.

The hook at the end of the cable supporting her had been slipped through the bonds that tied her wrists together, now leaving her hands free. Reaching up, she grabbed the point where the steel cable met the top of the hook. Her hands felt like slabs of meat from the reduced circulation, but she forced them to do her bidding, knowing that all she had to do was hold on for a minute or two and then it would be all over.

Once she was satisfied that she had a decent grip on the top of the hook, she used what strength she had left in her arms to pull downward while at the same time swinging her legs in a jackknife position up over her hands. She wrapped one foot over the other, pinning the cable between ankle and shin and taking her weight momentarily off her hands.

Her stomach and back muscles shook with the effort to hold herself there, but she knew they would hold for a moment, and a moment was all she needed.

The second the downward drag on her wrists eased, she jerked them upward, lifting the ropes that bound her free of the hook.

Hands now free, her body knifed back downward, and she let herself go with the momentum, somersaulting as she fell so she hit the floor feetfirst.

She'd imagined executing a perfect two-point landing, like a gymnast coming off the jump at the end of the uneven bars. In reality, her feet hit the damp floor and shot out from beneath her, sending her sprawling on her side against the cold tile with a dull smack.

Luckily she didn't hit her head.

She lay there for a few seconds, willing the pain away and waiting for some feeling to return to her hands. When it did, she pulled her sword from the otherwhere and used it to cut herself free.

Annja climbed shakily to her feet and hurried over to the door. A glance out the window showed her she was just in time; a woman in a white lab coat carrying a specimen collection tray was coming down the hall. She was only a few yards away and would have seen Annja peering through the glass if she'd been looking up and paying attention rather than scanning the paperwork on the clipboard in her other hand.

One should always watch where they were going, Annja thought with a grim smile as she flattened herself against the wall next to the door, sword at the ready.

The nurse wasn't expecting to find anything but a helpless prisoner, and so she took several steps into the cell before she seemed to realize that the room appeared to be empty.

It was almost too easy. Annja pushed the door closed as she came out from behind it, the sword in her hands already swinging toward the woman's skull.

For her part, the woman must have sensed something at the last moment, for she turned in Annja's direction, her mouth hanging open in a look of surprise that might have struck Annja as amusing in some other less-threatening situation.

As it was, all she felt was a flash of satisfaction as the flat of her blade struck the woman along the side of her head, sending her toppling to the floor of the cell. The small basket of supplies went skittering in all directions as she lost her grip.

Annja brought the blade back up, ready to deliver another blow should it prove necessary, but she needn't have worried. The woman was unmoving against the floor, down for the count from Annja's first strike.

Ignoring the unconscious woman for a moment, Annja stepped over to the door and glanced out through the window, wanting to be sure that the sound hadn't carried and reinforcements weren't on the way.

The hallway outside her cell was still empty.

Satisfied that she had a few moments in which to make her escape, Annja sent her sword away, then returned to the woman's side and quickly searched her. The pockets of the woman's lab coat were empty, but Annja found an electronic key card hanging on a lanyard around her neck. She took that and the lab coat itself, knowing she was going to need both to get out of here. Then she dragged the body against the wall so it couldn't be seen easily from the door.

Satisfied with her preparations, she used the key card to unlock the door, slipped out into the hall and pulled the door shut behind her.

She found herself in a narrow hallway with doors on either side identical to the one she'd just passed through, right down to the window and key card–operated locking mechanism. Unlike her room, all of the others were dark. She continued past them without looking inside, quelling her curiosity in favor of finding her way out.

At the end of the hall was an elevator. She pressed the call button several times, but it didn't illuminate. Closer examination showed her a slot below it that was just large enough to accept the key card in her hand.

Annja gave it a try.

The card was sucked out of her hand by some internal mechanism, and for a moment she thought she'd lost it, but then the unit buzzed and spit the card back out. Moments later she heard a hum from behind the wall, indicating the approach of the elevator.

Please be empty.

It was.

There was only one button on the control panel—Up, presumably—and so Annja pressed it.

After a moment, the doors closed and the elevator began to rise.

24

If Annja had to guess, she would have said that the elevator went up only a floor, maybe two, but she really had no way of knowing how fast or how far it traveled.

When the doors slid open, she found herself looking out onto another hallway, one that reminded her of a medical facility or hospital corridor more than anything else. With nowhere else to go, she headed down it at a brisk walk.

Doors were spaced evenly along the corridor, and when she peered in through the windows she found either offices or lab units. Lights were on in a few of them, but she didn't see anyone moving about inside, and the few doors she tried were all locked. She thought she might be able to gain access with the key card but didn't see a benefit to delaying her escape just to have a look around. She'd come back with some help once she gained her freedom.

The hallway ended in a T intersection, and when she reached it Annja paused, glancing up and down the hall. Both directions looked the same as the corridor she'd just come from, and for a moment she was uncertain which way to go. Then she was reminded of the old adage about always turning left in order to get out of maze, and she figured that was as good a move as any other.

Annja had moved down two more hallways in the same manner without encountering anyone when she was startled by voices coming from somewhere ahead of her.

She stopped and listened.

After a few seconds it was clear that they were getting closer.

A glance down at her disheveled appearance didn't make her confident that she could pass scrutiny, especially not if the staff were small enough to know one another. She needed to get out of sight, and she needed to do it quickly.

Annja moved to the nearest door and tried the handle.

Locked.

This door, like all the others before it, had a key card access slot. Without hesitation she swiped her card. After a moment, during which Annja thought she might need to resort to more active measures to get the door open, the control beeped softly and the lock clicked open.

Annja opened the door and slipped inside, closing it behind her as swiftly as she dared. She called her sword to hand and stood off to one side, her gaze locked on the door handle. If it started to turn, she'd have to act quickly to keep from being discovered.

The voices grew closer…closer…closer still, until it

was clear they were on the other side of the door. She thought she recognized Radecki's voice, though she couldn't be sure. It took all her will not to open the door and confront him then and there, but she knew that if she did she would drastically cut her chances of escape.

Concentrate on getting out of here, she told herself. Deal with him later.

It was good advice and she might have even taken it, if she hadn't turned at that moment and looked through the large plate-glass observation window that formed the rear wall of the conference room in which she stood.

What lay beyond drew her attention like a moth to a flame.

The observation window overlooked a large room that was lit by massive overhead banks of electrical lights that left nothing in shadow. Portable beds, the kind one might see in an emergency medical ward, were arranged in four different pods throughout the room, five beds to a pod. Monitors and other medical equipment were arrayed in clusters at the head of each bed. Annja recognized the standard telemetry units for measuring heart rate, blood pressure and respiration, but there were quite a few others with which she wasn't familiar.

Fourteen of the twenty beds were occupied. It looked as if all of the patients were women, though it was tough to tell from here. Technicians in white lab coats moved back and forth between the pods, tending to the patients.

Though the lights were off, Annja was worried that one of the technicians might look up and see her, so she made sure to stay several feet back from the observation window. This, of course, limited her view of what was going on, something she found increasingly frustrating the more she watched.

The voices in the hallway finally moved on, but Annja was too wrapped up in what was going on below her to leave yet. She stood there watching for several minutes, trying to get a sense of what the technicians were doing to the patients under their care. Something about the scene didn't seem right. It wasn't any specific action she could point to, just a vague sense of unease that seemed to linger over it all. It was as if the patients were all screaming in her head, though she could see that they weren't making a sound.

It was creepy, to say the least.

Annja stepped a little closer to the glass and that was when she realized she wasn't alone in watching the happenings below. A light was on in another office, overlooking the medical facility from the opposite side, and a woman stood by the window, gazing downward.

Annja recognized her immediately—Diane Stone.

Seeing her, Annja was reminded of Stone's earlier comments about the extraction process and being behind in the production schedule.

The question was what, exactly, were they extracting from these women?

Annja was determined to find out.

Stone suddenly raised her head and looked in Annja's direction.

Her instincts told her to duck away, but Annja did just the opposite, holding herself rock steady, knowing that moving now would invite discovery. She reminded herself that she was surrounded by the darkness of the room and was standing back far enough from the window that the lights below shouldn't give her away. A sudden flash of movement would ruin that illusion.

She can't see me. She's just feeling the weight of my stare. Stay calm and she'll look away.

After a moment, that was exactly what Stone did. She turned away from the window and walked to the desk behind her. Annja watched her for a few minutes more, but she didn't want to press her luck. If the woman began to feel uncomfortable, she'd likely send someone to investigate, and that was the last thing Annja needed.

The clock was ticking; eventually her disappearance would be noticed and the halls around her would be full of guards trying to track her down. If she was going to get out of here, now was the time, but she couldn't bring herself to abandon the women below, not without knowing what was going on.

She needed to get into the medical ward without being seen.

As she stood there, pondering how she was going to manage that, the technicians began to gather at one end of the unit, near a large nursing station that appeared to serve as the command center. The handheld tablets they'd been using to make notes and examine patient charts were pushed into docking stations set into the desktop, most likely to recharge them for the next shift. The staff stood around chatting for a few more minutes, then began making their way to a set of stairs at the far end of the ward.

Moments later that same group passed by the conference room in the hall outside.

Annja smiled. If they could get to the hallway so quickly, she could make her way to the ward even faster.

She glanced at Stone's office. It, too, was dark. At some point in the past few minutes, Stone had apparently slipped out.

It was time for Annja to make her move.

She stepped over to the conference room door and listened for a moment. When she didn't hear anything, she cautiously opened it and stuck her head out into the hall.

The coast was clear.

Making her way to the end of the hall, Annja quickly located the stairs the staff had used and descended to the medical ward.

25

The medical staff had dimmed the lights when they'd left, but Annja was able to see well enough to make her way across the room. She ignored the nursing station and its collection of tablet computers for the moment and moved over to the first cluster of patients.

As she approached, Annja expected one of the patients to turn her head and look at her, but none of them did. They just lay there, unmoving. Not a twitch or a sigh or even a restless limb.

Annja felt a chill pass over her; if she hadn't just seen the technicians tending to the patients, she would have thought they were dead.

Neither was a particularly pleasant thought.

She moved closer until she stood right next to one of the beds, and nearly recoiled when she saw the state of the patient resting within.

The woman was horribly gaunt, her flesh stretched tight across bones that stuck out like daggers. Her eyes were sunken in her head, her lips shriveled to nothing more than thin gray lines and her skin was the color of a New England November sky. Much of the woman's hair had fallen out, and Annja could see bandages wrapped around the woman's fingertips, most likely where she'd begun losing her nails.

If it hadn't been for the steady rise and fall of the woman's chest, Annja would have been sure that she was dead. As it was, she wondered just how much longer she had to live.

The woman was wired into a variety of monitoring devices, with electrodes attached to her head, face and chest. Two different IV lines were pumping fluids into her left arm, but the IV bags themselves didn't indicate what medication they contained.

As she stepped away from the IV bags, a loud click came from the other side of the bed. The click was followed by the hum of activating machinery.

Curious, Annja walked around the bed to investigate.

What she saw brought her up short.

A pumping device, similar to those used to remove the fluids from a body during the embalming process, sat on a small cart. Tubes running from the pump and filled with a pinkish fluid disappeared beneath the sheet covering the woman's lower body. Another tube, this one filled with a deep red liquid, ran back out from under the sheet to a collection container resting on the lower level of the cart.

An image of the strange puncture wounds on Marta Vass's thigh sprang to mind, and Annja reached forward and lifted the sheet that was covering the woman's body with trembling hands.

Just as she'd suspected, the first tube ran from the machine to a plastic port set into the woman's inner thigh, right about where the femoral artery would be. The second tube ran from the same spot on the woman's other thigh back to the collection unit.

It wasn't hard to figure out what was happening. The device was pumping some clear-looking fluid into one side of the woman's body and forcing her blood out the other. From the bruises Annja could see up and down the woman's legs, it was clear this wasn't the first time it had happened.

Stone's question rang in her head: *When will the harvesting procedure begin?*

From the next bed in the pod came a click similar to the one she'd heard moments before, followed by the same hum of machinery starting.

Then another. And another and so on until there was a humming sound coming from each bed in the group.

With growing horror, Annja turned and looked at the other patients lying in the beds nearby. All of them were in similar condition, gaunt and skeletal, like starvation victims, except here their life and vitality were being stolen away by the ticking machines at their sides.

Annja wanted to tear the tubes out of their flesh, but she didn't dare. Who knew what would happen if the pump was abruptly shut off?

She stood there, frozen in place, uncertain as to what to do.

It took her a moment, but she managed to shake off her paralysis and turn to face the next pod of patients. Afraid of what she would find but knowing that she had to look anyway, Annja headed in that direction.

This group wasn't as bad as the first, though Annja

would have been hard-pressed to call them healthy. Their skin was jaundiced and appeared tight in some places, mostly around the mouths and eyes, but there was none of the sunken, wasting-away look that characterized the first group of patients.

Annja stepped over to one of the beds. It was occupied by a blonde woman who looked to be in her early thirties. Her hair was brittle, but she still had most of it and she seemed to be breathing a little bit easier than the others.

Annja bent down next to her.

"Hello?" she said. "Can you hear me?"

There was no response from the woman. Not even a twitch of recognition that someone was close by.

Annja tried again, a little louder this time.

"Can you hear me? I'm here to help you."

Still nothing.

Reaching out, Annja took the woman's hand in her own. Her skin was cold, as if she had ice water running through her veins.

The woman didn't respond to her touch.

Annja was starting to have some suspicions about just what was in those IV bags. Sedatives fed directly into their bloodstreams on a regular basis were sure to keep the patients—cut the nonsense, she thought, call them what they are: prisoners—unconscious and therefore under control at all times.

It would also keep them from protesting their own slow but steady deaths.

A white-hot rage burst into flame deep inside Annja. Not only was someone murdering women, but the victims were also being tortured to drive a company's profits.

She was going to put a stop to this or die trying.

Annja gently laid the woman's hand back down on the bed and was about to turn away when something about the patient in the next bed caught her attention.

She frowned and stepped closer.

The woman looked familiar…

Annja racked her brain for where she might have seen her before. The woman was dark haired with sharp features made all the more angular from what she was experiencing at the hands of her captors. Annja guessed her age at about twenty-five. The woman's eyes were closed, but Annja had the feeling they'd be a deep brown…

Her eyes. That was it!

Annja had seen this woman staring out of a photograph in Novack's file. The image had been a haunting one, the photographer capturing the woman's mournful expression at just the right moment, and it had stuck with Annja as a result. So had the woman's name— Belinda Krushev.

Belinda was one of the woman Novack had claimed were missing. The police, of course, disagreed. According to the official report, she'd most likely run off with her boyfriend, who'd gone missing at the same time. Since they were both over the age of eighteen, the police had told the families there was little they could do. That had been the status quo for almost a year until Novack had come along and added her to his list as a possible murder victim.

Looking down at her now, Annja was pleased that Novack had been only partially correct. Belinda might have fallen victim to foul play, just as Novack had suspected, but there was still time to keep her from the list of those Stone and company had killed.

Having found one of the women on Novack's list, Annja guessed there were probably more. She moved from bed to bed, staring at the women's faces, trying to match their features with her memories of the photographs in Novack's files. She'd managed to identify five other matches when she came to the bed containing the ward's newest patient.

Csilla Polgár.

The woman looked much like she had when Annja last saw her, though there were several fresh bruises on her face. Like the others, Csilla was hooked up to both a pair of IVs and a blood pump, though in her case the pump unit hadn't yet been switched on.

Annja stared at Csilla in disbelief, astounded that she was here rather than in police custody.

Inside her head the pieces of the puzzle began to click together.

Stone was running some kind of research and development operation to generate an expensive and much-desired product. That much was clear from what Stone had said back in Annja's cell. Whether Stone was working on behalf of Giovanni Industries or just using them as a cover, Annja didn't know.

The operation required something that was only found in a select group of women, and given what she was seeing around her, most likely found in the women's blood. Extracting it was apparently an all-or-nothing process, otherwise Stone and company wouldn't be kidnapping the women and then faking their deaths to keep anyone from looking for them.

The women, of course, were not dead, not yet at least, but there was little doubt in Annja's mind that was how they'd end up once Stone took whatever it was she needed from them.

Radecki, and most likely the medical examiner, Petrova, were in on the operation. Annja was convinced of that. There was no way for them to have pulled this off without someone on the police force and in the medical examiner's office. The autopsy reports she'd seen had been signed off by Petrova, so he was the logical culprit. Others might be involved as well, particularly within the police and other emergency services, though Annja had no way of knowing that for certain yet.

And she couldn't prove anything. Like Novack before her, she'd be laughed out of the department if she went to the police now. She needed something concrete, something that would prove she wasn't making wild-card accusations against a multibillion-dollar corporation with more lawyers than she could shake a stick at.

Annja's gaze lifted from Csilla's bed to the observation windows overlooking the medical facility.

She knew just where she could find what she needed.

26

Radecki sat at his desk, staring at the clock. He'd told the nurse to bring Creed's sample directly to his office so he could personally oversee the processing of the test results.

That had been half an hour ago.

How long did it take to draw some blood? he wondered with more than a little impatience. Either the nurse was goofing off—something she'd pay dearly for if he found out that was the case—or something had gone wrong.

Given how much trouble Creed had been so far, Radecki would bet on the latter.

Best if he went down and had a look for himself.

Radecki opened the top drawer of his desk and removed the stun gun he kept there. He'd used it a couple of times to subdue some of the women they'd taken from the streets, and he liked the way it put down even the most aggressive targets. He thought it might be handy should Creed prove difficult. He slipped the weapon into his pocket, then got up and walked out of his office.

The halls were empty because the few employees working at this hour were assigned to the residential wing until the next shift. That was fine with him; he couldn't stand interacting with the idiots Stone hired to handle the drudge work. How anyone could convince themselves that they were involved in legitimate research, given what they were doing to these women long-term, was beyond him, and yet those half-wits had apparently managed to do so. Radecki didn't believe that self-delusion was an acceptable indulgence.

Many of the technicians had been promised a hefty bonus should they reach the stated goal of artificially replicating the catalyst in the patients' blood. Radecki knew better. That bonus would never be awarded, never mind cashed. Success or failure, the working stiffs would end up with their contracts terminated in the most literal sense of the word, and he would be laughing as he cleaned up the mess.

He suspected that Stone would get rid of him as well, when the time came, so he'd taken steps to protect himself. The guards employed throughout the facility were his men, not hers. If worse came to worst, he was confident they would follow his orders rather than Stone's. If the operational structure was ever put down on paper—which it wouldn't be, not as long as Radecki was in charge of project security—Stone's name would certainly be at the top of the chart. But as with many kingdoms down through the ages, the real power was not in the hands of the one sitting on the throne. Radecki played chancellor to Stone's queen. He stood behind her, hidden in the shadows, and he was quite happy with the arrangement.

Lately, however, she'd started to make him nervous. He suspected that her behavior was a byproduct of the formulation they produced, one of the reasons he wasn't in a hurry to try it out himself. Stone had first been exposed to the test product—a deep red cream that reminded Radecki of lotion—by accident, but when she'd seen how it rolled back the hands of time, making her skin look years younger, she had started using it on a regular basis.

And therein lay the rub.

From what he could tell, the cream was not only changing her on the outside—making her look like a woman two decades her junior—but it was changing her on the inside, as well. Now, he was no scientist, but even he knew that sudden, drastic changes, even beneficial ones, to any single aspect of a complex system had the potential to throw the entire thing out of whack. And he was starting to see that very thing with Stone. She was making brilliant leaps of deductive logic and advancing the project, yes, but she was far more short-tempered and aggressive, often to the point of violence, than she'd been six months ago.

The formulation was taking a toll.

He just hoped she could hold it together long enough to figure out how to artificially produce that one key ingredient. So far they'd been able to locate enough women with the genetic marker and harvest what they needed, but they couldn't go on doing that forever. They were already finding it difficult to select appropriate targets, and if Novack and Creed were any indication, they couldn't keep their operation hidden forever.

At least Novack was out of the way, he thought with a satisfied smile as he boarded the elevator. Soon Creed would be, too, and he could relax and wait for it all to be over.

Radecki took the elevator down two floors and got off on the lowest level of the complex, where the test subjects were held. At Creed's cell he glanced in the window as he reached for his key card, only to have his heart skip a beat when he saw that Creed was no longer hanging from the hook where he'd left her.

He pulled out the stun gun and switched it on, then swiped the key through the card reader. When the lock clicked open he went through the door quickly, glancing to either side to keep from being ambushed.

The nurse he'd sent to take the blood sample, Phillips, lay on her side against the nearest wall, out of sight of anyone looking into the room from the hallway. She was still breathing and didn't have any apparent injuries, so he didn't give her more than a passing thought. He'd send someone down to help her back to the dormitory section and that would be that.

Right now, he had to find Creed.

The ropes that had bound her lay in the middle of the floor, neatly cut in two.

There was no sign of the prisoner herself.

Radecki cursed beneath his breath, then turned and hurried out of the room. He needed to find Creed before Stone realized she was missing. If Stone got it into her head to come down and question the prisoner and found Creed had escaped, all hell would break loose. It was just the kind of setback that might send her completely over the edge.

Any other escaped prisoner would make a beeline for the exit, if they could find it, that was, but he had a hunch Creed would be different. She'd been dogging their heels ever since she'd rescued one of their discarded subjects and he didn't see any reason that she'd give up now. Not while she was right here, in the heart of their operation.

If anything, he expected her to keep hunting for answers now that she was so close to them.

That meant she could be anywhere in the complex. The place was too big to search effectively on foot, but thankfully he didn't have to resort to such extreme measures.

There were better, faster ways of searching the facility and they didn't involve the chance of running into Stone in the process.

Radecki headed for the elevator and the security control center on level B.

27

Stone's office.

That was where she would find the answers she needed; Annja was certain of it. Now all she had to do was get there.

She looked down at Csilla's bruised face.

"Don't worry, I'll be back for you," she told her, taking the woman's hand in her own and giving it a gentle squeeze. She had no idea if Csilla could hear her, but she didn't feel right just leaving her alone without saying something. If Csilla was aware, even peripherally, beneath all the drugs she was being given, Annja didn't want her to think she was being abandoned.

"I'm going to get some help, but I'll be back," Annja told her. "Just hold on."

It was hard to turn around and walk away, but Annja did it anyway. If she was going to put a stop to this, she didn't have a choice.

At the far end of the ward was another staircase, similar to the one she'd taken earlier. Annja hoped it would lead her to the offices overlooking that portion of the ward.

Her hunch proved correct.

Conscious that the clock had started ticking the moment she'd set foot outside her cell door, Annja hurried along the hallway, passing several doors until she came to the one she thought was Stone's.

Taking the key card from around her neck, she slid it through the slot.

There was a low beep, but the signal light on the lock remained red instead of turning green. She tried it again, deliberately sliding the card at a slower pace, but ended with the same result.

The door stayed securely locked.

Annja worried that the card reader was tied into the security system and that repeat failures might trigger an alert of some kind, so she stopped trying after the second failed attempt.

The card would have made things easier, but she didn't need it to get inside. She had her own special tool for that.

She shot a quick glance up and down the hall to be certain no one had come along while her attention had been on the lock. Then she called her sword to hand, pulling it from the otherwhere with just a thought. As always the weapon made her feel more powerful, more confident, and she felt her spirits pick up just by gripping the hilt in her hand. She put the tip of the sword into the space between the door and the jamb, right where the electronic lock was situated, and then she drove the weapon forward while bearing down to the left.

The blade went through the lock with ease, and the door popped open with sharp crack.

Annja glanced around, concerned that the sound might have been overheard, but when no one came to investigate she smiled in satisfaction and stepped inside the room, flipping the light switch with one hand while closing the door with the other. When she saw that she was alone in the room, she released her sword, sending it back to the otherwhere to wait until she needed it again.

The office was large, with an oversize desk, a couch with matching leather chairs and a bar. A door to the left of the desk opened onto a private bathroom. The back wall of the room was made of glass, and through it Annja could see the medical ward she'd left behind just moments before.

A switch near the desk controlled the window blinds, and Annja used it to cut off the view from downstairs. Once that was taken care of, she turned her attention to the desk in front of her.

Stacks of file folders and photocopied articles from scientific journals lay in messy piles atop its surface, right next to the computer keyboard and flat-screen monitor. Annja picked up a few of the articles and glanced at the front pages, noting that they had titles like "A Multi-trait Meta-analysis for Detecting Pleiotropic Polymorphism" and "Integrating Multiple Genomic Data Elements to Predict Disease-Causing Nucleotide Variants in Exome Sequencing Trials."

Nothing like some light reading for the afternoon, she thought sourly.

The articles weren't going to be any help. They were clearly referencing genetic studies of some kind or another, but they weren't proof that Stone was kidnapping women and killing them.

She tossed the papers back down on the desk, and in doing so must have accidentally nudged the mouse because the computer screen came out of sleep mode.

Intrigued, Annja pulled out the desk chair and sat down. She dug through the stacks of paper on the desktop until she found the mouse, and then began clicking through the files, looking for anything interesting.

Stone had left several windows open, so Annja started with those. The first few files were spreadsheets showing purchase orders and budget expenditures. She glanced at them but quickly moved on. Next up were half a dozen scientific papers, all focused on bovine spongiform encephalopathy, otherwise known as mad cow disease. She stopped there for a moment, trying to make a connection between the missing women and MCD, but eventually moved on because she just wasn't seeing it.

That was when she found the video.

It had been paused halfway through and showed a weary-looking Stone sitting in front of the camera. Intrigued, Annja clicked Play.

"…morphed into a new formation before failing entirely. I'm directing the staff to focus on the left-hand peptide chain, hoping that running its characteristics to ground can give us some insight on the right-hand chain, which is the important one."

Annja used the mouse to slide the control back to the starting point.

The video stuttered for a moment and then smoothed out.

"This is update number three hundred and forty-seven," Stone began. "Thursday evening, just after midnight."

Day before yesterday, Annja thought. She kept watching.

"Our attempts to artificially replicate and stabilize the prion continue to meet with failure, but I'm determined to push through to the end. Today's activities centered on getting the left-hand chain of the prion molecule to stabilize…"

Stone went on for several minutes, summarizing the steps her team had taken in the lab that afternoon.

Annja slid the control forward to a spot later in the video and let it play again.

Stone was still speaking but had moved from science to marketing. "Supplies are low—I understand that—but as I've told you, I cannot speed up the process any more than I already have. We have a full complement of donors at the moment, so we should be able to continue producing what we need for the next several weeks. In the meantime, we're searching for additional carriers we can bring into the program.

"We're close to a breakthrough—I know it. I just need a few more weeks. I will have better news in my next update."

With that, the video ended.

Annja right-clicked on the file and called up its properties. When she followed the path it had been saved under, she discovered that it was stored in a folder marked…Project Báthory.

Why am I not surprised?

She followed the path to the folder where the video was stored and discovered more than three hundred additional video files.

Each of the files was named with a six-digit number that corresponded with the date on which the video was recorded. A few had an asterisk at the end of the numeric sequences, separating them from the rest. Annja found the first of those, dated over three years ago, and opened it.

Stone's face filled the screen, and Annja gasped in surprise when she saw it.

In this video Stone looked ten years older than she had in the more recent one. She had deep lines on her face, crow's-feet around her eyes and her hair looked limp and lifeless—a far cry from the smooth skin and vibrant hair that Stone exhibited now.

It was as if they were two separate people.

"Personal update number one," Stone said, and Annja thought she could hear a quaver in the woman's voice.

"It has been twelve hours since I accidentally exposed myself to the Báthory prion taken from the test subjects. I've decided to make these personal diary entries to correspond with my official updates in order to document any changes that might occur as a result of the exposure.

"My vital signs are all steady at this time. I've ordered a full blood panel to be taken so it can be used as a baseline comparative moving forward. I'll keep track of any issues I encounter where and when possible."

Stone looked away from the camera, and a moment later the video ended.

Annja's thoughts churned as she closed that video and selected another. This one was also marked with an asterisk, but it was dated six weeks after the one she'd just viewed.

It began the same way, but in this video Stone's condition had markedly improved. She not only looked better, but her energy levels were practically off the charts.

"I feel fantastic! Better than I have in years, actually." Stone was sitting at her desk, smiling at the camera. Gone were the lines on her face and the tired, exhausted look in her eyes. She practically sparkled with vitality.

"My most recent blood test shows that the prion is activated and is replicating damaged tissue at a startling rate. I feel as if I've lost ten years overnight, as if I could get up and run a marathon right now with no training whatsoever. My thought processes are clearer, with less distractions, too. Better yet, I've experienced no ill effects.

"Given these results, I've created a temporary delivery vehicle in the form of a body lotion and have decided to continue treating myself moving forward. If we can find a way to bottle this, we'll be billionaires overnight."

Stone rambled on for several more minutes, detailing the changes she was seeing in her physical form, but Annja stopped listening, her thoughts lost in the realization of what she'd just heard. Stone's mention of the prion they were trying to replicate was the key.

A prion was an infectious particle composed of abnormally folded proteins that tended to cause progressive degeneration in the central nervous system. Rather than multiplying in the host organism the way viruses do, prions induced normal, healthy proteins to convert to an abnormal version of the same particle. Prions were the culprits behind diseases like mad cow and Creutzfeldt-Jakob.

But Stone seemed to be suggesting that they'd discovered a prion that worked in the exact opposite fashion. Instead of converting healthy proteins to unhealthy, abnormal ones, this prion was reviving the proteins that were breaking down due to age, bringing them back to their original healthy state. By altering the proteins within the cells, they were, in effect, changing the cells themselves, reversing the effects of age and disease from the ground up. If she could find a way to control the process, Stone could quite literally prevent the human body from aging. It was a stunning achievement.

Still, the devil was in the details, and Annja knew that for all the good this project might do in the long run, there was a dark side to it, as well. The very name that had been given to the project—Project Báthory—spoke of the darkness and pain at the center of it all. Clearly Stone had continued with her research and produced a viable product, which she was selling to the highest bidder. But like Báthory before her, Stone was using the blood of innocents for the sake of her own

personal agenda, and Annja wasn't about to let that
continue.

She *couldn't* let it continue.

The monitor was wireless, but it didn't take Annja
long to find the computer's tower sitting on a shelf next
to the desk. She pulled the tower down, unscrewed
the side plate and then tore the hard drive, a rectangular case about the size of a large cell phone, free of its
mounting bracket. She left the now-useless tower where
it was and slipped the hard drive into her pocket.

She was just coming around the side of the desk
when there was a knock at the door.

"Hello?" a male voice called out. "Director Stone?
Are you in there?"

Before Annja could say anything, the door began
swinging open.

28

When Radecki arrived in the security office, he found two men on duty. As luck would have it, they were the same two men—Gregor and Chovensky—who had tried and failed to scare off Creed the other night in Čachtice.

He smiled when he saw them; they would be perfect for the job.

"Get me the feed from the containment level for the past thirty minutes," Radecki ordered.

Chovensky jumped to comply. He clicked through several screens and hit a few keys, then spun the time signature dial backward, rewinding the video. "Coming up on the central monitor now," he said, pointing.

Radecki leaned closer and said, "Back it up to the point where you see me coming out of containment cell six."

Chovensky fiddled with the controls and finally an image popped up on the monitor in front of them, showing Radecki and his two companions stepping out the door of the containment cell.

"That's it! Right there."

"Got it," Chovensky said.

"Okay, now advance it slowly."

The camera only had a thirty-degree arc, so Radecki wasn't surprised to see his digital self, along with his two companions, walk down the hall and disappear while the camera stayed trained on the door to the containment cell.

Chovensky moved to pause the feed but Radecki stopped him. "No," he said. "Let it run."

The security guard did so, and the three men watched the empty corridor for a few moments.

"Speed it up a little," Radecki said.

Chovensky complied. The tape skipped along until a figure entered the screen from the left side and approached the door to containment cell six.

"Slow it down now."

At regular speed, the figure resolved into that of Nurse Phillips. Radecki watched as she approached the containment room and then used the key card around her neck to open the door. Phillips stepped inside the cell.

"Leave it running," Radecki ordered.

The rooms had originally been designed as storage spaces, so there weren't any cameras in the cells themselves. The best he could do was watch the corridor and see what happened from there.

Less than five minutes after Phillips entered cell six, the door opened again, this time from the inside. It wasn't Phillips who stepped into the hallway, but Creed. She was wearing Phillips's white lab coat and appeared to have something in her hand.

"Can you zoom in on that?" Radecki asked.

Chovensky worked the controls, zooming in and enhancing the image at the same time. When he was finished, Radecki could easily see what it was that Creed was carrying.

Phillips's key card.

Not good.

"Start it up again," Radecki said. "Let's see where she goes."

This time, both men got in on the act. Chovensky worked the first camera, running the feed until Annja stepped past the lens and was therefore out of sight. At that point, Gregor took over. Since the cameras were time synced, he could switch to the next one in line, moving down the hall without dropping Creed from sight. In that fashion they followed her down to the end of the hall and then watched as she used the key card to call the elevator.

The elevators didn't have cameras in them either, but Chovensky and Gregor were already calling up the feeds from the cameras outside the elevators on the other levels as Radecki said, "Find her. I want to know where she went and where she is now."

There were a tense couple of minutes as the two men negotiated the various possibilities, but it wasn't long before Gregor said, "Got her! Conference Level B."

He put the feed up on the master monitor so they could all see it.

Annja emerged from the elevator and began making her way down the hall. As before, the men followed her with the cameras, watching as she wandered down several hallways, apparently searching for a way out.

Radecki found himself hoping she'd discovered the exit. It would be so much easier arranging a fatal accident if she was outside in the real world rather than locked down here with them.

But it wasn't to be.

About five minutes after getting off the elevator, Creed looked back with some anxiety on her face and then swiftly moved to the closest door.

She swiped the key card and, when the lock flashed open, slipped inside the room, easing the door shut in her wake.

Gregor spoke up before Radecki could voice the question.

"Conference room, second floor. The one that overlooks the medical ward."

They watched as three employees walked past in the hall outside the room and then waited several more minutes for Creed to emerge, to no avail.

Perhaps she was still in there.

He was thinking of heading in that direction when the screen in front of him fluttered several times and then went dark.

"What happened to the feed?" Radecki demanded as he felt his pulse begin to race. If he lost her now...

Gregor grimaced. "That camera's been on the blink for the past week or so."

"Why wasn't it fixed?"

"Authorization hasn't been approved. It was submitted earlier this week but the director hasn't signed off."

Another sign that she's slipping, Radecki thought. "Find her!" he said. "I want to know where she is in this facility at this very moment."

"Yes, sir."

Radecki pulled out a chair and sat down while his men began scouring security tapes, trying to locate their missing prisoner.

29

With nowhere else to go, Annja did the only thing she could think of. She quickly stepped into the bathroom and shut the door.

She was just in time.

She could hear the newcomer's voice growing louder as he came into the room.

"Director Stone? Are you all right? I saw the door was damaged and...Director Stone?"

There was silence for a moment, followed by approaching footsteps and then a knock at the bathroom door.

"Director Stone? Are you all right?"

Annja reached into the otherwhere and drew forth her sword, even as she rapidly weighed her options. She didn't particularly like any of them, truth be told, but she had a hunch that whoever was out there wasn't going to go away until he made sure Stone was okay.

Covering her mouth with her hand to muffle her voice, Annja called out, "I'm fine."

"Okay, no problem, then. I'll just wait here."

Come on!

Annja had been hoping her visitor would leave once he discovered that "Director Stone" was in the restroom, but no such luck. She would have to go out there and deal with him.

She took a deep breath and opened the bathroom door.

Her visitor had opened the blinds and was standing near the window, looking down into the medical ward. He was curly haired and wore a white lab coat over dark slacks.

"I hope you don't mind," he said, keeping his eyes on the patients below. "I brought the latest pathogen reports and thought we might go over…"

He turned and saw Annja standing there, sword in hand.

She nearly smiled, the expression on his face was so comical. She didn't blame him for his shock, though. A woman wielding a sword and standing between him and the safety of the hallway was probably the very last thing he'd expected to see when he'd got up this morning.

Or any morning, for that matter.

"Close your mouth before you swallow a fly," she told him wryly.

His jaw snapped shut with a loud clack.

Annja had planned on tying him up and leaving him locked in the bathroom, but now she had other ideas. He'd mentioned pathogen reports, which meant he probably knew exactly what was going on around here. He could fill in the blanks in the narrative she'd constructed.

"Sit down in that chair and don't move," she told him, pointing to the leather desk chair she'd just been sitting in. "You and I are going to have a little chat."

He glanced at the chair and drew in a deep breath.

"Who are you? What are you doing here? You shouldn't be in the director's office. I'm going to call security and see to it…"

He'd started toward the door, thinking perhaps that the weapon was just for show and that Annja wouldn't have the courage to use it.

She quickly disabused him of that notion, flicking her wrist and sending the very tip of the blade lashing toward his face, cutting a two-inch furrow across his cheek.

"I said sit down," she told him as his eyes grew wide and his hand clamped over the injury on his cheek. From where she stood, Annja could see the blood well up between his fingers and run in little rivulets across his hand.

He sat.

"What's your name?" she asked him.

"Theo. Theo Owens."

"What do you do here, Theo?"

He shook his head, wincing at the resulting pain from the cut on his cheek, but he ended up answering her anyway.

"I'm the assistant lab director."

"Lab director, huh? Sounds pretty important."

He looked at her, his eyes blazing. "Don't you mock me! You have no idea what we're doing here!"

But she did, and she let him know it in no uncertain terms.

"You're kidnapping women and using them against their will in an illegal drug trial. Something I fully intend to put a stop to."

"You wouldn't dare!" he said, sitting up straighter and glaring at her.

Annja smiled. "Try me."

"No, you can't. You don't understand. What we're doing here has worldwide significance."

Annja nearly laughed, but she decided that he might just stop talking out of spite, and that was the last thing she wanted. Instead, she said, "Do tell."

"The prion research we're doing here can literally turn back the clock. Solve problems such as cancer, senility, simple old age. With the products we're developing, we'll be able to ensure that the best and brightest of us live lives considerably longer than we do now."

"The best and brightest?"

His brow furrowed in confusion. "But of course. Who else would you give it to?"

She ignored the question; if he didn't already see the "us versus them" theme inherent in his statement, she wasn't going to educate him.

"You're using those women against their will."

Owens missed her tone apparently, because he said, "Yes! Yes, we are, I know that! But you don't understand—we need to do it! We'd be morally remiss if we didn't!"

Morally remiss? Are you bloody kidding me?

Somehow she didn't think he was.

He went on. "This is clearly a situation where the good of the many outweighs the civil rights of these few individuals. The prion we're studying is only found in those of a particular bloodline that dates back to the 1600s, a bloodline that's becoming more and more diluted with each passing generation. If we don't act now, the prion may very well be altered through genetic changes that we have no control over, breeding out the one quality that we need to solve the problems plaguing our society today! We must act, and we must act now!"

Annja couldn't believe what she was hearing. That anyone could have so little respect for the lives of others made her sick, and she had to look away for a moment to keep her temper in check and not carve him into little pieces for his arrogance.

When her attention shifted away from him momentarily, Owens made his move.

He surged up out of his seat, shouting something incoherent as he tried to get to the door, perhaps thinking that if he could get out into the hall he might be able to summon help.

For a split second Annja was caught off guard. She hadn't imagined that Owens had it in him, and yet here he was, making a break for it. Instinct caused her to raise her sword, but she realized even as she did so that she was probably going to need this sick son of a gun to get out of this place, especially if she intended to rescue the women.

So she stuck out her foot just as he went rushing past. Owens's shin hit her outstretched ankle, and he toppled over like a runaway freight car, slamming face-first into the carpet.

To his credit, he didn't stay down, but immediately rolled over and tried to get back to his feet. Unfortunately for him, Annja reacted quicker than he did. She stepped in front of him, blocking his way with her sword.

"You really shouldn't have done that, Theo," she told him.

A few minutes later Owens was back in the swivel chair, though this time his hands were bound behind his back with the cords Annja had cut from the window blinds.

30

"Got her!" Gregor crowed.

Radecki was out of his chair and next to Gregor's in a heartbeat. "Where is she?" he demanded.

"Coming out of Director Stone's office," Gregor said, pointing at the screen where Annja could be seen emerging from the room behind a man in a white lab coat.

"Who's she with?" Radecki asked, tapping the image with his finger. "And is that a sword she's carrying?"

The newcomer turned out to be Theo Owens, one of the geneticists working on the project under Stone. His hands were tied securely behind his back. As Radecki looked on, Creed gave Owens a shove that sent him stumbling down the hall. She was clearly forcing him to take her somewhere.

And the instrument she was using to enforce that request was, indeed, a sword. Where it had come from or how she'd gotten it, Radecki didn't know. He didn't remember anything like that being in Stone's office, but perhaps it was a new addition. Maybe Creed had picked it up from somewhere else in the complex before getting to Stone's office. Either way, the game had changed now that she was armed.

"Keep them in sight. I want to know where they're headed."

Gregor did as he was told, using the cameras to keep an eye on the duo as they made their way down the hall. Rather than taking the elevator, they headed for the stairs, which allowed the security officer to keep them in sight at all times as they descended to the floor of the medical ward. Once there, they made a beeline for one of the patients in pod three.

Radecki crossed the room to the weapons cabinet, took a set of keys from his belt and unlocked the door. He removed a pistol in a shoulder holster and a stun baton, keeping the former for himself and giving the baton to Chovensky before relocking the cabinet.

"Where are they now?" he asked as he slipped the shoulder holster on and checked that the gun was loaded.

"In the medical ward," Gregor replied.

Radecki nodded. That would make sense; Creed seemed to have a hero complex. Must be going for the donors.

He took a pair of two-way radio headsets from the rack below the cabinet and tossed one to Chovensky.

To Gregor he said, "We'll be on channel nine. I want you to keep her in sight at all times and radio me if she starts to go anywhere, understood?"

Gregor nodded. "Got it."

"Chovensky, you're with me."

The big man grinned and nodded.

Time to put an end to this, Radecki thought as he swept out the door with Chovensky in his wake.

ANNJA KEPT HER sword low but still pointed at Owens's back as they headed down the corridor. He appeared docile now, perhaps having learned his lesson back in the office, but Annja was taking no chances. He was going to help her get Csilla and then lead them out of this place, or he was going to get hurt. It was that simple.

Owens led her back down the stairs she'd come up only a short time earlier and into the medical ward.

"Now what?" he asked, glaring at her over his shoulder.

"Over there. Pod three," Annja said, pointing with the tip of her sword.

He hesitated. "What do you want at…?"

She gave him a shove to get him going. "This isn't Twenty Questions. Move!"

Owens did as he was instructed. He did it reluctantly, but he did it. When they reached the patients' beds, he looked at her and raised an eyebrow as if to say, *Well*?

Annja inclined her head toward the last bed in the pod. "Over there. Csilla Polgár. I want you to turn off the machine and unhook her from it."

"Now, just a minute! You can't…"

Annja didn't let him get any further. She backed him up against the bed and shoved the tip of her sword under his chin, forcing his head back as far as it would go. "I can't *what*?" she asked in a low, menacing voice.

Go on, give me a reason, she thought.

Theo must have sensed how close to the edge she was, for he clamped his mouth shut and didn't say anything more.

She leaned in. "I'm getting tired of having to ask for everything twice, do you hear me?"

He nodded. It wasn't much of a nod, but then again it was hard to nod vigorously when the blade of an ancient sword was thrust under your chin.

"So do it."

She stepped back, pulled the sword away from his throat and used the edge of the blade to cut the bonds from his wrists.

His hand immediately went to his throat, is if to prove that it was still intact. He coughed once, and then moved to do as she'd asked without another word.

As Annja looked on, Theo went to work. First he checked Csilla's vitals by looking at the monitors she was hooked up to. Then, apparently satisfied with what he saw there, he moved around to stand next to the pumping device attached to the side of Csilla's bed.

He glanced at Annja, seemed about to say something, and then decided against it. Instead, he flipped the switch on the side of the pump.

The pump ran through another cycle and then stopped.

Annja nodded with satisfaction.

"First the leg tubes, then the IV," she told him.

She did her best to keep an eye on him while also watching the entrances at either end of the ward. It wasn't easy. But she didn't trust him enough to turn her back on him. For all she knew he'd slip Csilla something when she wasn't looking, and all this would be for nothing.

The incoming transfer tube was attached to Csilla via a plastic port that had been surgically implanted in the vein of her left thigh. Theo donned a pair of latex gloves and removed the line, but then he hesitated.

"I don't have the equipment I'd need to remove the port and suture the artery properly closed," he told Annja.

"So leave the port in place for now. Just be sure that it's sealed and capped properly," she replied.

"You're the boss."

Annja let the sarcasm slide. The important thing was getting Csilla out of here before anything else happened to her.

She glanced around at the other patients, wishing she could take all of them with her. She simply didn't have the manpower—or the transportation—to pull it off at the moment, but she made a vow that she'd be back for them before long.

Just stay alive until I can get help, she told them silently.

A glance toward the entrances at either end of the ward showed them still empty.

When Theo was done with the intake tube, he turned his attention to the outtake one. Again, he carefully removed the tubing and then sealed and capped the access port. After that it was a simple matter to take out her IV.

"Done," he said, stepping back. He stripped off the surgical gloves and tossed them on top of the pump.

Annja looked around the room, finally spotting a wheelchair in the pod next to them.

"Go get that chair and bring it over here."

Theo did as he was told.

"Gently lift her up and put her in the chair, please."

Annja looked on as Theo slid his arms under Csilla, lifted her out of bed and put her down in the wheelchair. Csilla's head lolled to one side, and he did his best to make her comfortable.

"What's the best way to get out of the facility?" Annja asked.

Theo didn't have to think about that one. "There's a garage down on sublevel three, with a ramp that leads up to ground level. You should be able to get a vehicle from there."

"Then start pushing the wheelchair in that direction," she told him.

31

As Radecki approached the door to the medical ward, he keyed the microphone on his headset.

"Talk to me, Gregor. Are they still inside the ward?"

The microphone gave the guard's voice a tinny cast but Radecki had no problem hearing him. "Yes. Creed just forced Owens to remove the transfusion gear from one of the patients, and now they're putting her in a wheelchair."

Radecki gritted his teeth. Not only was Creed planning to escape, she was trying to steal one of their subjects.

There was only one logical way to do that.

"Are the cameras in the garage operational?" he asked Gregor.

"Yes."

In an instant, Radecki decided to get there ahead of them. He explained as much to Gregor, adding, "Keep following them with the cameras. If they're headed in a different direction, let me know immediately."

"Understood."

With a signal to his companion, Radecki turned and

headed back the way they had come, taking the staircase at the end of the hall down three floors to the garage.

If Creed expected to find a huge garage—with plenty of vehicles to choose from—she was about to be disappointed. The highly sensitive nature of the work being doing here meant that those involved with the project, with the exception of Stone, Radecki and one or two others, were housed in the complex. As a result, there was no need for an extensive garage.

Stone and Radecki parked their personal vehicles in the garage, and Radecki and his team maintained three Suburbans for the collection work they had to do periodically.

The keys were routinely left in the ignitions, so Radecki sent Chovensky to collect all of them. Then both men stepped into the small office to the left of the elevator, leaving the lights off and the room shrouded in darkness, to watch for Creed's arrival.

THE GARAGE WAS rectangular, with the elevator at one end and the exit ramp at the other. Parking spaces ran down either side of the room, with the center open for travel. There was space for ten, maybe twelve vehicles, but at the moment there were only five—three dark-colored Suburbans, a deep crimson-colored Mercedes and a silver Land Cruiser. All five were parked next to one another close to the elevator.

Almost there, she thought. Just a few minutes more and they would be free. Then Annja could get on with the business of making Stone and her colleagues pay for what they'd done. Annja couldn't wait to see the look on the woman's face when the authorities came to take her away.

Of course, there was the little issue of not knowing who she could trust among the local authorities. If men like Tamás and Petrova were in on the conspiracy, it stood to reason that others were, as well. If she went to the police, she'd be putting herself and Csilla at risk until she knew just who those "others" were.

First things first, she reminded herself. Get Csilla out of here and then worry about bringing the law down on Stone's head.

The fastest way of getting out of here would be to steal one of the automobiles, preferably one of the SUVs as there'd be room for Csilla to lie down in the back. Unlike the Mercedes or the Land Cruiser, which looked like personal vehicles, the SUVs, with their identical configuration and color, seemed like corporate vehicles. If they were, the keys would probably be around here somewhere, as the company would want to make it easy for its employees to gain access.

Television shows might make hot-wiring a car look easy, but this was the real world and Annja certainly hadn't mastered that particular skill. She needed those keys.

Owens was apparently thinking the same thing, because he looked back at Annja and said, "The security team usually just leaves the keys in the ignition."

Annja smiled; that was the first bit of good news she'd had all day.

"Lead on, then, Theo, lead on."

Owens headed for the trio of SUVS, pushing the wheelchair ahead of him. When he reached the first one, he parked the wheelchair behind it and walked over to try the driver's door.

Anxious to be out of there, Annja did the same with the second one in line.

She found the driver's door locked, so she bent down, using her hands to keep the glare out of her eyes, and peered in through the window.

She couldn't see the keys.

Damn!

She straightened, and in that instant her instincts kicked in. Annja jerked her head to one side, and the punch that had been intended for the back of her head glanced off the side of her skull.

It was enough to spin her around so that she ended up with her back to the SUV.

She put out a hand to steady herself against the side of the vehicle, shaking her head to try to clear it.

Her opponent came into focus even as he rushed toward her in another attack. He was a big Slavic-looking individual with close-cropped hair and arms that looked as big around as Annja's thigh. Annja recognized him as one of the guards who'd accompanied Radecki to her cell.

The man threw a whopping left haymaker that would have done some serious damage if it connected, but Annja was alert now and she saw the blow coming. She waited until the last second and then jerked her head to the side.

The guard's fist shot past the edge of her cheek and

hammered into the car window, shattering it into fragments.

Annja didn't hesitate, but went on the offensive. She spun forty-five degrees toward her opponent and delivered a punishing strike to the thug's kidney, then followed that up with a heel stomp to the top of his foot.

The guard howled in pain but didn't go down. He turned to her with rage in his eyes.

Annja expected him to lash out with his fists, and she prepared herself to block, only to have the man move in on her instead. He stepped forward and wrapped his arms around her in a big bear hug, lifting her up off the ground.

Then he started to squeeze.

Annja knew she was in trouble the minute he wrapped those meaty arms around her. His biceps were like cords of steel, easily able to crush her ribs if given the opportunity, and with her feet off the ground there was no way for her to get the leverage she needed to break his hold.

He squeezed tighter, forcing the air out of her lungs, and grinned down at her as if to say, *I've got you now.*

She reared her head back and then snapped it forward, smashing her forehead into the guard's nose with all the force she could muster.

There was an audible crack as his nose broke.

He let go, his hands going to his face, and Annja took advantage of the opportunity to drive a knee up toward his groin.

That blow never landed, however, for he brought his own leg up, blocking the strike and taking the knee against his thigh. It still hurt, she knew that, but it wasn't the debilitating blow she'd hoped for.

He made that clear seconds later when he began hammering her with his fists, throwing face strikes and body shots with remarkable alacrity, moving at a speed that was unexpected given his large size.

Annja blocked the majority of them, her forearms and hands moving as fast as her opponent's, but the few that got through told her she wouldn't be able to keep this up forever. Her blows were doing less damage than his, and that differential would eventually hand the confrontation to him. She needed to end this quickly if she wanted anything left in the tank for what was to come.

No sooner had the notion occurred to her than he managed to slip a punch past her defenses and she took a fist high on the right side of her face, snapping her head around and sending her to the floor.

Dazed by the blow, Annja was just pushing herself up off the cement floor, trying to get back to her feet, when the first kick caught her on the left side of her rib cage. She felt one of her ribs snap beneath the force of the blow. The kick lifted her up and bounced her off the SUV's tire before she dropped back on the floor.

If she stayed there she was going to get kicked to death.

Move, girl, move!

She scrambled back to her hands and knees, only to take another kick to the stomach. Her breath left her in a great rush, and when she tried to inhale again, she found she couldn't; he'd hit her solar plexus dead-on with the toe of his boot, temporarily paralyzing her diaphragm.

She fought to inhale, her entire being focused on getting that next breath and filling her lungs with air. Distantly she was aware of the guard continuing to kick away, but with all her attention focused on not suffocating she could barely summon the strength to defend herself.

Breathe! Come on, breathe!

Another kick slammed into her, and then all of a sudden her lungs were inflating as her body finally decided to listen to her brain. She sucked life-giving air into her system.

She could sense her opponent pulling back his leg, getting ready to deliver another blow.

Not this time.

As the kick came in, she spun around and grabbed his leg, trapping it against her torso, and pulled backward, yanking him off his feet.

He hit the floor hard, and she threw herself atop his body, pinning him to the ground with her knees. As he reached for her neck, Annja reared up over him, her hands held together over her head.

When she thrust her hands downward a second later, they were no longer empty.

The sword plunged into the middle of his chest, only stopping when it struck the cement floor on the other side. The guard stared up at her with surprised eyes and then died, alive one minute and gone the next.

32

Annja let her sword vanish back into the otherwhere and then climbed slowly off the dead man. She was bruised and battered but alive.

The sound of running feet caught her attention and she stumbled around to the back of the SUV to see that Owens had abandoned Csilla's wheelchair and was now making a run for the elevator.

Oh, no, you don't!

She started after him, only to catch sight of Radecki coming out of a door she hadn't noticed earlier, a few feet from the elevator. He was pointing something in her direction.

Annja threw herself behind the SUV just as the rear window exploded, sending glass flying.

"You're not getting out of here, Creed," Radecki yelled, "so why make this difficult?"

His voice echoed in the confined space of the garage. If she hadn't seen him, Annja would have been hard-pressed to know where the sound was coming from.

"You should have just gone home when Tamás told you to, you know? That would have saved a number of people, yourself included, a lot of trouble. But that would have been too easy, huh?"

Annja rose to a crouch and cautiously tried to look through the SUV's window, but the tint was so dark she couldn't see anything.

"No, you had to stick your nose where it didn't belong, and so here we are."

Yeah, and you sound all broken up over it, too, she thought as she got down on her hands and knees to look underneath the car.

She couldn't see much of Radecki, just his shoes, but that was enough to pinpoint his location. As she looked on, he began slowly walking toward the SUVs.

Annja didn't think he was coming to wish her well.

As he approached, she slowly backed away from him, moving around the side of the vehicle to keep herself out of his sight. When he stopped near the side of the vehicle, Annja got the sense he was about to stoop and look under it, so she moved to crouch behind the tire.

Annja needed to act quickly. She couldn't stay where she was—Radecki was coming around the front of the vehicle, headed in her direction. She couldn't circle around the back, because that would expose her to Owens. With nowhere else to go, she slid beneath the SUV next to her, pushing herself sideways with hands and feet until she came out again on the opposite side.

That put her behind the very last vehicle in the row, out of sight of both men for the moment. She crouched there below the window, her feet hidden from view by the rear tire.

She heard Radecki call out to Owens. "Where did she go?"

"She's around the other side. Between the first two vehicles!"

Wrong.

But that was fine with her. She listened closely, heard Radecki moving between the first and second vehicles, heading for the rear. She waited until he reached the SUV's bumper and then moved to the far front corner of her own.

A glance beneath the cars showed Radecki moving toward her, and she knew it was time. Her heart was racing and her hands itched for her sword, but she didn't draw it out. She wanted to get the gun away from him and take control of the situation, but she didn't want to kill him.

She was going to have to do this the hard way.

Radecki slowed as he got close to the front of the SUV, raised his gun and then spun quickly around the corner, expecting to see Annja hiding in front of the second vehicle.

Except she wasn't there.

Annja was already surging toward him. As he turned and brought his gun up, her foot lashed out in a perfectly timed crescent kick that struck the inside of his wrist, knocking the gun aside even as he pulled the trigger.

The shot went wide, ricocheting off the Suburban beside her, but Annja barely noticed as the bullet swept past. She planted her foot as it came down, using it as a fulcrum to spin her body the rest of the way through the arc and delivering a smashing elbow strike to Radecki's jaw.

The blow drove Radecki against the front of the SUV, and Annja moved in on him, pinning him in place. She grabbed his right hand and slammed it against the grille of the car—once, twice, three times—until his fingers went numb and he had no choice but to drop the gun.

Annja kicked it under the SUV.

Radecki was disarmed, but not out of the fight. He reversed Annja's grip on his wrist and caught hers instead, spinning her around and locking his other arm around her throat, pulling her back against his chest in the process.

"I'm going to make you pay for that," he said in her ear as he pulled his arm tighter, choking her.

Annja's lungs started to burn seconds after he grabbed hold of her. She was already exhausted from her fight with the guard, and she couldn't take much more of this abuse. She needed to get out of his grip and she needed to do it quickly, or she'd be unconscious and completely at his mercy.

She couldn't pry his arm free, not with the way he had it locked up against his other one, so she didn't even bother trying. Instead, she reached into the otherwhere, wrapped her hands around the hilt of her sword and dragged it into the real world.

The blade flashed into existence, the hilt clasped tightly between her two hands, and Annja drove it backward, running the flat of the blade against the edge of her body as a guide, hoping to skewer her assailant where she stood.

Fortunately for Radecki, Annja's aim was a little off. The position of her body and the growing dimness in front of her eyes as the air was choked out of her caused the blade to shift to the left. Instead of running through the center of his gut, the blade simply slashed through the fatty tissue on the outside of his torso.

It hurt—hurt a lot, no doubt—but it wasn't fatal.

The strike did accomplish her objective, though. Radecki loosened his chokehold, and that was enough to allow her to break his grip entirely.

She spun away from him, bringing the sword up and around in a whistling arc, then slashing downward in the kind of blow designed to split a man in two.

Except the man in question was no longer where he'd been a moment before. Radecki had dived to the right, and instead of cleaving him in half, her sword slashed into the hood of the vehicle with the shriek of tearing steel.

Radecki turned his dive into a rolling somersault and came up on his feet, facing Annja. He was bleeding from the wound in his side, but it didn't look bad enough to take him out, an observation he proved when he charged her as soon as he was back on his feet.

Her sword was embedded in the SUV's hood, and she tried to tug it free.

It wouldn't move.

It was stuck, good and fast.

Radecki had already closed half the distance between them. She had only seconds to act.

Annja was about to order the sword to vanish,

thereby freeing it from its metal trap, but decided against it. She had a better idea.

As Radecki charged toward her, arms ready to grab her again, Annja waited until the very last second and then leaped up into the air, using the sword as a fulcrum to support her weight. At the top of her arc, she kicked outward with one foot.

The toe of her boot struck Radecki right on the temple.

He crashed into the front of the vehicle and went down without a sound as Annja landed.

Radecki lay there on the floor of the garage, unmoving.

Finish him now before he can do more harm.

For a moment, Annja considered doing just that. She let go of the sword, and as she did it flashed out of existence and then popped back into her hand, ready to deliver the fatal blow.

Radecki had helped kidnap and murder dozens of women. He had shown no remorse and would certainly continue doing so if Annja couldn't stop him.

In Annja's view, Radecki certainly deserved to die for his actions.

But Annja was not judge, jury and especially not executioner.

As near as she could tell, she'd been called to bear the sword as a representative of justice, truth and righteousness. Killing Radecki—no, murdering him— would be a violation of all the sword and its original bearer stood for and of her own tacit agreement to continue that tradition.

However much she might want to do so, killing him now while he lay defenseless would be wrong.

She turned away, and in doing so caught sight of Owens frantically pushing the elevator call button while looking back at her with frightened eyes.

Annja knew Owens would sound the alarm, but it would take time to coordinate a response. She intended to be long gone by that point.

It was time to get out of here.

She ran over to Csilla's wheelchair, grabbed the handles and began pushing it as fast as it would go as she ran for the gate and the ramp to freedom that lay just beyond.

Thirty feet…

Twenty feet…

Ten feet…

Almost there.

Something punched her hard in the leg, knocking her feet out from under her. She fell forward, unbalancing the wheelchair in the process and sending it crashing to the floor. Annja could only watch in dismay as Csilla toppled to the ground.

After a moment, Annja was finally able to identify the sound echoing in her ears—a gunshot.

33

Radecki found his gun, Annja thought absently as she looked down at her leg in a semidaze. The outside of her thigh was bleeding freely, but she didn't feel much pain.

Then again, she couldn't feel most of her leg.

You're in shock, a voice said in the back of her head. You're in shock because you've been shot. That's why you don't feel anything.

As fuzzy as her thinking was, she knew that if she'd been shot, someone must have done the shooting.

Looking back, she saw Radecki leaning against one of the Suburbans, one hand holding the gun pointed in her direction and the other clamped over the bleeding wound in his side. She was wondering why he hadn't just killed her with the first shot when he fired again.

The shot went wide, the bullet hitting the concrete more than a yard to her right.

It took her a moment to put two and two together; Radecki was shooting with his off hand!

Thankfully he wasn't that good with his left.

Frustrated he tried again, but when that bullet, too, missed, he threw the gun away in disgust. Pulling something out of the inside pocket of his coat, he began walking purposefully in Annja's direction, calling over his shoulder to Owens as he went.

Annja clamped a hand over her own wound and tried to stand, only to collapse back on the floor, her leg too numb to support her weight.

As if that wasn't enough to deal with, a sudden rattling sound from close by caught her attention, and when she looked up in the direction of the ramp she discovered the source.

The gate over the exit ramp was slowly descending!

Another glance behind her showed Radecki walking inexorably closer and, over his shoulder, the figure of Owens standing near the gate controls, a triumphant smile on his face.

It was the smile that did it.

There was no way she was letting these two beat her. *Not today, not ever.*

She could feel the blood trickling out between her fingers. It was going to get worse if she exerted herself, but staying here was not an option. She'd bleed to death if they didn't kill her first. She had to get on the other side of that gate.

Pushing herself up onto her hands and knees and letting her injured leg drag behind her, Annja began crawling forward.

"She's getting away!" Owens shrieked.

Thank you, Captain Obvious, Annja thought. And damn right I am!

Behind her, Radecki started a kind of limping run in an effort to catch her.

Annja crawled past Csilla's wheelchair, and the sight of it caused an ache to well up from her heart. She'd tried to help, and in the process she'd dragged the woman into even greater danger. Now she was abandoning Csilla where she lay. The fact that she had no choice, that if she didn't get away she couldn't help Csilla or any of the women back in that medical ward, didn't help remove the sting and shame leaving her behind.

She kept going anyway.

The gate was less than a foot above the ground by the time she reached it.

She knew if she hesitated, all would be lost, so she went for it.

Annja dropped to her stomach and crawled forward as fast as she could, doing her best not to think about either the homicidal maniac running up behind her or the steel gate lowering itself toward her unprotected body.

Radecki was shouting at her, but Annja couldn't understand what he was saying over the clank and clatter of the gate. Nor did she care. All of her attention was focused on getting clear of the several hundred pounds of steel descending toward her. She'd worry about Radecki later.

She reached out with her arms, braced them against the floor and dragged herself forward until her head and shoulders cleared the gate.

Clank.

The gate dropped an inch.

She did it again—reach, grab, drag—pulling her torso through.

Clank.

Another inch.

The steel edge was less than four inches off the ground at this point. Annja's heart was beating wildly, the pounding rhythm filling her ears.

Hurry up!

Clank.

A mere three inches or so left.

She bent her left leg, pulling it clear, but couldn't do the same to her right thanks to the bullet wound in her thigh.

Come on! One more time! she screamed at herself.

Annja pulled and her leg slid forward beneath the gate's edge just as it dropped the rest of the way to the floor…

…and caught the sole of her boot beneath it.

Sensors built into the bottom of the gate kept her foot from being crushed as the machinery controlling it shut down the moment the gate encountered an obstruction.

That was the good news.

The bad news was that she was stuck.

Annja reached back, grabbed her lower leg and, ignoring the pain, tried to tug her leg free.

Nothing.

Come on, you can do this.

She braced her good leg against the gate, gritted her teeth and pulled on her other leg a second time.

Still nothing.

She was stuck hard and fast.

Annja looked up and found Radecki standing on the

other side of the gate. As she looked on he raised his hands and slowly, mockingly, began to clap.

"A marvelous attempt," he said with a grin. "Really top-notch."

Her reply was less than politic.

Radecki grinned. "You had a good run. For a while there I thought you were even going to make it. But now it's time to bring this little charade to an end."

He squatted down, reached under the edge of the gate with his hand and pressed the stun gun he was holding against the back of her trapped leg.

Five hundred thousand volts of electricity surged through her body, making it shiver and shake against the floor of the garage. The last thing Annja saw before she descended into unconsciousness was Radecki's face, grinning at her.

34

Annja regained consciousness slowly, as if drifting up from the depths of a deep sleep. Her thoughts were fuzzy, incomplete, and more than once the waves washed over her and dragged her down again for a time. In her more coherent moments she had the sensation of movement and would occasionally hear people talking over or around her, but she couldn't make out what was being said. Each time, she was washed back beneath the tide and lost track of her surroundings again. Gradually the real world intruded, and at last she found herself back where she belonged.

Back in the real world.

She was unsurprised to find herself being carried along between two men, their hands gripping her under the arms and lifting her partially off the ground while her legs dragged along behind her.

What was surprising, on the other hand, was her discovery that she couldn't move her head.

It was like having a disconnect somewhere between her brain and her muscles; the latter were being told what to do but they weren't listening to the commands her brain was giving or they were unable to carry out the task.

And it wasn't just her head.

The same held true for her arms.

And her legs.

And her hands and feet.

She couldn't move at all—not even a twitch of a finger!

Annja would have groaned aloud at the discovery, except she couldn't move her mouth.

Thoughts of all the terrible things they might have done to her to cause this condition ran unbidden through her head, and she could feel panic starting to well up from somewhere deep inside her. She knew that if she let it out she might not be able to get it under control.

Calm down, she told herself, calm down. Temporary paralysis was one of the side effects of sustaining a heavy electrical shock. Your control will come back; you just have to wait it out.

In the meantime, she could gather information about where she was and figure a way out of this mess.

Her paralysis wasn't the only difficulty she was experiencing. Her head was pounding and she was having trouble organizing her thoughts. Her mouth was full of the taste of burned metal and she felt as though she'd been drugged, but these were all symptoms of electrical shock, as well. Like the paralysis, they would disappear with time.

Look on the bright side, she told herself. At least she could still see and hear.

It might have been a more rewarding observation

if she could see something beyond the floor beneath their feet.

And yet, on second thought, that might be helpful after all, she realized. Gone was the institutional tiled floor that she'd seen after escaping her cell. In its place were flagstones held together by some kind of mortar, and the crumbling nature of both made it clear that wherever they were, the place had to be at least several hundred years old.

She'd been moved. That was clear.

But to where?

They could be anywhere, but something told Annja they hadn't gone far. The women's disappearances had all happened in one general area, in and around Nové Mesto, which suggested that Stone had wanted to be near the source of her prion supply. And while there were literally dozens of medieval ruins in that area, only one had any real relevance to the situation.

Only one that Annja had spent hours wandering around, so that the look and feel of the place had settled into her bones.

She recognized it now.

Csejte Castle.

With her head hanging down and her hair falling over her face, her captors probably didn't know she was conscious, a fact that was borne out just moments later when her two captors started talking.

"What are we doing here?"

The voice came from the man on her left. It took her a few seconds, but she recognized it as belonging to Owens.

"We're taking care of a problem. Something that should have been done the minute she stuck her nose where it didn't belong."

There was no mistaking the voice of the man on her right.

Radecki.

Owens apparently didn't like the sound of that. "You brought me in to supervise the lab. I'm not some hired killer."

Radecki laughed. "No? Then you're an even bigger fool than I thought. A hired killer is exactly what you are. Or did you think all those women survived the things you've been doing to them?"

"That's different!" Owens answered hotly. "What I've done has been in the name of science! This is... cold-blooded murder!"

Radecki came to a sudden halt, causing Annja's head to jerk about as Owens took another step. She instinctively tightened her neck muscles to avoid injury and was stunned when she felt them respond.

"I don't care what you call it," Radecki said in a deceptively calm voice. "You will do as you're told or I'll hook you up to one of your own machines and let it suck you drier than the Gobi Desert. Understood?"

Owens was smart enough to realize he'd gone too far. "Understood," he said, without complaint this time.

They started walking again, dragging Annja along, and she used the cover of the movement to test her body's responses. It seemed the numbness was slowly going away. She could move her mouth and facial muscles now, as well as her neck.

It must have been the stun gun, she thought. Now the effects were wearing off and she was starting to regain some control.

The question was whether she'd get back enough control in time to get her out of this mess.

As they dragged her along the passageway, Annja focused all her attention on the fingers of her left hand.

Nothing happened.

She tried again, turning her head slightly so she could see her fingers as she directed her thoughts at them, willing them to bend, just a little bit.

They didn't respond.

Her hands were still as good as dead.

It's okay. You'll get there. Just gonna take some time.

But she didn't have time to spare.

Owens and Radecki dragged her around corners, along several passageways and down a flight of stairs. They had to stop several times along the way to give Radecki a chance to rest; the wound in his abdomen was obviously making it difficult. They continued down another hallway until they reached the end, at which point they entered a room.

Annja recognized it right away, and she felt her heart rate accelerate as she considered what Radecki intended for her. Based on where they were standing, she knew it wasn't going to be good.

A large sunken tub sat in the center of the room and took up most of the space, leaving a two-foot walkway surrounding it on all sides. At the far end of the tub, a metal support structure shaped like an inverted Y rose from the edge, standing stark and alone in the beam of their flashlights.

"What is that?" Owens asked.

Annja didn't need to wait for Radecki's answer to know she was looking at the iron framework from which Elizabeth Báthory had allegedly hung her victims while their blood drained out of them into the bath below.

Seeing it confirmed Annja's suspicions that they were at Csejte Castle.

It also told her in no uncertain terms that she was in serious trouble.

"Over here," Radecki said, and led the way around the side of the tub to the base of the Y. When they reached it, he said, "Put her down and help me with this."

Annja was left lying on her back. Her head lolled to one side, pointed away from where the two men were working. She was literally in the dark, as they took their flashlights with them.

That was fine with Annja; it gave her a chance to turn her head toward them under the cover of darkness. She waited a moment to make sure neither of them had noticed and then cracked her eyes open the tiniest bit, just enough to see what they were doing without advertising that she was conscious.

Owens was squatting next to the Y, his back to Annja. He appeared to be tugging at something. Radecki stood nearby, holding both lights so Owens could see what he was doing. Annja didn't need to see them to know what was happening; she'd examined the device pretty thoroughly when she'd been filming the other day.

At the base of the Y was a mechanism that controlled the frame's movement. When a thick iron pin was removed, a hinge allowed the Y to be lowered to the ground so the latest victim could be strapped into place. Once that was completed, the Y could be raised back up and the pin returned to its rightful place, holding the Y upright and allowing the victim's blood to drain downward into the bath.

It took Owens a few minutes to get the pin out, but after that it was relatively smooth sailing. The two men lowered the frame and then turned back to get Annja. She quickly closed her eyes and let her head and right hand hang limp like the rest of her limbs, not wanting to give anything away until she was ready to make her move. It wasn't easy; it took everything she could muster not to fight them off the minute they laid their hands on her.

They stretched her out atop the frame, with her spine against the center post and her feet together at the base. Annja knew that if she was going to get out of here she couldn't allow them to secure her in place, so she cracked her eyes open just enough that she could keep them in view while preparing to make her move. Her legs still wouldn't obey her, but her right arm was almost fully under her control and her left arm wasn't too far behind. All she needed was a few more minutes.

Radecki stepped out of sight for a moment, and when

he returned he was carrying several short lengths of rope, each about a yard long.

Her time had just officially run out.

35

Owens grabbed her by the ankles while Radecki readied the ropes. Neither of them was paying any real attention to her. It was the perfect opportunity to take control of the situation.

Now or never.

Radecki suddenly stood up. "Finish tying her feet," he said to Owens. "I'll take care of her hands."

Radecki stepped over her legs and squatted down in the space between her outstretched arm and her torso, intent on lashing her wrist to the brace. This close she could see that he had bandages wrapped around his lower torso, no doubt covering the stab wound she'd given him earlier.

He didn't even spare her a glance…had no idea she was conscious.

She considered summoning the sword but decided against it. Her left arm was still weak, and if she dropped the sword, she'd lose the element of surprise.

Annja couldn't let him tie her down, so sword or no sword, she had to make her move and she had to do it now.

As Radecki reached for her arm, she snatched it back, causing him to start in surprise and turn in her direction. As his body opened up, Annja drove a fist right into the spot where she'd stabbed him earlier.

Radecki's howl of pain filled the room, echoing off the stone walls as he involuntarily hunched over his injury. That brought his head down and forward, which was exactly what Annja had hoped would happen. Before he had time to recover, she drew her arm across her body and then snapped it back out, slamming the base of her fist into Radecki's temple.

The cop dropped flat, clearly dazed. Annja had hoped the blow would be enough to render him unconscious, but she wasn't that lucky. Even as she looked on, Radecki pushed himself up on his palms, shaking his head, clearly trying to get back up.

Oh, no, you don't.

Annja brought her arm up, ready to deliver another blow, only to have her aim thrown off at the last moment. As a result, her fist careered off Radecki's shoulder instead of slamming into his temple.

"I've got her! I've got her!" she heard Owens shout.

Looking down toward her feet, Annja saw Owens squatting there, his hands around her ankle, and realized that he must have pulled on her leg in the moment before she'd struck. She still couldn't feel that limb, so she'd had no idea that he'd laid hands on her.

But she knew now, and she was none too happy about it. Watching him holding her leg down and shouting for his partner sent a white-hot fury raging through her veins.

She reacted almost without thought, and her foot was halfway to Owens's face before she'd even realized she could feel her left leg well enough to kick with it.

Owens probably didn't know what hit him. One minute he was shouting to his partner and the next Annja's boot was striking him square in the bridge of the nose, breaking it with an audible crack. Unfortunately for him, he was crouched at the edge of the sunken tub when the kick landed and, as a result, he tumbled to the bottom of the bath.

The meaty thud that reached Annja's ears just seconds after Owens disappeared didn't bode well for the man's health. Annja didn't know how badly he was injured, but either way it seemed Dr. Owens was no longer a threat.

Annja turned toward Radecki, only to discover the hard way that he wasn't out of the fight quite yet when he smashed her across the jaw with a vicious haymaker.

Annja saw it coming at the last second and rolled her head with the blow so it didn't have as much impact. She blocked the next punches and then managed to sneak one of her own past Radecki's defenses, rocking the man's head back just as he'd done to her moments before, dazing him.

Annja took advantage of that brief lull to try to scramble to her feet, only to have her right leg collapse under her, still too numb to hold her weight. She ended up sprawled on the floor, staring at Radecki.

He didn't waste any time capitalizing on her misfortune. Radecki lurched to his feet, pulling something out of his pocket as he did so, and threw himself atop her. For a moment Annja thought he was just trying to pin her to the floor, but then she felt something jab her thigh.

Looking down, she found an autoinjector device sticking out of her leg.

He'd drugged her!

Not again.

Suddenly frightened, Annja batted the injector away and stared up at him.

"What did you do?"

Laughing, Radecki leaned back, a smug grin on his face. He was already starting to relax, as if the fight was over and Annja just hadn't realized it yet.

Adrenaline was pouring through her system, both in reaction to the fight and her fear of whatever Radecki had injected her with, and it did what time alone had not yet managed to do—it freed the rest of her muscles from their reaction to the stun gun. As Radecki's grip on her loosened, Annja fought back.

She reached up and grabbed Radecki's arm, pulling it sideways so he started to turn as he fell toward her. At the same time she scythed her legs up, ignoring the pain in her right thigh, wrapping one leg around his head so that his neck was trapped in the crook of her knee. She locked her foot behind her other knee and began to squeeze her legs together as hard as she could while pulling his arm forward across her.

For a second Radecki only stared at her with a confused expression on his face, but as she began to bear down, using her legs to choke the air from his brain, the danger of his position finally set in. He reached around the back of his head and tried to pull Annja's legs apart, to release the crushing pressure that was starting to build on his neck, but her hold was cinched in tight, and it was going to take a lot more than the strength Radecki had in a single arm to break it. He wasted a few precious seconds trying and then, when that didn't work, began to flail at her with his free arm. His position made it hard for him to land a blow with any significant force, though, and as the seconds ticked by his strikes became weaker and weaker.

Eventually, they stopped altogether.

Annja held on for another second or two when Radecki slumped across her, wanting to be sure he wasn't faking it. She counted to ten and then released her hold, pushing his now-limp body off her own and wondering as she did so if she'd managed to kill him.

As it turned out, she hadn't. When she recovered enough to check his pulse, she was grateful to find one. It was thin and shaky, but it was there. Officer Radecki would live to stand trial after all—a fact that Annja found rather uplifting given the circumstances.

She limped over to the discarded injector and picked it up, looking for some indication of what it might have contained. A label or something similar would have been very helpful, but the sleek gray case of the injection device was devoid of any markings. It didn't even have a manufacturer's label. She slipped it into her pocket anyway; maybe a lab test might reveal something later.

If there was a later.

Whatever Radecki had injected her with was starting

to take effect. She could feel herself getting woozy, and her vision was starting to blur. She needed to get medical attention and she needed to do so quickly.

The fact that she didn't know what had been in the injector complicated things. Radecki could have been trying to kill her or he could have been trying to knock her out. Frankly, neither option was all that attractive.

She limped back to Radecki's unconscious form and knelt down to search him, coming away with a digital key card, a cell phone and a set of car keys for her trouble. She pocketed the key card and the keys, then swiped the screen on the phone with her thumb. To her surprise, it wasn't locked. Even better, when the screen lit up she saw four green bars in the upper right corner, indicating a healthy signal.

Annja stood up and moved away from Radecki's unconscious form, not wanting to be too close to the man. She stared at the phone's lit screen for a moment, debating, and then tried to dial a number from memory. The keypad seemed to shimmer and dance as the drug continued to make its way through her system, and it took her three tries to get it right.

There was a moment of silence after the call was answered.

"Nové Mesto policajné oddelenie," a bored male voice finally said.

"Detective Tamás, please."

"Just a moment," the duty sergeant replied, then put her on hold. Calling Tamás was a calculated risk. Until recently, she'd thought he was directly responsible for the deaths of Havel Novack and Marta Vass, never mind being a willing participant in the cover-up of nearly two dozen additional murders. But after overhearing the discussion between Radecki and Stone, Novack's true killers, she'd come to believe that she'd misjudged the police detective. Tamás likely still wanted to speak to her regarding the Novack house fire, so Annja was confident she could get him to make the trip out here.

At least now she had proof those women hadn't just disappeared. They'd been kidnapped. Annja reached into her pocket for the hard drive, only to find that the device was gone. Radecki had probably searched her for weapons after he'd knocked her out.

The detective's voice startled Annja out of her ruminations.

"This is Tamás."

"Do you know who this is?" Annja asked, not wanting to give her name over the open line.

Tamás was silent for a moment, and then said, "Yes."

A wave of dizziness washed over her, forcing Annja to wait until it passed. It was getting harder for her to pull her thoughts together, and she could feel her sense of the here and now slipping away. Her dizzy spell must have been stronger than she thought, for when she came back to herself she could hear Tamás speaking into her ear with concern.

"Hello? Are you still there?"

"I'm here," she said as the room ballooned in front of her and then settled down again.

She must have been hit with some kind of psychotropic.

"Are you all right?" the detective asked.

Annja quelled the urge to shake her head, and settled for pacing to keep herself focused, despite the pain in her leg. The last thing she wanted to do was collapse unconscious.

"No, I'm not," she told him. "In fact, I need your help, as do the several other injured women I just left behind. I found them, Tamás. Novack's missing women. I found them and they need your help."

"What? What are you talking about?"

Annja turned, intending to retrace her steps, and nearly screamed in surprise when she found a bloodied Radecki standing directly behind her.

He lashed out with his left hand, knocking the cell phone from her grip, and then followed it up with a snap punch to her face.

Normally Annja was quick enough to slip a punch like that, but whatever Radecki had jabbed her with was wreaking havoc with her reaction time as well as her senses. She tried to jerk her head to one side, a move that had helped her evade many a punch in the past, but this time she was too slow, and instead of sailing harmlessly past her face, Radecki's fist slammed into her cheekbone.

The pain was so overwhelming she saw stars, and in that moment she was helpless.

Her heart was beating madly, no doubt sending whatever he'd injected her with pumping wildly around her circulatory system. Soon Radecki could stand back and watch her fall.

If she was going to survive this, she needed to do something before she lost all her strength.

Radecki picked up a piece of rope and advanced toward Annja. She covered her head with her arms and hunched over, hoping Radecki would think she'd given up. Annja couldn't see much of anything in that position, but she could see his feet, which meant she knew where he was.

When he got close, Annja shot her foot out without warning, delivering a near-textbook front snap kick to the man's groin. Radecki doubled over, his hands cupping his groin. He was staring at her with hatred, his face red with pain.

Radecki let out a bellow and charged toward her.

Annja watched him come.

She didn't have the strength for another prolonged fight; the last one had left her battered, bruised and exhausted. She needed to end this decisively, here and now. If she didn't stop him, she likely wouldn't survive this next confrontation.

She was only going to get one shot at this.

She waited for Radecki to close the distance between them, waited for him to build up so much momentum there would be no chance of turning aside or stopping short, waited until he was almost atop her...

Then she reached into the otherwhere, wrapped her hand around the hilt of her sword and pulled it forth into this side of reality with a wordless shout of defiance as she thrust it forward.

The blade entered his stomach just to the left of his navel and, cutting through everything in its way, came thrusting out his back as his own momentum carried him forward until the hilt of the weapon was pinched up against the front of his gut.

For a moment, he hung there, impaled on her sword, staring at her. His eyes were filled with hatred and disbelief, then Radecki gurgled once and died, a thin stream of blood running out the side of his mouth.

Annja released her sword back into the otherwhere and let his corpse drop to the floor at her feet.

36

It was all Annja could do to stand there a moment and catch her breath. Her head was pounding and her heart was beating wildly. One eye was so swollen she could barely see out of it, and she was pretty sure her cheekbone was fractured, if not broken outright. The difficulty she was having taking a deep breath told her Radecki had probably cracked a few of her ribs, as well.

But at least she was alive.

If only Tamás would get here quickly...

Tamás!

She spotted the cell phone fetched up against the far wall and stumbled over to it. Picking it up, she put it to her ear.

"Detective?"

Nothing.

A glance told her why; both the case and the screen were cracked. The phone must have been damaged when Radecki swiped it out of her hand.

Now what?

She had two options, she supposed. Try to find help

on her own, or wait, hoping that Tamás had taken her call seriously and was on his way right now.

She slumped against the nearest wall, trying to make up her mind, when the sensation of being watched alerted her to someone else's presence.

Annja glanced up, startled, and found Diane Stone standing in the doorway. Stone was dressed semicasually, wearing a white lab coat over jeans and a T-shirt.

"A rather impressive display," Stone said. "From conjuring the sword out of thin air right down to slaughtering Radecki with it. I must say I'm surprised."

The drug coursing through Annja's system bent and distorted the words slightly, so it took her a moment to understand what Stone was saying. The predatory look in the woman's eyes was clear.

Out of the frying pan and into the fire.

Having already been seen once, Annja didn't hesitate. She slipped her hand into the otherwhere and drew her sword.

"Stay back," she said, brandishing the weapon before her. "I'm warning you."

Stone laughed. "Or what? You'll cut me with that thing?" She marched forward until she stood about two feet in front of Annja. "Go ahead," she said.

Annja's flesh crawled at Stone's nearness, as if her body instinctively knew that the woman standing before her was, in part, unnatural. Annja felt the almost overwhelming urge to run, to get as far away from the woman in front of her as possible.

Sensing her distress, Stone smiled a shark's smile,

full of hunger and teeth. "Cut me or I'll take that blade from you and use it to cut your hand off."

Annja's survival instinct flared. Before she knew it she'd flicked her wrist, slashing the very tip of the sword across Stone's cheek. The near razor-sharp weapon opened a long gash in the woman's smooth skin.

That was going to leave a nasty scar, Annja thought with a sense of drugged detachment.

Stone, on the other hand, didn't even flinch. She wiped at the blood with the back of one hand and said, "Is that all you've got?"

As Annja looked on, the gash in Stone's face stopped bleeding on its own and began to knit itself back together. Starting from each end and working toward the middle, the cut went from an angry, bloody red to a faded pink to nothing at all in the space of thirty seconds.

Annja shook her head. That couldn't be. Nobody healed like that. It must be the drugs making her see things.

But it wasn't the drugs, and somewhere, deep down inside, Annja knew it.

"I know you saw my research," Stone said. "I know you can understand what I've created. The prions are far more powerful than even I anticipated. Now there is almost no injury I can't recover from!"

To prove the point, Stone abruptly stepped forward, impaling herself on the blade.

Annja gasped in horror and instinctively jerked her arm back. There was a wet sucking sound as the blade pulled free of Stone's flesh, causing the other woman to grunt in pain. Blood flowed freely down her leg.

Without proper medical treatment, it was a fatal injury.

Or it would have been, on any other person. Stone just stood there, stoically enduring the pain while the wound healed itself. The first had taken mere seconds; this one took several minutes, but in the end the result was the same—the wound might as well have never existed.

Stone caught Annja's gaze. "Now that that's been settled, we're going to have a little chat about your bloodline and that sword of yours," she said, still smiling that crazed smile.

With the drugs coursing through her system, addling her brain and playing with her senses, Annja knew she would be no match for Stone in a physical confrontation.

Instead of fighting, she did the one thing her body had been screaming at her to do since Stone had set foot in the room.

She ran.

Annja released her sword, letting it vanish into the otherwhere, and then lurched forward, slamming into Stone and knocking her aside as she headed for the exit.

"Oh, good!" Stone called from behind her. "At least you're going to make this interesting!"

Annja didn't bother to answer or even look back as she slipped out the door and headed down the hallway beyond as fast as she dared. It wasn't easy; her thigh was throbbing and the ground seemed to keep slipping away, leaving her to stumble about off balance. More than once she careened off a nearby wall, but each time she did what she could to use the collision to her advantage, pushing off the wall and propelling herself down the hall.

Getting to the ground floor should have been easy; she'd memorized the layout of the ruins prior to filming her episode and had explored the grounds pretty thoroughly while seeking out the best backdrop for each scene. But every corridor looked like the one before it, and Annja soon found herself hopelessly lost.

Behind her, she could feel the looming specter of Stone's presence getting closer with every moment.

The next corridor ended in an aged wooden door, and Annja skidded to a stop in front of it. She could hear footfalls coming toward her at a measured pace. A memory of her dream from the other night flashed through Annja's mind, and she shuddered at how prophetic it all seemed now.

She's gaining on you; stop wasting time and move!

Pulling open the door, Annja found a set of circular steps rising upward.

Go! Go! Go!

She went.

Annja began climbing them as fast as she could, holding on to the steps in front of her as she forced her feet to keep moving upward. She went up step after step, seemingly forever, and then nearly tumbled backward when she suddenly reached the top. A quick grab for the door kept her from falling head over heels back down the stairs.

She could hear footsteps behind her, so she hauled the door open and ran through it. She found herself in another corridor with a doorway at the far end.

That's got to be the way out, she thought, and headed for it as fast as her drugged body would carry her.

There was still no sign of Stone when Annja reached the doorway, so she hurried through, crossing half the room before pulling up short. Too late, Annja recognized that she was standing in the ruin of the room where Elizabeth Báthory had spent the last several years of her life. A literal dead end if there ever was one.

She spun about, intending to retrace her steps, only to see Stone in the doorway, blocking her retreat.

The other woman smiled. "Looks like the end of the road."

Annja backed up, looking for another exit. The room was empty, like all the other rooms inside the castle ruins, but this one had a window.

Perhaps there was a way to climb down, she thought.

The fact that she was having difficulty seeing was irrelevant; she had no other options except to surrender, and that wasn't something she would do. She wouldn't last a week in Stone's hands.

Annja stumbled over to the window—an oversize affair easily three feet wide and at least four feet high— and looked out, frantically searching for some means of escape.

But there wasn't one.

Or, at least, none that she could manage in her current condition.

The window looked down at least two stories onto the rocky escarpment the castle had been built on, and while there were plenty of handholds in the crumbling rock, there was no way Annja could negotiate the climb. Not with her head spinning and her senses reeling. Trying would be tantamount to suicide.

She turned away from the window, only to find Stone standing right there in front of her, practically toe-to-toe. Annja jerked back in surprise; she hadn't heard Stone approach and certainly didn't expect her to be standing so close.

The move almost proved to be her undoing.

Annja's heels struck the wall, unbalancing her, and she teetered on the edge of the very window she'd just turned away from.

It was Stone who saved her.

The other woman reached out with lightning-quick reflexes, grabbing Annja about the throat and pulling her in close, away from the window's edge and the long drop just beyond. Annja dazedly realized that the prion treatment must be augmenting Stone's strength as well, for the woman stood there holding her an inch off the ground with just one hand.

"Now, about that sword…" Stone said.

The room was starting to spin, and Stone's face seemed to loom close and then pull back again in time with the motion. Annja's thoughts were equally jumbled; she knew she should be doing something, reaching for something to get her out of Stone's clutches, but for the life of her she couldn't remember what.

At her side, her right hand opened and closed,

opened and closed, without her even being aware of it until Stone pointed it out.

"That's right," the woman said with a cold smile. "Find that sword for me."

But it wasn't going to be that easy.

"Let her go!" a man shouted.

At first Annja thought she'd imagined the voice, that the drugs were starting to make her hear things, but then Stone's head turned in the direction of the door and Annja felt the first spark of hope. There might be a way out of this after all.

"I said, let her go!" the voice shouted again, and Annja saw Detective Tamás standing in the doorway, pointing his service weapon at Stone.

Pointing at her as well, she dimly realized. That wasn't good.

"Well, if it isn't Detective Tamás," Stone said, amusement in her voice. "Come to save the day at last?"

Tamás's voice was steady as he said, "I'm not going to tell you again. Let Ms. Creed go and step away from the window."

"My dear detective, I wouldn't have gone through all the trouble of capturing her if I was just going to let her fall out a window. That would be a waste, don't you think?"

Stone was still holding Annja upright with her right arm, which meant Annja's body was blocking Tamás's view of Stone's left side. That wouldn't have mattered much if Annja hadn't seen Stone slowly moving her left hand toward the small of her back.

Even with her fuzzy thought processes, Annja recognized that such a move didn't bode well for Tamás. Or herself, for that matter.

As things started to gray out around her, Annja summoned the last of her strength and made her move.

"She's got a gun!" she shouted, while simultaneously bringing her right hand across her body in a circular motion so that it struck the inside of Stone's arm, right where the key nerve meridians met in the lower wrist.

The blow was enough to break Stone's hold on her neck, and Annja felt herself falling to the floor even as she heard the echo of a gunshot fill the room.

As she struck the stone floor, Annja looked up to see a red flower blossom on the front of Stone's lab coat.

How pretty, she thought dazedly as she watched the force of the shot push Stone backward.

Stone's legs hit the lower part of the window just as Annja's had moments before, except there was no one to save her.

The last thing Annja saw was darkness finally closing in and Stone's shocked expression as she flipped over the windowsill and disappeared from view.

37

Nové Mesto Hospital

Annja awoke to find herself lying in a bed surrounded
by medical equipment and monitoring devices. The
steady hiss of a pump sounded from somewhere nearby
and her heart jack-hammered into overtime as Annja's
still-fuzzy brain told her she was back in the medical
ward under Stone's control.

With her mind screaming at her to get up and get
out, Annja tried to do just that, only to discover that her
wrists and ankles were secured to the bed with wide
leather restraints.

A high-pitched keening noise filled her ears as she
fought against the restraints, pulling and tugging and
pushing to no avail. In some distant part of her mind
she realized that she was the one making that sound,
but she was unable to bring herself back from the brink
as her fear began to overwhelm her...

"Hey, hey! Easy!" The voice cut through her fear
like a lighthouse in heavy fog, and she looked up to see

Detective Tamás entering the room, his hands up in the universal gesture for her to calm down.

"You're in a hospital in Nové Mesto. You're safe," he said, coming toward her. "You've got nothing to worry about."

"If I'm safe, why am I strapped down?" she asked, pulling on the restraints that held her wrists in place. Her voice was calm, but she knew she was close to the breaking point. All she had was Tamás's word that she wasn't back in that facility under Stone's control, and she wasn't sure she could trust him. Not entirely anyway.

Sensing her distress, Tamás moved immediately to her side and began undoing the strap that held her arm to the bed. "The restraints were for your own safety. The antitoxin they gave you causes significant muscles spasms. They didn't want you to injure yourself if you started flailing about."

Once he'd freed one arm, he moved around to the other side and released the other, then started working on the restraints around her ankles.

Annja watched him for a moment and then asked, "Do you believe me now?"

"Yes. And the next time you show up in my office with some fanciful tale for me to consider, I promise I won't simply dismiss it out of hand. I'm sorry I doubted you and Havel. If I hadn't, some lives might have been saved."

Annja shrugged; frankly, she probably would have doubted her story, too, if she'd been in his position.

Tamás went on, "Dr. Owens started talking the minute we brought him into the interrogation room and hasn't shut up since. He gave us directions to the facility, and we sent in a team about six hours ago to round up anyone inside. My men are interrogating them as we speak."

Annja didn't care about the lab workers; she had a far more important issue on her mind. "And the women?" she asked. "Did you get the women out?"

The detective nodded, but there was no joy in his voice as he said, "Yes, but the prognosis isn't very good for the majority of them. They've had their blood drained so many times it's a wonder any of them are still alive."

"What about Csilla? How is she?"

Tamás didn't say anything, just shook his head. She clenched her jaw against the rising tide of emotion. She'd tried so hard to save that woman, and now she didn't know whether to hit something or cry.

The detective didn't miss her reaction to the news. "If it makes you feel any better, we've recovered enough evidence to damn Officer Radecki twenty times over. Had he lived, he never would have seen the outside of a jail cell again."

Annja already knew that. After what he'd done, she would have made sure of it.

A sudden thought occurred to her.

"What happened to Stone?

Tamás glanced away. "I don't know."

"What do you mean you don't know?"

"I hit her with at least one, maybe two shots and then watched as she went out that window. No one should have been able to survive a fall like that. And yet, by the time I finished getting you the medical attention you needed and made my way around the tower to where she'd fallen, there was no sign of her."

Tamás turned to look at her, and Annja could see the confusion on his face, plain as day.

"How does a woman who's injured like that just get up and walk away?"

"Maybe she didn't," Annja said. "Maybe someone else spirited away her body." She didn't believe that was what happened, not by a long shot, but Tamás might. It was, after all, the most logical explanation.

But Tamás was already shaking his head. "I had the place cordoned off completely. No one but law enforcement personnel were allowed on-site and then only with my say-so. No one could have gotten her body out of there without being seen."

Annja saw the hole in his argument and used it to her advantage.

"But we already know Radecki was dirty. Is it such a stretch to think that he had help? That someone else on the force was working with him?"

It wasn't, not really, and it didn't take long for Tamás to acknowledge that. The idea actually seemed to energize him, and it wasn't long before he took his leave so he could get back to the investigation, saying he would check in with her later.

Annja didn't blame him; for someone with a policeman's mind, the intricacies involved in this case would be practically irresistible.

After Tamás left, Annja sat looking out the window, watching the sun sink behind the hills west of the city, and thought about the fact that she'd lied to the detective.

She did know what had happened to Stone.

Stone's body hadn't been spirited away by another person. In fact, Annja would bet that Stone hadn't died of her injuries at all. Stone had impaled herself on Annja's blade, and Annja had watched the resulting gash heal right before her eyes in a matter of seconds.

So was it such a stretch to think that Stone had used that same ability to heal whatever injuries she'd sustained in the fall and had simply gotten up and walked away on her own?

Annja didn't think it was.

Which meant Stone was still out there.

Somewhere.

Annja didn't doubt that she'd see Stone again. The woman didn't seem to be the type to leave loose ends lying around.

She'd lay low for a while, waiting for things to cool down as the authorities were distracted by other, more recent incidents, and then she would make her move.

Except this time, Annja would be there to stop her.

The broadsword once carried by Joan of Arc flashed briefly into existence and then disappeared again.

Puncture wounds were one thing, Annja thought. But Stone might not find it so easy to heal if her head were separated from her body.

The next time Stone showed up, Annja would be ready.

38

Three weeks later...

"If you would follow me, please."

The hard-looking man who'd been waiting for her at the Prague train station didn't say anything more as he turned and made his way down the hall. Stone didn't mind; she wasn't much in the mood for conversation anyway, at least not with the likes of him. She rose from her chair and followed, her thoughts on the conversation to come.

She'd never met her mysterious benefactor, and she could feel her heart unexpectedly racing as the moment of doing so drew closer with every step she took. She'd originally been approached through a mutual third party, Simon Kovács, and it had been hard to argue with both the freedom and the money she'd been offered. The project had been directly in line with what she'd already been working on, and she recognized the brilliance of the suggested line of inquiry almost immediately. She might not have been privy to her employer's identity, but that was a small price to pay to be afforded veritable free rein to pursue her research the way it needed to be pursued.

She'd sent the weekly video reports to Kovács and occasionally received an email in reply suggesting certain courses of action or methods of approach. She'd taken those in stride, understanding that operating in such a fashion was a requirement of the work they were doing. They were on the cutting edge of science, and sometimes that meant pushing past the ethical boundaries society had erected around such endeavors. Stone had expected some success, yes, but she never would have imagined things would turn out the way they had. She supposed all of the scientific greats—from Copernicus to Watson and Frick—must have felt the way she did now at some point or another, that giddy sensation that went along with victory when it was finally pulled from the towering piles of previous defeats.

Granted, the past three weeks had been difficult. Those first few hours spent crawling through the underbrush, dragging her broken legs behind her while trying to stop the flow of blood from the bullet wound in her chest, had nearly proved to be too much for her. She'd found a cavity in the rocks large enough to fit her body inside and had lain there in the dirt for the hour it took the prions to knit her tissue and bones back together again.

Escaping under the cover of darkness, Stone had made her way to Budapest, where she'd called the emergency number she'd been told to memorize at the start of her employment. Two hours later she'd boarded a black helicopter with a dragon logo on the nose and was flown to a remote estate outside of Vienna, with instructions to stay there until called for. The estate had been fully stocked with food and liquor, and she'd enjoyed her time there, hidden away from the world and the events unfolding in Nové Mesto.

Until this morning, when she'd been summoned to Prague.

They reached the end of the hall and a set of double doors. Her minder knocked once, then opened the door.

"He's waiting for you inside."

"Thank you," she said, nodding, and then walked past him and into the room beyond.

It was a lavish study, furnished in dark woods and leather but with a touch of modern styling that helped it rise above the banal.

A man stepped out from behind the massive granite desk in the corner of the room and came toward her, his hand extended in greeting.

"Dr. Stone, a pleasure to meet you at last. My name's Garin Braden."

Her host was a tall, athletic man with long dark hair, a goatee and dark eyes that shone with confidence. She found herself attracted to him immediately, a response that was entirely unlike her, and she was momentarily nonplussed.

"The, ah, pleasure is all mine, Mr. Braden."

He smiled as he shook her hand. "Please, Garin is fine."

He led her over to a leather chair pulled up in front of his desk and indicated that she should sit, before resuming his seat on the other side.

Braden wasted no time getting down to business. "I understand the project has undergone a setback."

Stone flushed; she wasn't used to having her failures talked about so openly.

"Yes, that's true," she replied, covering her discomfort with studied nonchalance, "but it's nothing more than a minor inconvenience."

Braden raised an eyebrow. "You call the loss of a five-million-dollar facility and all the staff a minor inconvenience? How…interesting."

Stone knew she was right and pushed ahead. "We could lose ten such facilities and still be ahead of the game." She held up the small leather case she carried. "All the data was pulled from the computers before the authorities arrived, and it's stored right here on this drive. We can start fresh anywhere you want and at any time. I assure you, the money we'll earn from this project will buy another such facility ten times over."

"I see. Mr. Kovács has kept me informed of your progress, but I'm not entirely sure what happened three weeks ago. Perhaps you could bring me up to speed?"

She sighed. "A woman managed to disrupt our operation unexpectedly. I was able to save the research from falling into the wrong hands, however, so we can move forward again as soon as you give the word."

Braden continued gazing at her steadily as he asked, "Does this woman have a name?"

Stone hesitated. She had the sudden sense that she should tread carefully, but she had no idea why. At last, she said, "Her name is Annja Creed."

"Is? I take it she has yet to be dealt with?"

"Yes, but it's only a matter of time. Every loose end will be taken care of."

Her host nodded. "As they should be. Tell me, what of the research? It has been several weeks since your last report to Mr. Kovács."

Stone smiled. "Let me show you what we've accomplished."

She reached across the desk and picked up the stiletto-like letter opener lying there. Braden didn't say anything as she pulled up one sleeve and slashed the blade across the outside of her forearm. Blood welled up in a thin line.

"Watch," Stone said.

Braden looked on noncommittally as first the blood stopped and then the cut itself closed right before their eyes.

"My healing ability is growing more powerful every day. I've healed broken bones, punctures, even a bullet wound."

"Have you now? And all that's a result of those tiny little prions floating through your veins?"

She leaned forward, eager to share her success. "Yes! I'm just days away from creating a synthesized version of it, as well. We've been giving our clients a harvested version from the blood of the living, but without continued injections the prions…die off, for lack of better terminology. But with a synthetic version, we can keep them in place indefinitely."

Stone's face was flushed with excitement as she said, "Think of it! We're talking virtual immortality here!"

Braden smiled. "I'd say that calls for a drink, don't you?"

Before she could answer, he rose from behind the desk and moved over to the drink cart standing against one wall. "Brandy all right?" he asked over one shoulder as he pulled out two snifter glasses.

"Yes, that would be just fine."

She could hear him making the drinks—the sound of ice dropping into the glass followed by the soft gurgle of the pouring liquid—but when he turned around he only had one glass in hand.

"Actually, I much prefer whiskey," he said, taking a sip, "and since I'm drinking alone I might as well indulge."

Her mind was still trying to process what he'd said when he brought his other hand up, and Stone found herself staring down the barrel of a handgun.

"What are…?"

That was all she managed to get out before the sound of the gun filled the room and she knew no more.

GARIN REMAINED WHERE he was, though he did lower the gun. He gazed curiously at the body across the floor from him, paying particular attention to the bullet hole in the center of the woman's forehead as he calmly sipped his drink.

A thin line of blood slipped down the flesh of her face, but that was the only sign of activity he could see, even after fifteen minutes of waiting.

He sighed.

Apparently she hadn't been as close to virtual immortality as she'd thought.

The room was filled with the smell of cordite and bodily waste. The rug behind Stone's chair was now littered with blood, bone and brain matter. Garin hardly noticed any of it. After living for six hundred years, the sight and stink of death had become almost commonplace.

The Báthory project had been a long shot from the start. He'd heard about Stone's research and had decided to bankroll her efforts in the event that her discoveries might shed some light on his own longevity. He'd even suspected that the bloodline she'd been tracing might come full circle; he'd sown his oats far and wide in those early years, and it wasn't a stretch to think Stone might have confused a German bloodline for a Hungarian one. But none of that mattered in light of what she'd actually achieved.

There was no way the fools of this day and age were ready for something so powerful. Not by a long shot.

And Kovács... When Garin had learned that his executive director was concealing Stone's more brutal methods, he'd brought the man in for a final meeting before permanently ending their relationship.

He put down his now-empty glass and walked over to the body. Stone's hand had clenched at the moment of death, and he had to pry the leather case containing the hard drive from her grip. Straightening, he leaned over his desk and pressed a button on the intercom. A moment later there was a discreet knock on his door.

"Come."

His man, Griggs, stepped inside the room.

"Sir?"

Garin gestured at the mess in the chair across from him. "Ms. Stone's appointment is over. Get a team in here to see her out and clean the place up."

Griggs didn't blink an eye; he'd no doubt heard the gunshot and was the last man who would question his employer's actions.

That was one of the things Braden appreciated in a man like Griggs—he knew his place in the food chain, and his discretion was absolute.

"We're headed back to Munich. How soon can the chopper be ready?"

"I can have it warmed up on the pad in ten minutes."

"Excellent."

He glanced at the body one more time and nearly laughed. Stone had probably gone to her death thinking she'd been executed for her loss of the research facility, but the actual reason was much simpler than that.

She'd threatened Annja, and that was something Garin did not tolerate unless he was the one doing it.

Not that Annja couldn't have handled the woman on her own, but then again, it was the principle of the matter.

He headed for the door, the leather case holding the extent of Stone's research clasped firmly in one hand.

* * * * *

COMING NEXT MONTH FROM

GOLD EAGLE®

Available April 7, 2015

THE EXECUTIONER® #437
ASSASSIN'S TRIPWIRE – *Don Pendleton*

American high-tech ordnance has gone missing
en route to Syria. Determined to destroy the
stolen weapons before they can be used,
Mack Bolan discovers nothing is what it seems
between the Syrian regime, the loyalists and the
beautiful double agent working with him.

SUPERBOLAN™ #173
ARMED RESPONSE – *Don Pendleton*

A rogue general sets out to stage a coup in
the drought-stricken Republic of Djibouti.
Hunted by the police and the army and targeted
by assassins, Mack Bolan won't stop until
the general and his collaborators face their
retribution.

STONY MAN® #136
DOUBLE BLINDSIDE – *Don Pendleton*

The killing of US operatives in Turkey threatens
US–Turkish relations. While Able Team moves to
neutralize the threat in the States, Phoenix Force
heads overseas, where they discover the dead
agents are just the beginning.

COMING SOON FROM

GOLD EAGLE®

Available May 5, 2015

THE EXECUTIONER® #438
THE CARTEL HIT – *Don Pendleton*

Facing off against a Mexican cartel,
the Executioner races to secure the lone
witness to a brutal double murder.

DEATHLANDS® #122
FORBIDDEN TRESPASS – *James Axler*

While Ryan and the companions take on a
horde of hungry cannibals, something far
more sinister—and ravenous—lurks beneath
their feet...

OUTLANDERS® #73
HELL'S MAW – *James Axler*

The Cerberus warriors must confront an alien
goddess who can control men's minds. But are
they strong enough to eliminate this evil interloper
bent on global domination?

ROGUE ANGEL™ #54
DAY OF ATONEMENT – *Alex Archer*

A vengeful fanatic named Cauchon plans to
single-handedly resurrect the violence of the
Inquisition to put Annja and Roux on trial...
and a guilty verdict could mean death.

SPECIAL EXCERPT FROM

A greedy obsession leads to deadly retribution...

Read on for a sneak preview of
DAY OF ATONEMENT
by *Alex Archer*

The floor was cold and damp against her face.

There was a familiar smell.

"A crypt," Annja said, without realizing she'd spoken the thought aloud.

"Most perceptive," the woman said.

The light began to move. The woman placed an oil-filled lantern on top of a great stone sarcophagus close to where Annja lay bound.

Annja tried to get a better view of the woman standing in front of her. She was toned but petite, which meant she wasn't the unwashed mountain of muscle that had slammed her into the wall. There was no way this woman would have been strong enough to overpower her, even with the benefit of surprise.

Annja managed to work herself into a sitting position, propped up against the wall; only it wasn't a wall, it was another sarcophagus. The carvings dug into her spine.

"How long was I out?" Annja asked.

"Four hours, nearly five. You must have the constitution of a horse. That dose should have put you down for the best part of a day. Unless he managed to screw that up, too." The woman's eyes flicked to one side for an instant, an involuntary motion.

Annja followed the woman's gaze and saw a dark heap in the shadows. "Is he dead?" she asked.

The woman nodded. "I should hope so." She made the shape of a gun with her fingers and thumb.

Did this woman really value life so cheaply?

"And me? Am I just another loose end to be put out of my misery?"

"You? Oh, no, not at all. You are *far* more important than that. I am sure my brother will tell you all about it when you meet him."

"Brother?"

"Enough with the questions. This isn't a quiz show. One more and I'll tape your mouth shut. I really have no interest in listening to you. You're almost as bad as your friend."

"What friend?"

"The pretty one. Garin."

"Have you killed him, too?"

"Killed him? Of course not. Why would I? He's vital to what's happening. He's been most helpful."

Annja thought of everything Roux had told her about the midnight visit and the theft from the vault and muttered, "I'll kill him."

"That's entirely up to you, but not until we're finished with him."

Don't miss
DAY OF ATONEMENT by Alex Archer,
available May 2015 wherever
Gold Eagle® books and ebooks are sold.

GERAEXP54